DARK CHOICE

A LANCE BRODY NOVEL (BOOK 7)

MICHAEL ROBERTSON, JR.

ISBN: 978-1-7360939-6-2

DARK CHOICE

PROLOGUE

THE OFFICE where Elliot Gibbons spent most of his waking hours held none of the fun and excitement and charm that existed outside its building's walls. It was drab and screamed corporate boredom: the colors all grays and beiges, the furniture all metal and plastic and cheap. There were no windows, but a few framed pictures of the park hung on the walls, and sometimes if Elliot got bored and he stared into one of those pictures long enough, he could hear the squeals of delight from children as they grew dizzy on the Spinning Goblets, and he could see the Wheel of Adventure start its slow rotation, giving wide-eyed and smiling guests the best view of the park and all the land beyond.

The fat paycheck and twice-a-year corporate destination celebrations that he and his wife got to attend did make the mundane surroundings and long hours a bit more palatable, but now, as Elliot sat behind his desk with a burning pain in his stomach that he was beginning to suspect might not be the result of too many cups of coffee over the last decade but instead a stress-induced ulcer eating him from the inside out, he considered the reality of what he had feared was coming and had finally arrived just this morning via an early-morning phone call from the New York office.

He was trying to think what he was going to tell his wife when there was a soft knock on the office door and Elliot pulled his vacant stare away from one of the pictures. "Come in," he said, louder than he'd intended. He shrank away from the sound of his own voice.

The door pushed open and a horse walked in carrying its head under its arm. Well, not the entire horse, just the front half. Jack Webber closed the door behind him with a kick and then sat down in one of the chairs facing Elliot's desk. He set the horse costume head in the chair next to him, and the way its lifeless beady eyes stared at Elliot made him feel like the horse was judging him. Jack wiped his forehead with the back of one furry arm. "Heard you wanted to see me? Is it important? If it's not, can I come back in ten so I can go change out of this stupid thing?" He leaned forward, and droplets of sweat landed on Elliot's desk.

"I can't believe you put that thing on," Elliot said, unable to suppress a smile despite his mood.

Jack shrugged. "Either I did or we would have had to cancel the midday show. Too many callouts today. Hell, poor Jeremy Riggs has worked a double every day this week. Oh, and we need to hire a new maintenance man. Teddy quit. So we're down two. We've already got one ride operating past its maintenance schedule, and another two shut down because of malfunction. I'm assured they're both semi-easy fixes, but with less hands, it's taking longer and..."

Jack stopped, seeing the look on Elliot's face. "What is it?"

Elliot stared at his brother-in-law—and assistant director of operations—for a long time. Jack had been hired on as a favor to Elliot's wife's sister (which had netted Elliot tons of brownie points with his own wife, and a cherry-on-top blow job) after Jack had been let go from one of the big rental car companies during a corporate restructuring. Elliot had thought the guy would just phone it in for a while until something better came along, but he'd been wrong. Jack had been a go-getter from the start, with a big brain that could unravel logistical and financial puzzles while also charming vendors nearly out of their pants. Hell, sometimes Elliot wondered if Jack should be the one sitting in the big chair instead of him.

Right now, Elliot would have much preferred that to be the case.

"It's done," Elliot said. He leaned back in his chair, which gave off its familiar squeak. "I got the call this morning."

Jack's face fell. He looked over to the horse head on the chair next to him, as if it might have better news, or was going to tell him this was all a big joke. When the horse failed to offer any support, Jack looked back to his brother-in-law and said, "Done, like for good? Or just until..." He couldn't even figure out how to finish the sentence.

"Done for good," Elliot said. "One accidental death on a ride, maybe we come back from that. It happens. It's never easy, but it happens. But two in the same year, Jack? Plus a handful of staff injuries ... some small, sure, but a few big enough to threaten major litigation?" He shook his head. "Between insurance payouts and settlements, the media blowback, and a drop in attendance so large it looks like we've experienced some sort of apocalypse, we've just ... bled out. And the big boys in New York aren't going to infuse us with any more blood."

Jack sat stone-still, and Elliot could practically see his mind working. Elliot glanced to the horse head, found it still staring at him, and then quickly looked away. He'd never liked those damn things. They gave him the creeps.

"What about us?" Jack asked, a hopeful tone rising in his voice. "Can we relocate to another—"

Elliot was already shaking his head. "Severance package and see ya later, thanks for nothing. We're on our own."

Jack looked down at his feet, two comically oversized horse hooves. When he looked back up, Elliot was surprised to see tears in the man's eyes. "Jesus, what am I going to tell ... *Christ*, what a loser I am. I've lost two jobs in less than..." He shook his head and then met Elliot's eyes. "What happened, Elliot? I mean, what the *hell* happened?"

Elliot wished that he had a better answer, but all he had was the truth as he knew it. For nine of the ten years he'd served as director of operations for Arthur's Adventureland, they'd never had any major issues. A few hiccups now and then, a few empty lawsuits from folks looking to make a buck, but nothing major. Their safety ratings were always high, the health department had always been impressed, and guest satisfaction ratings year after year were high enough for Elliot to pocket a nice Christmas bonus. He—and later, Jack—had run a tight ship, and it had all seemed to be working so well. Until...

Until the bottom fucking fell out.

Suddenly, Jack stood up, the chair toppling over backward. "You know who I blame? I blame the staff!"

Elliot stood up too, gesturing for Jack to calm down. "No, Jack. It's not their fault."

Jack's eyes lit up with a fire Elliot had rarely seen, if ever. "They talk too much. Ever since that first guy got killed, they've been talking nonsense. Spreading all these rumors about how the park is cursed, how they hear screams at night when the park is closing down, how they *see* things moving around in the shadows—like we're ... like we're fucking *haunted*."

Elliot, of course, was aware of all of this. But he knew it had nothing to do with why the park was really closing. People had died and been injured, the revenue dropped, profits disappeared, and a rebound was unlikely. The PR team had put on a master class in disaster recovery, the marketing team had worked overtime, but bottom line: folks weren't coming to the park anymore. The staff had read the writing on the wall, and the good ones were getting out before the ship sank.

Those were the facts.

Jack was incensed, his anger sudden and strong like a geyser. "Gossip and bad press!" he yelled, pacing behind the chairs. He stopped and spun around to face Elliot, his face twisted in an ugly smile. "Hey, here's an idea. Let's flip this whole thing on them. Halloween's coming up, right? Let's lean into it. Go all out and invite everyone to come to the only truly haunted theme park in Texas. Half off for all ghost hunters!"

Elliot stepped around his desk, put a hand on Jack's shoulder. The man was breathing hard, his chest rising and falling so fast that Elliot was sure his brother-in-law was on the verge of a full-blown panic attack. "Jack," he said. "It'll all be okay. What do they always say? One door closes and another one opens? Look, you're getting a nice severance, you've got a strong resume and, shit, we both know you're smart as hell. You would have gotten my job over me if you'd gotten here first." He gave Jack a playful nudge and forced a laugh.

Jack sucked in a big breath of air and held it, then let it out long and slow. He cleared his throat, nodded his head. "You're right. I'm sorry. It's just ... I'm sorry."

Elliot was about to suggest the two of them go out for a late lunch together, milk that corporate credit card for all it was worth while they still could. But before he could speak, Jack turned and walked out of the office, leaving the horse head behind in the chair where he'd left it and saying, "I've got to get out of this thing. It stinks to high hell."

Elliot gave a nod and watched his brother-in-law leave. "We'll talk more later," he called after him.

But they wouldn't talk more later. Or ever again.

"I really appreciate you doing this, Jeremy," Jack Webber said to the young man who'd spent all week pulling double shifts. The park had been closed for over an hour, and storm clouds loomed on the blackened horizon. A hurried breeze brought with it the scent of funnel cakes and cotton candy. Jack looked at the guy—a kid, really, no older than twenty-three or so—and envied him, wanted to go back in time to that point in his life. A time before the wife and the kid and the mortgage and ... and all the bad luck that had come after. Jack Webber wasn't old, exactly, having just celebrated his forty-first birthday last month, but after the news Elliot had delivered to him today, he *felt* old. The idea of starting over again was already exhausting him. And to make matters worse, his pride was hurt.

Pride. That was what he'd always liked about working for the park—the fact that if he did his job right, lots of people would be able to come and spend the day and have a great break from their reality. Could smile and laugh and forget all their troubles.

Jack Webber was not smiling or laughing now.

"It's fine," Jeremy said, but Jack could tell the kid was already regretting agreeing to this, probably too afraid to say no to one of the park's big bosses.

I'm not your boss anymore, kid. You just don't know it yet.

"Just for like, what, five minutes, right?"

Jack nodded. "Five minutes is fine." What he didn't say was he just wanted one last look at the place from high above, one last chance to revel in the memories. He'd always enjoyed the view from the top of the Adventure Wheel. After the Texas Star at the state fair, the Adventure Wheel was the largest Ferris wheel in the state. You could see for miles at its apex, but Jack only wanted to look down and see the place where he'd once felt so important.

"Cool," Jeremy said. "I'll start her up and then run back to my locker and grab my stuff and then come back. That long enough?"

Jack nodded again. "Fine."

They walked together up the ramp, their footsteps sounding hollow and loud without the normal din of park activity to drown them out. Jack climbed into the waiting gondola and closed the door behind him. Jeremy fastened the latch, double-checked that it was secure, and then gave Jack a suspicious look, as if a sudden realization had cast a blanket of doubt over this whole business.

"You, uh, know that I'm not supposed to leave this thing unattended with people on board, right? I mean, isn't that like, against regulations and, uh, like, the insurance stuff? Is this a test? Am I going to get fired?"

Jack shook his head. "I'm not firing you, Jeremy." *No, Elliot will do that soon enough.* To make things a little easier to swallow, Jack pulled his wallet from his back pocket and handed the kid a twenty. "Like I said, I really appreciate you doing this."

Jeremy eyed the twenty-dollar bill like he expected it might bite, but eventually the temptation won him over and he stuffed the bill into his pocket and said, "Okay, back in a few," and turned away, heading down the ramp like he was trying to outrun his ability to change his mind.

Jack watched the kid turn the key on the control panel and then press the button to start the ride. The Adventure Wheel jerked to a start but quickly smoothed out its motion as Jack's gondola moved backward, the cool air growing colder as it sliced past him as he rotated up and away from the platform and began to rise into the sky. When he reached the top, his gondola centered at the wheel's highest point, there was another jerk as Jeremy must have punched the Stop button and everything fell still. Jack looked over the side and saw the miniature version of Jeremy jogging away from the ride, off to the staff locker room.

Up here, it was quiet. Like the earth below, all sounds had fallen away, and Jack was left with nothing but the gentle breeze and the looming clouds creeping closer and ... his thoughts. He slid down in his seat and leaned his head back and closed his eyes, breathed in deeply, filling his lungs with cold air. When he breathed out, he tried to let all his stress and anger and anxiety out with it. He'd gotten so mad earlier, in Elliot's office. It wasn't like him, wasn't like him at all, and he felt ashamed. To act the way he had to his own brother-in-law, the man who had gotten him this job when he'd been at one of his lowest points—it was understandable, but inexcusable. Elliot was family and had always been there for him. He needed to apologize.

Hell, maybe when the severance packages came in they could all go on a little vacation together—try to drink and laugh away the whole thing. Elliot, though mostly boring and unadventurous (ironic, given the park's name), had a unique ability to always be optimistic, and that was the sort of company Jack needed right now. And Elliot had connections, too. This place hadn't been his first gig—no, he'd worked for a major food distributor and a hotel chain before settling down at the park (though all of those moves had been his *own* decision, and each time for more pay), and every conference or convention Jack ever attended with the man, Elliot always seemed to know just about everybody. Yeah ... Elliot would find a job, no problem, and Jack had no doubt the guy would put in a good word for him anywhere he could.

Everything would be alright. There might be some uncomfortable days ahead, full of conversations nobody ever wanted to have, but there would be light at the end of the tunnel.

See, this is exactly why I needed to come up here, Jack thought. *Best twenty bucks I've spent in a long time.*

The Adventure Wheel shook hard, a single time, like a strong gust of wind had suddenly slammed into it out of nowhere. Jack's gondola rocked back and forth after the impact, and Jack pushed himself upright again and peered over the side, expecting to see Jeremy back at the control booth.

But the booth was empty. And the wheel didn't move again.

Jack looked further over the edge, saw nobody, then slid across to the other side of the bench seat, the side closest to the outside of the park. He looked over the side and again saw nothing unexpected.

"What could have...?"

And that was when the feeling overtook him. His insides suddenly chilled, like somebody had snuffed out a candle, and all the optimism he had worked to build up in the last couple minutes vanished, a slate wiped clean. A new word was written on the slate, big and bolded and repeated over and over and over again.

Jump Jump Jump Jump Jump

JUMP

There was another jolt of the Adventure Wheel and it snapped Jack out of his despair-filled trance, just as his gondola rocked with a newfound weight. Jack spun around from where he'd been peering over the edge and came face-to-face with a tall woman with bright white hair and wearing a black trench coat.

"Who are ... how did you...?" He fumbled for words. Fumbled backward in his seat. Because not only was it impossible (*How did she get here?*), but he could feel the ugliness coming off the woman, a scent like spoiled milk that was creeping inside him, souring his mind.

"Shhh," the woman said, holding a bone-white finger to her lips. "You've had a long day. Why don't you rest now? Everyone will understand."

Like a blur, with a speed that Jack's brain did not have time to compute, the woman shot forward and grabbed him by his waist and flung him over the edge of the gondola with ease.

As he fell, screaming and pinwheeling, Jack had just enough time to realize that the sound of his own scream was joining others, a chorus of pain and agony growing louder as the earth rushed toward him. A second before he splattered to his death, Jack would have sworn that the ground below began to open like a giant eye, an angry red light spilling from the cracks. The eye was the source of the screams, and it was hungry for him.

How about that? Jack had time to think, right before impact. *The place really* is *haunted.*

Then his body broke in every way it could break and the red eye closed around his soul.

[1]

Lance Brody said nothing.

In the driver's seat, the Surfer cruised the Plymouth Horizon along the highway with one hand on the wheel, and the thing called Patrick Cain rode shotgun. The Reverend sat tall and straight in the back seat next to Lance like a dutiful parishioner attending Sunday service. Every so often he would close his eyes and his chin would tilt down and he would doze off, looking like he'd suddenly decided to fall into silent prayer. The four of them—three hunters and their prey—had ridden silently in the too-cramped car all through the night, as if the events that had led them to this moment together had drained them, and now that the adrenaline had faded they were left in a state of muted recovery and contemplation. It was only when Patrick pointed to a highway exit sign just as the sun was cresting the horizon and the Surfer had obediently driven the car off the ramp and into the parking lot of a fast-food restaurant that the first words were spoken.

"Pit stop, boys!" Patrick said, sparking to life, like the four of them were a group of college roomies on a spring break road trip. "Time to piss and fuel up!" He turned in the seat, his leather jacket making a sucking sound as it pulled free from the upholstery, and through a menacing grin he looked at Lance. "Our sun-bleached friend here"—he jerked a thumb toward the Surfer—"will take you to the men's room so you can do whatever. Nothing funny, okay? I think we can all agree we're past that. You made your choice." He laughed, and a bit of spit flew from his mouth. Lance stared at the boy who wasn't really a boy at all, gave him no reaction. Zero emotion. "I'm going to grab us some food," Patrick said. "We can eat on the road."

Patrick nodded to the Surfer and then turned and grabbed the door handle to get out. "Coffee," Lance said, his voice flat and groggy.

"What's that, friend?" Patrick turned back around, that menacing grin even larger.

Lance cleared his throat. "Get me a large coffee. Black."

He didn't wait for an answer or any response at all. Lance opened the back door and unfolded his long legs out of the Plymouth and stretched his back. He walked straight into the restaurant without waiting to see if the Surfer was following. It didn't matter. He wasn't going to do anything stupid. Wasn't going to try to run out the other side of the building or start shouting for help. It would do no good. Nobody could help him. He wasn't even sure he could help himself. His ancient flip phone was in his pocket, but the battery was long dead, and its charger had been left behind along with Lance's backpack. Besides, there was no number on earth he could call to make things any better.

Because whatever evil was inside the boy named Patrick Cain had been right. Lance had made his choice. Or more specifically, it felt as though the Universe had led him to it, had been guiding him every step of the way, putting people and things into motion until all the pieces were in alignment and it was time for...

For my purpose, Lance thought, feeling the certainty of it all, the weight of realization that had fallen on him just last night in Paul and Breanne Michie's living room. The time had come, and something big was coming with it.

But as usual, Lance had no idea what. Some things never change. The Universe always seemed to have a card up its sleeve. All Lance knew now was that whatever it was—whatever was coming—it felt definitive. It felt ... *final*.

One side would win, the other would lose.

Lance was trying not to focus on those implications, on what scale the damage might be measured.

He was standing at the urinal when the door opened behind him and the rubber *slap slap* of the Surfer's flip-flops announced his arrival. Lance flushed and washed his hands and left without even acknowledging him. The Surfer followed him out, silently stalking, through the restaurant and back to the car, where the two of them took their seats again. Patrick and the Reverend came out several minutes later, their hands full of bags and cups. The Reverend got into the back seat and handed Lance his coffee and one of the bags, which was full of breakfast sandwiches. Lance took two biscuits from the bag and handed it back. Had one nearly gone before the Surfer had the car out of the parking lot.

They were two hours down the road when Lance finally felt sleep coming over him. Despite the food and the large coffee—which he'd nursed as long as he could before gulping down the last quarter of it—the fact was Lance had forced himself to stay awake through the night and now his body was shutting down.

He felt his eyes slide closed and his head leaned over against the window and the slightly off-rhythm hum of the tires on the asphalt began to lull him to sleep. He felt his mind begin to relax, to drift off, to open up and...

Lance!

Leah's voice. Blasting through his head like a megaphone.

Lance! Tell me where you are!

Lance bolted upright, suddenly wide awake again. But he wasn't the only one who'd noticed.

"Stop!" Patrick Cain shouted, and the Surfer slammed on the Plymouth's brakes hard enough that the tires screeched and cars blared their horns and swerved around them, narrowly avoiding an accident while the Surfer brought them to a complete stop on the shoulder of the road.

Patrick glared at Lance, the evil in his eyes like black orbs swallowing all the light around them. "*No*," he hissed. "Shut her out, Lance. Cut her off."

Lance stared back, silent. Processing the idea that Patrick had heard Leah, too. Or maybe...

He felt her.

"I was serious when I said I was doing you a favor before, by letting her live," Patrick said. "Don't you see that? I could have killed her and still gotten what I wanted. Don't make me change my mind, Lance. There are others. Others like them." He pointed to the Reverend and the Surfer. "All I have to do is say the word and they'll track down your little girlfriend and make her wish she'd never met you." He smiled that ugly, toothy smile again and said, "I don't really need to go into more detail, do I? You can work it out for yourself."

Lance could.

The car was silent for a full minute. Patrick stared at Lance and Lance stared right back. On the highway, cars flew by in blurs of color and bursts of noise. Finally, Lance nodded once. He closed his eyes, reached out into the wavelengths and found that connection between Leah and him. The one that had only recently grown to its full strength, surprising them both. He sent his message.

Stay away. Don't come for me. Then, because he could think of no other fitting send-off, he spoke the truest thing he could find. *I love you.*

Then he closed the iron gates of his mind, shutting out this world and others beyond.

With the connection severed, Patrick must have been satisfied, because he nodded once to the Surfer and then they were moving again.

Lance felt terrible. Hated himself for what he'd done. But he also took solace in something he'd learned. The way Patrick had reacted when Leah had reached out to Lance, it had been more than just anger. Lance Brody had spent a lifetime becoming very adept at reading people, and even though the thing called Patrick Cain was not entirely human, it was forced to communicate through human speech and emotions. Lance had seen panic along with that anger, and in Lance's experience, panic bordered on fear.

They're afraid of her, Lance thought and smiled. *She's dangerous to them.*

He took this thought with him and held it tight as he once again attempted to get some sleep. The Universe was still dealing the cards, and Lance would have to make his bet and play his hand when the time came. Until then, all he could do was wait.

But the wait would be excruciating. Because today brought

with it a feeling that he'd been working hard to forget, the feeling he'd experienced the day after the Reverend and the Surfer had killed his mother and Lance had fled his hometown. It was like drowning, only not in water but loneliness. Now, he'd lost Leah, the one person who had helped to fill that emptiness inside him, the one who'd made him feel as though he didn't have to walk through this world alone. Only this time there were differences. The biggest of which being that Leah was still alive.

And she was strong. Stronger than even Lance had thought possible.

They're afraid of her, Lance thought again, just as he slipped into sleep. *This isn't over yet.*

[2]

The idea had struck her just as Leah had pulled the Beetle into a large convenience store's parking lot, where she planned on filling up the car's tank and grabbing as many snacks and drinks as she could carry, because even though she didn't know what she was doing or where she was going, she knew that time was already working against her, and with every ticking second of the clock Lance was getting further away, closer to...

She didn't know what, but she knew it could only be bad. The image of the Reverend and the Surfer standing by in Paul and Breanne Michie's living room while the teenage boy they called Patrick had gripped Leah's hair and violently shoved her face toward the fire sent a surge of anger and dread through her. Not because of what they'd done to her, but because they'd taken Lance. Lance had been forced to choose, and what an unfair choice it had been.

Because Leah knew—she had *felt* it—that the thing that had been masquerading in the body of a young boy in a leather jacket would have killed her. Would not have hesitated to follow through on his threat.

Evil had no conscience and did not discriminate. It took what it wanted, and if the world burned, that was all the better. Leah's time with Lance had shown her this truth in ways no scholar or theologian ever could have. While they stared into the words on a written page, Leah had stared directly into the eyes of Evil and had lived to talk about it.

We *lived to talk about it*, she thought.

Because they had been a team—*were* a team. Lance had told her that he'd felt the good in her from the first day they'd met, and how he had recently begun to sense something more growing in her, a stronger sense of the Light—the same Light that Lance himself was blessed with and used to fight against the Darkness.

Leah had been unsure how to process this information, and whether or not there was any substantial truth to it. Because who was *she*, really? Why now, after she'd reached her early twenties, would a deep-seated and hidden power inside her suddenly make itself known? What had it been waiting for?

But the answer to that question was easy, she realized. It had been waiting for Lance. He always told her how he had felt that he'd spent most of his life being led along a path, that every decision he made was laced with suggestion from a guiding force. That things eventually would slide into place, align in the proper order, and the truth or the purpose would reveal itself before Lance had even realized what had happened. As he'd gotten older, he'd become better at understanding this and had learned to trust his instinct and his feelings for what they really were. But he admitted that he did not think he would ever fully understand his own gifts, and he often lacked the ability to control or use them at will.

But the things she'd seen him do...

He *was* getting stronger. Even Leah, who'd only been with him a short time, had been able to sense that in him. It wasn't always a tangible thing, something she could describe to somebody on the outside looking in, but a feeling, a ... *connection* between the two of them.

The connection...

Which was when the idea struck. She had just parked the Beetle alongside one of the concrete islands with the gas pumps, and she'd realized that with the trauma of everything that had happened and all the overwhelming emotions that had swarmed her as she'd discovered her new abilities, in her panic and grief at losing Lance, she had forgotten the most fundamental thing she should try.

The connection...

She'd been able to reach out to him with her mind before. They'd exchanged thoughts. How far was her own reach? How could she try?

There was no manual for this sort of thing.

But...

You're stronger than you think... Lance's words, echoing in her head.

Leah took a deep breath and leaned her head back against the seat. Closed her eyes and tried focusing only on her breathing, clearing her head of all thoughts except...

Lance.

She sent her mind out along the newly discovered wavelengths of the Universe, focused her energy on Lance's soul. Called to him.

For a while, there was nothing, no trace of his existence. And she was worried, because Lance had explained to her how, as he'd gotten stronger, he *had* been able to control his mind, to be able shut out the rest of the world when needed, to shield himself from prying beings, those who were hunting him. Sometimes he succeeded, sometimes he didn't.

Is he doing that now? she wondered. *Is he protecting himself from—*

But then he was there. Like somebody had pulled back a curtain for a great reveal, she felt him, his mind plugging into the wires. The sensation warmed her heart, sent a tingle through her soul like only love could do.

Lance! she called, rushing toward him.

Lance! Tell me where you are!

And for a second, she knew he had heard her. She felt his mind latch onto her words, felt the connection buzz with energy. But then ... nothing. He said nothing. For what felt like an eternity the line was nothing but static, and a palpable sense of dread began to seep into Leah.

Stay away. Don't come for me.

His words sliced through the silence and into her heart, searing flesh.

But then, a soothing salve. *I love you.*

And then he was gone. The connection was severed, and all trace of Lance had vanished as suddenly as it had appeared.

Leah opened her eyes, her heart beating fast in a combination of anger and fear.

He shut me out! (The anger)

They must have made him ... threatened him. (The fear)

But no, he wouldn't have shut her out to save himself. He would have done it to...

Leah slammed the Beetle's steering wheel with her palm. "He's doing it to protect me!" She slammed the wheel again. "I don't *need* protection, Lance! How many times do I have to tell you that!"

Outside, a man next to her who was pumping gas into his Jeep turned to look at her. Leah caught him looking and stared back until the man looked away, embarrassed.

"Calm down," Leah told herself, taking deep breaths and trying to slow her heart. "Lance would stay calm."

"Not always," a voice next to her said.

An icy chill shot through Leah and she sat frozen for a second before slowly turning her head to the right. A ghost was sitting in the passenger seat.

[3]

LANCE MIGHT HAVE SPENT every day of his life with perpetual visitations of spirits and visions of things from beyond our world, but Leah had experienced her very first encounter only just that morning—before she'd even had any *coffee*—and she had to work to keep her composure after she turned and found the dead woman sitting in the Beetle's passenger seat. It would have been startling even under normal circumstances, to believe she was alone and then suddenly discover she wasn't, that somebody else was with her in what she thought was a private moment, their voice shocking her out of her own thoughts. But, when you factored in that the surprise newcomer was a ghost, and that they'd simply appeared with no warning, no preamble, it only made things more uncomfortable.

But as Leah's mind worked through all this, tried to process and slow down and remember who she was now, what she could do, trying to grasp a WWLD (*What would Lance do?*) mindset, she *really* looked at the woman seated beside her and thought about the words the woman had spoken (*"Not always."*) and all at once the pieces clicked together. Not only did the pieces snap into place, but Leah *felt* the woman beside her—her very essence, the goodness that seemed to radiate out and reach for Leah to wrap her in a warm, tight hug.

It was familiar, that essence. A lovely calming presence that felt so much like the way Lance made her feel, the way his own goodness had seemed to envelop Leah when they would lie together, entwined in each other, mentally and physically. This was the same ... but slightly different, two shades of the same color.

The emotion of the moment rose in Leah's belly, a warmth spreading out and filling her as she looked the woman over: the long skirt, the baggy sweater, the dark blond hair that fell just past her shoulders, framing her face—a face that was smiling back at Leah with kindness and ... *amusement*?

When Leah looked into the woman's eyes, she felt herself begin to cry, a hot trickle of tears on her cheeks.

"Don't cry," the woman said.

And Leah couldn't help it—she laughed loudly, and then cried harder as she struggled to say, "Lance told me you had an interesting perspective on crying. That he ... he..." Leah took a deep breath, let it out slowly and wiped her eyes with the backs of her hands. Cleared her throat. "That he never really understood it."

The ghost of Pamela Brody smiled wide and nodded. "He says that, sometimes, when he's not really ready to explain something. It's not his best trait, if we're being honest."

The reality of what was happening fell across Leah again like the sun emerging from behind a cloud, and it was so much to bear that she felt the tears begin to come again. She closed her eyes and took another deep breath and counted to ten. When she opened them, Pamela Brody was still there, her hair unmoving in the warm stream of air from the car's heater, her smile having been replaced with a small grin.

"You're his mom!" Leah exclaimed, then quickly slapped a hand over her mouth. "Sorry," she said, "It's just ... you're you ... and you're here!"

Pamela Brody said nothing.

Leah had so many questions—about now, about Lance, about everything. She tried to organize her thoughts, find the path to follow. But as she scrambled to make sense of the moment, one thing became very apparent. She was already beginning to feel better, now that she wasn't alone. If she couldn't have Lance beside her to work this all out with, his mother was certainly the next best thing.

What a strange way to meet your boyfriend's mom for the first time, Leah thought and felt her own grin spread across her lips.

"I don't understand," Leah finally said, deciding on which question she wanted to ask first. "I asked Lance if he'd ever seen you, you know, since the night you..." She trailed off, not sure how to phrase what had happened. The way Lance had described it all, he'd always spoken as if the Reverend and the Surfer had killed his mother, but the story itself had made it seem more like the woman seated across from Leah now had made her own choice, had made the sacrifice to save her son. To buy him some time. "He said he never has."

Pamela shook her head. "No, he hasn't."

"Why? I mean, why are you here now, with me, and not with him?"

Pamela Brody tilted her head to the side, gave Leah a look that said *You really don't know?* Then she smiled what Leah could only describe as a mother's smile and said, "He doesn't need to see me, because I've never left him."

Now Leah tilted her head, confused. "What?"

"He thinks it's just his own subconscious, his own memories, when he hears my voice. But it's me ... the part of me that will always live on in him. There's a piece of every mother's soul inside their children. It lives on in them, even after we're gone." Pamela reached out and rested a hand on Leah's arm. There was no physical sensation of touch, of course, the woman's hand disappearing through Leah's own flesh and bone, but Leah felt the warmth inside her, a surge of compassion. For a moment, she would swear she could smell something sweet, like lavender and ... honey. "But you know all this already, don't you?" Pamela asked. "Because you've always been able to feel your own mother inside you. She gives you strength. Always has."

Leah felt the start of fresh tears, only these were calmer, more languid expressions of her own understanding that everything Pamela Brody was saying was true. She nodded once and could do nothing but laugh at the happiness she felt. She'd never known the woman seated across from her in life, but Leah found she already loved her. These few brief moments had already shown her a big reason why Lance was the person he was. Why he was the person Leah loved.

"I've always been with him," Pamela said again. "He's very smart, but sometimes he misses what's right in front of his face." Then she added, "Though I suppose grief will do that to a person. You see, despite Lance's ability to help *others* with grief, he's not very good at handling his own. He's never had to be."

Leah considered this, then nodded as it all added up. "Because you were his first big loss. He loved you more than anything."

"And now he loves you."

Leah sighed and then leaned back in her seat. The two women were quiet for a minute while a few snow flurries twirled lazily in the breeze outside. The warm feeling Leah had experienced was beginning to dissipate, the slow creep of dread beginning to return as the reality of the bigger picture took shape again in her mind. "So ... why are you here again? With me?"

"Because you need help," Pamela said. The grin never seemed to leave her face.

Leah scoffed. "You got that right."

"From the day he was born, Lance always had me by his side. We learned about his gifts together. Earlier, when I told you he wasn't always calm, I meant it. That boy has a temper. He tries hard to suppress things, to compartmentalize and pack away. He tries to push his own emotions aside because he doesn't think they're important. He thinks that by taking time for himself, he's taking away from helping others. But of course" —she shrugged—"that's impossible to keep up. Eventually, he explodes. I was there to bring him back down to earth. We worked through all the bad ... and the good. Tried, and often failed, to make sense of what Lance is and what he can do. But together, we learned a lot. At the end of the day, the one thing I learned is that beyond all else, what Lance really needed was somebody to talk to, somebody he could trust and share his truth with. Because you see, it's an awful way to live, feeling like you're completely alone."

Leah nodded. Thought about all those days she'd spent working at her family's motel, her mother dead, her brother missing, her father not fully present—not the way she'd needed him to be—and how even though people came and went each and every day, it was as if nobody ever really saw her anymore. For a long time, Leah had always felt more like a...

Like a ghost.

Until Lance.

"We have to find him," Leah said, sitting up, getting down to business.

Pamela nodded. "Yes."

"So what do I do?"

Pamela's grin widened. "You sound like Lance."

Leah rolled her eyes. "Not helpful."

"Okay. Here's what I used to tell him. The Universe gave you your gifts for a reason. So use them. *Trust* them. Let them show you the way."

"I already tried reaching out to him. I found him ... sort of ... but then he cut me off. Shut me out. He can do that, you know? He's gotten a lot stronger."

Pamela nodded.

"So if I can't have him tell me where he is, if I can't *feel* him out there, how am I supposed to find him?"

"Trust your gifts. They'll show you."

"I don't know how."

"Remember when I said sometimes Lance would miss what was right in front of his face? Sometimes he would get so fixated on what he thought was the right answer, he'd miss the obvious truth in front of him."

Leah nodded. But she didn't understand. Said, "I see where he gets his ability to speak without making any sense."

When Pamela spoke again, her voice was full of nothing but patience, which was both comforting and also infuriating. She acted as though her son *wasn't* currently being held captive by three evil maniacs. "You've only tried looking for a direct connection to Lance to show you the way," she said. "You need to be open to other possibilities."

"I don't—"

"Try."

Pamela's tone left no room for interpretation. It was a command, plain and simple. The way Leah's own mother had told her to clean her room when she was a child.

The two women held each other's gaze for a few seconds, then Leah sighed, nodded, and leaned her head back against the seat and closed her eyes. She focused on nothing but the sound of the Beetle's heater blowing, let her mind fall into the noise. It caught her in soft hands, carried her away. And then she was gone, no longer inside her car in the convenience store's parking lot. She was drifting in a vast ocean of mindfulness, letting the waters take her where they wished, unencumbered. She let the small rippling waves pull her and turn her, completely at their will.

And then she heard it, far off in the distance. The sound of somebody pounding a great drum, a drum as big as a mountain in a faraway land. The sound reached her and Leah latched on and that was when she recognized the sound for what it really was. It wasn't a drum but a heart, beating loud. Asking to be found. The waves changed direction, began floating her toward the noise.

She was being pulled.

Leah opened her eyes and sat up. "I found something!"

Pamela Brody was gone.

[4]

THEY WERE HEADING WEST. That much Lance was able to figure out by simply watching the highway signs. He'd been doing a lot of watching, because there wasn't much else to do when you were trapped in the back of a car that was usually going no less than seventy miles an hour down the interstate. He watched the road, watched the buildings and farmland zoom by in a forever-shifting filmstrip, watched the people in other cars, wondered who they were, where they were headed, wondered if they had any idea of the Evil they were passing by.

Of course they didn't.

That was the thing about Evil. Most of the time it was right in front of your face, hiding in plain sight: the barista at the coffee shop who is always so polite and funny but has been stealing customer credit card numbers for years; the boys' high school gym teacher who everyone loves and who organizes the local special needs athletic events but installed a spy cam in the girls' locker room and sells the footage online; the long-haul trucker who drives countless hours to provide food and clothes for his family that he loves dearly but has also murdered seven women in the last three years and has hidden the bodies throughout the United States.

A man dressed in priest's clothing and a long-haired beach bum who look so comical together you have to laugh ... but whose single purpose is to hunt down those who fight for good and destroy them.

The body of a sixteen-year-old boy that was the embodiment of an Evil stronger and more vile than anything Lance had ever seen.

Lance had been watching his captors, too. Observing, taking the opportunity to really study them for the first time. The Reverend and the boy named Patrick were, if Lance was being honest, boring. They acted just as you'd expect anybody to act on a road trip. They shifted in their seats from time to time, they coughed and sneezed occasionally, they dozed off and slept with their heads against the window or leaned back on the headrest, they went to the bathroom and ate and drank when the group would make the occasional stop. All completely normal human behavior.

But the Surfer ... the Surfer did none of these things.

The thing dressed in the tank top and board shorts and flip-flops had sat slouched in the Plymouth's driver's seat ever since the moment the group had left the Michies' home just outside of Travelers Rest. One hand on the wheel, the other deeply tanned arm resting along the window, fingers sometimes softly drumming on the upholstery. They'd been on the road for two days now and the Surfer had not slept once, not eaten or drank anything, and, since he was always the one to accompany Lance to the restrooms, Lance knew the Surfer had not used the facilities a single time on their trip.

Lance knew what the Surfer could do. He'd seen it more times than he wished, and had been tricked by it more times than he was proud of. The Surfer could transform himself into the likeness of anybody he wanted. Shape-shifter was the word Lance had always been hesitant to use, because he thought it sounded like something out of a paranormal romance novel, but the truth was Lance's own reality—*everyone's* reality—was closer to fiction than not.

Bottom line was this: the last forty-eight hours had confirmed for Lance that, unlike the Reverend and Patrick, the Surfer was not a human at all. He was only something pretending to be. The shape of a human hiding a creature beyond comprehension underneath.

For a normal person, this might be a terrifying realization. For Lance Brody, it was just one more truth he'd have to accept and figure out how to deal with.

Lance tried switching his thoughts to something more pleasant than shape-shifting demons and the like. He thought about Leah, where she might be right now, and whether she had taken his warning and decided not to come after him. Lance smiled and chuckled to himself in the back of the car. *No way,* he thought. *She's coming. Nobody's going to stop her when she sets her mind to something. Certainly not me.*

While he thought about Leah, a very vivid and clear scene suddenly took shape in his mind, dropping into his thoughts so unexpectedly he actually flinched backward as if to avoid a blow. He was back at his and his mother's house in Hillston. Leah and his mother were there with him, and the three of them were in the small home's kitchen, gathered around the table. There was a cake in the center of the table, chocolate frosting and a single candle burning in the middle of it. Leah and his mother were singing Happy Birthday to him. On the counter behind them, the coffeemaker was gurgling as it just finished brewing a pot. The kettle was steaming on a burner and his mother's favorite mug was waiting with a tea bag next to the stove. The two most important women in his life finished the song and watched him expectantly, their faces all smiles. He looked at them, feeling the rush of emotions begin to overtake him. He quickly bent over and blew out the candle.

"Lance! You gotta go, or what?" Patrick's voice shattered the daydream to a million tiny pieces that scattered in the wind of Lance's thoughts. Lance found himself back in the Plymouth, which had at some point driven off the highway and was parked in front of another convenience store. There was a big neon sign in one of the windows advertising the Mega Millions jackpot, and it glowed behind Patrick's head like he was wearing the crown of the king of Las Vegas. The Neon Monarch. "You with us, friend?" Patrick asked, his eyes squinting at Lance like he was trying to catch him doing something naughty.

"I'm with you," Lance said. "Thanks for checking. I appreciate your concern."

Patrick stared at Lance for another second, his eyes narrowing even more, then, like a switch flipped, he smiled that ugly smile again and nodded. "Anytime, friend. Let's see what this shithole has on offer, shall we?"

Lance kicked open the car door and stretched his legs and turned and looked at the road. It was nothing more than a dusty rural route that sliced through mostly undeveloped land. For a moment, he retreated back into his thoughts, tried to find a few shards of that memory he'd just experienced. Wanted to go back to that place and stay there a little longer. Wanted to be with the people he loved.

But it wasn't a memory, Lance thought. *That never happened.* Leah and his mother had never met. His mother had been killed the day before Lance had even met Leah. He didn't have time to dwell on the meaning of it all; instead he chose to just accept the happiness he'd felt as he'd experienced it. He turned back and was headed to the store when he saw the small black sedan parked on the other side of the Plymouth. The engine was running and sounded like it had a cold, wheezing and rattling, with puffs of exhaust billowing from the tailpipe. A small boy, no more than four or five, stared at Lance through the back window. His face was dirty with dried snot, and his eyes looked puffy and tired. Despite this, the boy was smiling, showing small, cramped teeth. He waved at Lance, and Lance smiled and waved back.

"Lance..." Patrick's voice, coming from the front of the store.

Something inside Lance wanted to go to the boy. Wanted to...

What? What would you even do?

The sound of somebody clearing their throat caused Lance to turn to his left, where he found the Surfer standing, waiting.

Lance sighed, waved goodbye to the boy, and walked toward the store. He fought the urge to look back.

He'd just stepped up onto the curb in front of the store and was reaching for the door handle when the door suddenly flew open and a tall, disheveled woman emerged. She wasn't looking up, instead fumbling with a bottle of some sort of medicine she'd apparently just purchased. Her hair was a mess, pulled up into a sloppy ponytail, and she wore pajama bottoms with a baggy T-shirt. No jacket, despite the winter air. She walked right into Lance and her feet tangled in his, and as she started to fall, the bottle of medicine went flying from her hands. Lance, once a gifted high school basketball player, used his reflexes and long, strong arms to both catch the falling woman, pulling her into him, and reach out to grab the bottle before it could land in the parking lot.

And he was hit with it all. The images rushing through him like a strong hit of adrenaline.

The three jobs the woman worked to pay the bills—childcare one of the largest. The multiple bouts of bronchitis poor Miles had dealt with in the last two years, and how *those* bills added up so damn *fast*. How they didn't have health insurance, and the *good* medicine had run out and now all she could afford was the bottle of whatever Lance had just snatched from the air. And she felt like a failure, because she knew her only purpose in life was to take care of her son, who she loved more than she had known she could even love a person, and every day she woke up and fought hard and tried her best to do all the right things and every day it seemed like things got a little bit worse.

The woman had regained her footing, and when she stood up straight, Lance saw that her whole mood had changed. She stood back from Lance and stared at him with something akin to complete shock. Her eyes were wide and her mouth was frozen in a tiny circle, like she was maybe going to try to whistle. Then, to Lance's surprise, the woman's eyes softened and began to glisten with tears. Her entire face relaxed in relief, and the tears fell and she began to sob. Strands of hair fell down across her brow and into her face, catching in her eyelashes. "Oh, *thank you!*" the woman said and started to laugh. "Thank you, thank you, *thank you!*"

Lance stood silently. Stunned.

"He's going to be okay. Miles is going to be okay, isn't he?"

The words rushed out of her like she was playing the lightning round of a game show. "I've been so worried because he gets sick so much and each time it just seems to get worse and worse and oh God the way his chest rattles sometimes when he tries to breathe ... I just ... Oh, *thank you* for showing me. Thank you! I've seen it now. I've seen him grow up, I've seen how smart he'll be and how *fast* he'll be—his father played football. I've never told him that—and oh thank you thank you thank you!"

She leapt forward and wrapped Lance in a tight hug and then kissed him on the cheek. Her breath smelled like coffee and cinnamon gum. She left him on the sidewalk then, getting into the driver's seat of the small black sedan and driving herself and Miles back onto the dusty county road.

Lance never took his eyes off the car until it was out of sight, catching a glimpse of Miles turning and looking out the rear windshield and giving him one last wave.

"*What was that?*" Patrick's voice hissed from beside him.

Lance turned, his face blank and serious. "I don't know."

"Bullshit."

Lance shrugged and pushed past the boy, their shoulders bumping. "Believe what you want. If you think I understand everything that happens to me, you're not as powerful as I thought you were."

He stepped inside the store and headed for the restroom, trying to get a grip on what had just happened. Of course, getting those instant flashes of a person's life, and yes, sometimes their future, was something he was used to. It'd happened his whole life. But he couldn't remember a single time when he'd shown *somebody else* a vision. And the weirdest part was, he hadn't even known it had happened.

Another day with the Universe dealing him more cards.

Lance sighed and pushed into the men's room, wondering why he could learn so much about a stranger's future...

But so little about his own.

[5]

Lance had explained to Leah how, ever since he'd left his hometown, he'd basically let the Universe be his navigator. Despite his own actions—as large as bus ticket purchases and as small as choosing which street to walk down—Lance had told her that, for the most part, there had always been a gentle urging from the Universe behind each decision.

"Sometimes I feel like a character in one of those open-world video games people play," he had said to her once. "I have this illusion of freedom, but my choices and options are always going to be limited to what the game designer has set out for me to accomplish."

Leah had actually liked this metaphor. "It's like you have to complete one level before you unlock and move on to the next."

He had looked at her then, smiled. "Yes. Ever since the night Mom died, that's exactly what it's been like. Just a series of levels..."

Leah, taking the metaphor even deeper—because really, she'd jump onto any real-world comparison that could help explain what Lance was going through—asked, albeit a bit cautiously, "There's usually a big boss battle at the end of video games. The one ultimate bad guy. Beat the boss, win the game, right?"

Lance nodded. "True."

"So..." And it sounded silly, she knew that, but she had to ask. "Do you think you're going to have to face a final boss? I mean, you've certainly taken out your share of smaller bosses already, right? But do you think there's something ... bigger? Is there an end to the game?"

Lance had considered this for a long time. They'd been staying in a chain hotel among a cluster of several others just like it on a strip of highway by a regional airport, and the sound of a jet coming in to land had drowned out all other noises while Leah waited for his response. Finally, he said, "Death."

"What?"

"I think death is the final boss."

Leah said nothing.

"Death is everybody's final boss," Lance said. "And unfortunately ... it's undefeated."

They'd been lying in bed, and at this, Leah had rolled over and propped herself up on her elbow to look at him. "What are you saying?"

Lance had kept staring at the ceiling, where a smoke detector was winking its tiny green light. "I'm saying that in the end, we all lose the game. Which is why it's important to make the most of our time playing it."

"But what does that mean for you?"

He'd turned his head and looked at her then. "Leah, I'm not immortal."

"I *know* that, dummy."

He had nodded. "It means I'm going to keep doing exactly what I do now."

She hadn't known why, but she'd gotten slightly frustrated at this. Maybe it was because the truth of what he was saying weighed so heavily on their future together. "You're going to keep going around following the Universe's voice, doing its bidding until the day you die ... or quite possibly something *kills* you."

"Yes. Or until the Universe tells me I can stop."

This had surprised her, and she was a bit ashamed to admit that the prospect of such a thing happening excited her. "You really think that might happen? One day you might just get to ... what, retire?"

He shrugged. "In a realm of infinite possibilities, I can't see why it wouldn't be one of them."

They'd said no more after that, falling asleep to the sounds of planes taking off and landing, full of people who knew exactly where they'd be tomorrow.

That conversation had taken place less than two weeks ago, which might as well have been a different lifetime. That night in the hotel, Leah had hoped that one day she'd be able to more fully understand what it was like to be Lance Brody, to comprehend the impossibilities that seemed to be his life, and to share in his journey with him. But now, here *she* was, listening to the whispers of the Universe, letting the sudden urges and unexplained intuitions result in each next turn and new road.

Beneath the sounds of the radio and the traffic and the constant hum of the Beetle's tires and the chatter of her own thoughts, that pounding-drum heartbeat was always there, calling to her, pulling her closer and closer and closer.

For nearly two days she'd followed it west, stopping only to eat and sleep.

The Beetle had rolled through Pennsylvania, Ohio, Indiana and Illinois in nearly a straight line before making a slight climb north into Iowa and then, with that ever-present heartbeat in her subconscious growing a bit louder, the tug in her gut getting a little more forceful, like she was getting butterflies before a big first date, sloped back down into Nebraska. These were all states that Leah had never visited before, but she barely noticed any of the landscape or scenery passing by outside the car's windows. She was solely focused on getting to Lance, following the pull. Nothing else mattered.

She wondered if this was what it was always like for Lance, being so intent on his purpose that he couldn't stop to enjoy the beauty of things around him.

No, Leah thought, imagining all the good times they'd managed to have together in such a short period of time. *He's figured out how to balance it. Hopefully I'll figure it out too.*

But she wasn't going to give herself too much grief about it. The mission at hand was not exactly minor league. She was in hot pursuit of the Light's most powerful soldier, who was currently being kidnapped by three unique forces of Evil.

Man, Leah thought and smirked. *It really does sound like a video game.*

She was tired; her mind was wandering. She'd been driving for hours with no breaks, ever since that drumbeat had gotten louder. She knew she was getting closer. Looking back at the last couple days now, she realized what a blur they'd become. How she could hardly remember turning the steering wheel or pressing the accelerator. She hadn't consulted a single road sign or used her phone's GPS once. The entire trip had been...

Controlled.

It was damn freaky, if she was being honest, and again she marveled over how Lance had spent his entire life shrouded in this feeling.

She took a highway exit and figured she owed herself a break now, would pull into the first gas station or fast-food restaurant she could find and take care of things. She tried to think back to the last time she'd eaten and realized that she should definitely be hungry by now.

But I'm not, she thought. Which she found odd. Even odder still, when the gas station and convenience store appeared up ahead, she didn't slow the Beetle down at all. Nor did she when the row of restaurants came next. Instead, her eyes stayed looking straight ahead, driving past it all.

Two miles later, the commercial section of the town faded away and was replaced by flat farmland as far as she could see on the left and turnoffs for small residential neighborhoods on her right. Ahead, perched between two roads bordering a large expanse of land that was mostly a smooth black parking lot with a long one-story brick building set back from the road, an elegant sign advertised Fuller's Funeral Home and Crematorium.

Leah felt her heart plummet, her worst nightmare instantly becoming a possible reality. *He's dead. I'm too late and they've killed him and his body is in that building and ... what am I supposed to do now?*

The Universe's pull on her guided her to the Fuller's

Funeral Home and Crematorium sign ... and then past the turn-in.

Leah sighed heavily. She'd been sitting upright as she'd approached the funeral home, and now she fell back into the seat with great relief. She didn't want to look back, happy to be moving away from the funeral home and the quick burst of dread it had induced in her, but she could not squash the urge for one last flick of her eyes to the rearview. In that last glance, as the building grew smaller and smaller behind her, she saw a gray plume of smoke begin moving quickly across the funeral home's parking lot. No, not smoke. As Leah slowed the car and leaned closer to the mirror, she saw the gray smoke was actually a large cat that had begun to scamper away from near the funeral home's road sign and was now heading down the side of the building. She leaned back in her seat again and shook her head. *I'm a mess*, she thought. *I'm starting to see things.*

A quarter mile later, with that internal pull stronger than ever, she made a right turn into one of the neighborhoods and navigated streets lined with modest homes until up ahead, the last house on a dead-end street caught her eye, sitting back from the road across the cul-de-sac. The sun had settled below the horizon and the clouds were slate gray, giving everything the look of newspaper print, cold and lifeless. The house at the end of the street was a narrow two-story with gray vinyl siding and a dirty red minivan in the driveway. The porch lights were on, throwing weak yellow orbs against the gray to battle the just-arrived dusk, and a narrow flower bed ran along the length of the front of the house, peppered with neatly trimmed bushes and what was left of a few plants after winter had taken its toll.

Leah pulled the Beetle into the driveway, stopping and parking just behind the red minivan. As soon as she killed the ignition, two things happened. First, a dog started barking from somewhere behind them, small, high-pitched yips that carried across the neighborhood. Second, the drumbeat heart in her head stopped.

"This is the place," Pamela Brody's voice said from next to her.

Leah jumped in the seat so hard the Beetle rocked. "*Shit!* Can't you give me a warning or something?" she asked. But despite the scare, she was happy to see the ghost of Pamela Brody next to her. It had been a long trip with no company and she was happy to have somebody to talk to. "This ... isn't what I expected," she said.

"Things rarely are," Pamela said. The woman had her eyes trained on the front of the house. She nodded toward it. "Go."

And Leah was moving. She flung open the car door and jogged up the small sidewalk. Was halfway there when she realized she had absolutely zero plan, and then nearly stumbled as she came to an abrupt stop when she considered that if Lance was inside this house, then it was likely the Reverend and the Surfer and the boy named Patrick—*whatever* he *is*—would be inside too. And what could Leah do against any of them?

But...

This isn't what I expected.

Suddenly, everything changed. Leah felt as though the rug was being pulled from under her, like the Universe had played the ultimate bait-and-switch game with her head. She knew at once that Lance wasn't here.

Pamela Brody's words from the first time they'd met echoed in Leah's head. *Sometimes he would get so fixated on what he thought was the right answer, he'd miss the obvious truth in front of him.*

Leah had followed the Universe's pull, but she'd not stopped to think that it was pulling her toward something other than what she wanted.

Before Leah could think any more about where she was or what she was doing, the house's front door opened and a woman stepped out onto the stoop.

"Thank the stars! I knew you would come," the woman said, her eyes brimming with tears. "I've always known!"

[6]

THE WOMAN RUSHED across the sidewalk and hugged Leah like they were old friends who hadn't seen each other in years, maybe decades. She was about Leah's height, and very thin, but the arms wrapped around Leah's torso felt strong. The woman was wearing blue jeans with what looked like white and yellow paint speckled across the front of both thighs, and a red sweater that smelled of fabric softener and grease. Her hair was such a dark brown that it appeared nearly black in the fading light, and full of such beautiful natural curls that Leah was instantly reminded of the redheaded girl from the Peanuts cartoons who was always gushing proud about her hair ... though Leah couldn't remember her name.

The woman released Leah from the hug and then stood back and held her at arm's length, a gentle grip on each of Leah's shoulders. "My stars...," the woman said. "To finally see you. I just..." The tears came again, and the woman laughed and shook her head and released Leah's shoulders to wipe her eyes with the cuff of her sweater. "Goodness, Maya," the woman said, laughing again. "Pull yourself together. I'm sorry, it just, you know, with everything happening with Noah, well ... you understand." She wiped away the last of the tears and smiled at Leah. "Come on in," she said, turning and motioning over her shoulder for Leah to follow her into the house. "I hope burgers are okay."

Leah stood on the sidewalk and watched the woman all the way to the stoop, her head dizzy with confusion and...

Her stomach growled.

And hunger.

Maya reached the door and turned back and saw Leah still standing where she'd left her and said, almost as if she were embarrassed, "I can make something else ... if you'd like. I didn't really know what you'd want, but I figured, hey, everybody likes hamburgers, right? This is still America, last time I checked." She smiled, but Leah could see she was fighting back a fear that she'd done something wrong, offended Leah somehow.

Leah, who this woman named Maya had apparently been expecting for long enough to have prepared a meal for, and possibly

(*To finally see you.*)

much longer.

Leah stayed put for just a few more seconds, the light fading fast around her as the sun finished its descent. A breeze whipped around the house and Leah brushed her hair out of her face. None of this made any sense. This wasn't what she wanted. She wanted to get back in the car to go and find Lance.

But...

Leah doubted very much the Universe would have guided her halfway across the country to this house in a middle-of-nowhere Nebraska town if there wasn't a very good reason for it.

Her stomach growled again, and when it did, Leah walked

toward the house, telling herself she was about to do exactly what Lance would do.

Never turn down a free meal.

Inside the house, that smell of grease from the cooked hamburgers Leah had picked up on Maya's sweater intensified, and the aroma rushed a flip-book of memories through Leah's mind: diner after diner, truck stop after truck stop that she and Lance had stopped at during their time together as they had traveled up the East Coast. Somehow, the cloying scent of fried meat soothed Leah's nerves. Calmed and focused her.

I'm here for a reason, she remembered. *It's my job to figure out what that is. None of this is an accident.*

The house was small but tidy and full of bright colors. She entered into a foyer that was really nothing more than a small square of linoleum with a coatrack and a tiny rectangular table just in front of the stairs leading up to the second floor. To the right, the living room's carpet was still fresh with vacuum cleaner stripes, and the blanket on the sofa was folded neatly with two decorative pillows framing it on either side. In the corner of the room, wedged between the television stand and a long cabinet whose top was adorned with knickknacks, Leah saw that Maya still had her Christmas tree up, bursting with ornaments and colored lights. The sight of the Christmas tree caused a sharp pang of sadness as Leah remembered and then pushed away the memory of her and Lance's rental house in Travelers Rest, and how for a few short, special days everything had seemed so perfect.

Before it had gone to hell.

Leah saw all these things in the living room—the recently vacuumed carpet, the tidied-up sofa, the tree—and the point that Maya had definitely been expecting her—or expecting *somebody*—further hit home. But these were not the things that Leah found her gaze drawn to. Instead, she was completely focused on the walls.

She stood on that small square of linoleum in front of the stairs and slowly panned around the room. There must have been fifty paintings filling the living room walls, canvases of all sizes hanging almost haphazardly, as if their only job was to simply fill all available space. They continued on from the living room, lining both sides of the short hallway that led to what must be where the kitchen and dining room were, because that was where Maya was standing, a grin on her face as she watched her new guest absorb the surroundings. Leah looked ahead, saw that the paintings continued up the stairs as well. These were bigger works, the biggest that Leah had seen so far, as if the stairway itself was a private art gallery installation, a journey not just from one floor to another but through the artist's mind.

The subjects of these canvases covered the entire gamut of possibilities. Leah saw landscapes and abstracts and portraits. She saw everything and nothing, because the entire scene swirled your thoughts, wanted you to look everywhere and nowhere at the same time. It was a carnival fun house of art.

From the end of the short hallway, Maya said, "I'm a bit of a painter, if you haven't noticed. Oh"—she waved a dismissive hand—"silly me. I'm sure you already knew that."

Leah remembered the speckling of white and yellow paint she'd seen on the woman's jeans. "I see," was all Leah could force out. Tried on a smile of her own, hoped it didn't betray how uncomfortable she suddenly felt.

Maya laughed, motioned for Leah to join her. She vanished to the left and Leah heard the clattering of plates being moved, the rustling of a plastic bag. Leah walked down the hall, looking straight, ignoring the paintings that felt as though they were closing in on her. She followed the scent of the grease.

The kitchen, thankfully, was devoid of all paintings except one—a big yellow sun hanging above the sink window. But, Leah quickly noticed, that wasn't exactly true. The front of the refrigerator was decorated with several pieces of art fastened with neat squares of black magnets. Unlike the art on the walls, these pieces were not arranged in a splatter pattern but in two ordered rows going down the length of the fridge and freezer doors side by side. Also unlike the art on the walls, these pieces were not the work of a skilled hobbyist or professional. These were sloppy watercolors and paint-by-numbers. A few freehand sketches that looked like they were supposed to be superheroes. These were the work of a child, put on display by a proud parent.

Noah, Leah thought. *Outside, she said something about Noah.*

Maya moved in front of the fridge, blocking Leah's view as she pulled open one of the doors and grabbed bottles of condiments. She set ketchup and mustard and mayonnaise on the kitchen counter next to the stove, where she'd already laid out two plates and the bag of buns. Six burgers were piled on a third plate; the cast-iron griddle splotched with hardening grease was protruding from the sink where it had been tossed.

The sight of the food brought Leah's thoughts back front and center. She needed to focus on Maya. Accept the woman's hospitality and, for the time being, at least, be the person Maya thought she was. The expected guest. Hopefully, she'd be able to begin piecing together what any of this had to do with anything. The sooner she could do that, Leah figured, the sooner she could be on her way to Lance.

Maya had pulled two buns from the bag and set one on each plate, used a fork to place a burger on each. She gestured for Leah to join her. "Come help yourself," she said and then popped the top on the ketchup and squeezed some onto her own patty.

Leah fixed her burger and then sat at the table, where she could look out the sliding glass door that led to the backyard. Darkness had almost completely fallen, but Leah could still barely make out the swing set near the end of the property, just before a tall wooden privacy fence that bordered the yard. There was a pair of dirty child-sized sneakers on the doormat.

"I've got water, tea, milk, apple juice, uhh..." Leah turned and saw Maya once again in the fridge, digging around. "A couple wine coolers, if you want something stronger. Oh, and root beer."

Leah had consumed so many coffees and energy drinks over the last couple days that the thought of anything other than water made her stomach churn. She felt like she needed to flush out her whole system. "Water is fine, please. Thank you."

Maya filled a glass from a pitcher from the fridge and then grabbed a root beer for herself, brought the drinks to the table. Then, before sitting down, she headed over to a tall narrow cabinet that served as the pantry and returned with a bag of potato chips. "I was out of frozen french fries, so these will have to do. I hope you don't mind." She dumped chips onto her plate, held the bag out for Leah.

Then they ate. Leah, famished, wolfed the burger down so

fast she almost had no memory of even chewing it. "Grab another one," Maya said. "There's plenty."

Leah didn't hesitate. She ate a couple chips and then prepared another burger. When she turned around to head back to the table, Maya's eyes were on her, and Leah realized that the woman was watching her the same way a scientist might watch a new species—as if each move she made was a fascination worth documenting. She ignored the creepy vibe that came along with this realization. Sat down and worked on the second burger.

They ate in silence, Maya suddenly acting like now that Leah was here and she'd been fed, she wasn't sure what to do next. Leah stole glances at the woman while she ate, and in the bright kitchen lights she was able to make out the wrinkles around Maya's eyes, the strands of gray laced among that dark brown hair. She guessed the woman was early forties. And now that the chitchat had dwindled and the euphoria of Leah's arrival had seemed to have passed, Maya looked a bit sad. Like a harsh reality was about to come sliding back into place, one that she'd momentarily been able to forget.

Leah finished her second burger, polished off the chips on her plate. Maya was finishing up too, and the silence between them was beginning to become too much, striking Leah with a suffocating feeling, like the walls were closing in the way the paintings in the hallway had seemed to close in on her earlier. A moment was building in the kitchen, one Leah was supposed to take charge of. She could feel it, growing in her mind. A reason...

A purpose.

From the corner of her eye, Leah spied those dirty child's sneakers resting by the door. Turned and saw the neat rows of art stuck to the fridge. She pointed to the pictures and asked, "Noah did those?"

Maya was standing now. Reached down and grabbed both the empty plates from the table. She followed Leah's pointing finger to the front of the fridge and chuckled. "He did. A couple years ago, when he was seven or eight. Unfortunately, it looks like he did not inherit my artistic ability. He has no real interest in drawing or painting. Those were mostly done at school. The sketches near the top were when he thought he *might* want to make a comic book—I'd just taken him to see one of the *Avengers* movies—until he realized how much work it would be."

She carried the plates to the sink. Dumped them in with the griddle. "Which is fine," she said. "I'd never force him into something he doesn't enjoy. He likes reading, though, which is good. And sports. Though he's not great at those, either. Right now he's a bit small for his age." Maya sighed and shrugged her shoulders, still facing the sink, away from Leah. "Oh well, he'll find what he's good at, what he loves. We all do, right?"

Leah nodded. Asked, "Where is Noah now? I'd ... I'd like to meet him."

Maya went still, her hands hidden in the sink and her gaze fixed straight ahead, out the window. Leah felt it then, a sense of something coming from the woman that had not been there before, cutting through the cheer and pleasantness. It was...

Worry, Leah realized. *She's afraid of something now.*

"Noah's missing," Maya said softly, still looking out the window. Then she cleared her throat and turned to face Leah, a strange smile spread across her lips, like Leah's question had been a trick, or a test. "Isn't that why you've finally come, to help me find my son?"

[7]

Lance could feel the change in himself.

He was tired. Tired of being stuck inside the car with the three of them, tired of their silence. Each and every one of their little idiosyncrasies—the way Patrick cleared his throat often, the way the Reverend bounced his knee, the way the Surfer would run a hand through his long hair like a girl in a shampoo commercial—were driving Lance mad. He hated them, and he hated being trapped. Hated how ineffective he felt spending his hours doing nothing, watching cars and landscapes and taking naps for no other reason than to pass the time. All of this was hardening him, his insides hot with a rage slowly boiling. He was feeling less like himself and more like a shell, empty. He felt the anger building, his veins electric with it.

That's not you.

His mother's voice shocked him, an ice bath on a sweltering day.

Remember who you are. Remember me. Remember your purpose.

Her words were so clear it was as if she were right next to

him, whispering directly into his ear, which brought to mind a great swell of memories from when he was a child. When he would get angry or frustrated or simply fed up with everything, the weight of his burden too much for a young boy to handle—his mother would sit with him and pull him close, stroke his head and lean down and whisper into his ear, telling him how special he was, how proud she was of him, how they would figure it all out together and that he wasn't alone.

But I'm alone now, Lance thought, leaning his head against the window. He'd lost his mother, and now he'd lost Leah. Been forced to cut her off from his mind.

I'm here, his mother's voice again.

Lance sighed and closed his eyes. *I wish you were*, he thought, hoping to drift away into another nap, fall into a place where the anger hopefully wouldn't follow. He tried to focus on his mother's words—*Remember your purpose*—and they did actually help. Lance knew that whatever he was headed toward had to be part of the plan, part of the grand road map that the Universe had set out for him, maybe even long before Lance had been born.

But I don't understand any of it, he thought, feeling sleep come for him.

But instead of sleep, instead of dreams, Lance jolted as another vision—another memory that was not a memory at all—shot into his mind.

He was back in his and his mother's home again, this time in the living room. He and Leah were on the couch, their feet resting on the coffee table, Leah snuggled into him the same way Lance would snuggle into his mother on those days when he was a kid and she'd whisper into his ear. The lights were dimmed, and a bowl of popcorn rested on his lap. His mother was in the recliner, her favorite blanket pulled up to her chin. A cup of tea on the small table next to the chair. Lance was using the remote control to scroll through the list of movie options on Netflix.

"Nothing too long," Leah said, grabbing a fistful of popcorn from the bowl. "I have to work early in the morning."

Lance nodded and asked if they were in the mood for a comedy or a horror.

"Comedy," Leah and his mother said in unison.

Lance nodded. "Me too."

He found one that looked promising and clicked the Play button. Leah snuggled in closer, and the smell of her shampoo mixed with the butter from the popcorn created maybe the sweetest aroma ever. His mother sneaked a hand from under the blanket to take a sip of tea, and the movie started and Lance ate some popcorn and when Leah laughed at something on-screen Lance felt a warmth spread inside him, fell in love with how in love he was with this moment, with his life.

A car door slammed and the memory that was not a memory went black, the television switched off. Lance opened his eyes and saw that the car was stopped, empty except for him. Patrick and the Reverend and the Surfer were standing in front of the hood, waiting, watching him curiously through the windshield. Behind them, sitting alone in a dry and barren field at the end of a dirt parking lot, was a ramshackle building with a slanted wooden porch and the word BBQ painted in big red letters across the roofline. Lance looked left and right, saw a handful of other cars parked alongside the Plymouth.

He was hungry but didn't want to eat. He wanted to slip away again, go back to the living room with Leah and his mother to finish the movie. He wanted to go to bed in his own bedroom at home with Leah sleeping beside him and he wanted to walk with her to work in the morning and then meet her for lunch, maybe grab a coffee at Downtown Joe, and he wanted ... he wanted to go back to that place and never leave.

He wanted that life. Always had.

Instead, he pushed open the door and stepped out of the car and was greeted by warmth. It might have only been fifty or sixty degrees, but compared to the previous days' temperatures, it was practically like stepping into a heatwave.

Patrick Cain laughed, and Lance turned to see that ugly smile on the kid's face.

"Yeah," Patrick said. "Texas weather can be fucking weird."

Lance said nothing. Pulled off his hoodie and tossed it into the back of the car. It was freeing somehow, stripping down to his T-shirt. He felt lighter, different. Or maybe the sweatshirt just needed to be washed. He needed a shower. He needed a lot of things. But most of all, at that moment he simply felt like he needed to be *himself*.

Lance joined his captors and walked across the parking lot toward the restaurant, thinking about the vision he'd just had—the second one in as many days—and wondered if maybe he was losing his mind.

The restaurant was very much alive compared to the barren landscape on which it sat. Speakers mounted in each corner played country music—old-school stuff, not the new pop-flavored tunes—and gruff voices could be heard singing along from the kitchen, accompanied by a soundtrack of clattering plates and pans and silverware, and the occasional shout that an order was ready. The walls were covered with antique signage and old license plates and faded pennants of various Texas sports teams. The flooring was rough wooden planks, uneven and wobbly, overtop what must have been an open crawlspace below, causing footfalls to thud heavily and reverberate, the boards creaking and squeaking—the sound of horror films, the strange noise in the night that always made the guy or gal get out of bed to go investigate. The moment they realized they weren't really alone.

Perhaps fifteen tables filled the dining room, most of them occupied, and Lance and his three acquaintances sat at a round table in the front left corner, Lance with his back against the wall, pinned in. The Surfer on his left, the Reverend on his right. Patrick sat across from Lance, stared at him like he was an exhibit at the zoo. Lance stared back, didn't care. It was hot inside, the ceiling fans doing little to mitigate the heat, and Lance thought that during the hotter months people must feel like *they* were the meat being cooked when they came to eat.

"What are you thinking about?" Patrick asked, again with that tone that seemed to indicate he thought he was catching Lance in the act of something.

"Human meat," Lance said, just as their waitress arrived with their orders.

Patrick held Lance's stare for just a moment longer before turning and smiling at the waitress and thanking her as she set his plate in front of him. She did the same with Lance's and the Reverend's food, then put a hand on her hip and looked at the Surfer. "Sure I can't get you anything? You gonna just sit and watch your friends eat all this good food?" She smiled big, friendly.

The Surfer shook his head. Stayed silent.

"He has an eating disorder," Lance said, already shoveling pulled pork into his mouth.

The waitress's face fell. "Oh, I'm so sorry." She thought for a moment. "You know, I had a cousin who was bulimic and—"

"No, it's not that," Lance said. "He doesn't—"

"Thank you *so* much," Patrick Cain said, his voice letting everyone know the conversation was over. "I think we have everything we need."

The waitress nodded and said she'd be back to check on them in a few minutes and then walked off, the floorboards creaking beneath her steps, Alan Jackson filling the silence that was left in her wake. Patrick glared at Lance. Lance picked up his cornbread and took a bite, stared back.

"What are you doing?" Patrick asked.

Lance shrugged. "Just making conversation. You three are a bore to talk to." He went back to work on his food.

Truth was, Lance didn't know why he'd said what he said. Maybe it *was* boredom, or maybe it was just his passive-aggressive way of letting out some of the anger that was festering inside him. The anger ... and the confusion. Why not have a little fun at his captors' expense?

Five minutes later, Lance's plate was empty and he was hoping to ask the waitress if they had coffee. But then he heard the dog.

Somehow, over the sounds of the patrons' chatter and the noises from the kitchen and the music from the speakers, Lance heard the dog bark. Twice, and then four times in fast succession. He looked around the restaurant, saw that none of the other diners seemed to have noticed or cared. He looked at everyone at the table with him in the corner, found the Reverend and Patrick with their heads down, eyes on their food, and the Surfer leaning tipped back in his chair, arms crossed, looking straight ahead at nothing in particular.

It came again, the barking. Two more times, these sounding urgent.

And that was when Lance realized something familiar about the sound—not a recognition of the bark itself, but the way in which he was perceiving it. The barks were coming from inside his head, a voice of the dead.

Lance pushed his chair back and stood fast, causing the Surfer to stand too, the bodyguard ready to take action. The barking noise echoed in Lance's head again, and this time there was a pull along with it. A gentle tug toward the kitchen.

Lance slid behind the Reverend's chair, bumping the man forward, started walking toward the kitchen's swinging metal door, weaving between the tables.

"*Lance*," Patrick called after him. "Stop."

Lance rolled his eyes, turned and called, "Just headed to the restroom." But then he pushed through the swinging door and stepped into the kitchen. It was hotter back here, much hotter, and a few of the staff turned and saw him and none of them seemed to know what to say. Lance ignored them and his eyes locked onto the restaurant's back door, a big heavy thing with a push bar in the middle and a crooked illuminated exit sign hanging from the ceiling above. He took three quick strides and reached out and grabbed the bar and pushed, a cooler burst of outside air rushing in and greeting him. The sun was high in the sky and bright, and Lance stepped out and shielded his eyes against the glare, letting his vision adjust. The door slammed closed loudly behind him.

Standing on a rickety back deck with a set of two wide stairs in front of him, he was greeted with another bark, and this time the noise hit him from an actual direction, signaling the location of its source. Lance looked down to the bottom of the steps and saw a yellow Labrador standing and wagging its tail in a blur of speed.

More specifically, it was the ghost of a yellow Labrador, not a pup but fully grown, and staring directly at Lance.

Lance had not yet turned twenty-five years old, but he had a lifetime of experience in dealing with spirits that had yet to pass on. In that moment, he quickly scrubbed through a highlight reel of his encounters in his mind, trying to remember if he'd ever seen the spirit of an animal before. Nothing jumped out at him, so this might be the first. Looking at the Labrador, the way its eyes seemed to be pleading, Lance found he wasn't surprised. If any animal was going to have a soul, wouldn't it be a dog? Man's best friend?

This thought process took only a microsecond, Lance's brain spinning fast. Then gave the dog what it had apparently been waiting for—a simple recognition that Lance could in fact see it—because when Lance walked down the two wide steps and said, "Hi there," the dog jumped once in the air and then spun around in three quick circles, tail whipping back and forth even faster than before. Then it ran off, away from the deck and heading toward a single dumpster that was set back from the building, vanishing behind it. "Hey, wait!" Lance called from his mind, jogging in the same direction. The dog poked his head from the back of the dumpster as if to say *I'm still here* and then was gone again. Lance jogged the last few steps and rounded the corner of the dumpster. Found the dog sitting in the dead grass among a scattering of bits of trash that had escaped the bin.

Lance nearly tripped over the man's body.

Next to the dog, lying facedown in the grass, was a man

dressed in tattered clothing. Dirty jean shorts that looked several sizes too big, and a red T-shirt that Lance at first had mistakenly thought was covered in blood. There was a large hole in the right shoulder of the shirt, and Lance could see the markings of a tattoo on the skin beneath. The man's hair was shaggy, and a small breeze rustled the strands that here hanging down the back of his neck. One of the man's arms was outstretched in front of him, as if he'd been crawling and had been frozen midstride, or as if he'd been reaching out for something.

The dog barked again. Spun in another circle and then lay down in the grass next to the man's body, nuzzling its snout up next to the man's face, the dog's eyes glancing up at Lance.

"Right," Lance said, and he was moving again. He dropped down to his knees and reached for the man's shoulders and gripped them gently, feeling how frail they seemed beneath his fingers. Lance slowly turned the man over on his back, the one arm remaining outstretched above the man's head flopping over onto the grass with a sickening thud.

"Sir," Lance said, leaning in closer. "Sir, can you hear me?"

The man's eyes were closed, his lips chapped and cracking, his mouth slightly open and askew, as if he was puzzled. But ... he wasn't dead. At least not yet. There was a very subtle rise and fall to the man's thin chest, ribs visible beneath the fabric of the T-shirt.

Stroke, maybe? Lance thought. *Heart attack?*

He reached out to put a finger to the side of the man's neck to check for a pulse but stopped midway there. A necklace of thin rawhide was around the man's neck, loose and drooping beneath the collar of his T-shirt. Lance gingerly pinched the necklace between his thumb and index finger and pulled it up toward the man's chin. Something was attached to the necklace. A circle of dull metal that Lance at first mistook for a quarter with a hole punched into the top, but when he leaned in closer, he saw that the silver circle was actually blank except for one word etched into it.

SUNNY.

Lance's eyes darted up, saw the dog sitting in the grass by the man's body, staring back at Lance expectantly. Lance lowered his gaze and found the same strand of rawhide tied around the dog's neck, the same silver circle. Looked back to the version he held in his hand, and then back to the dog. Emotions rushed at him, a profound sadness for the scene he'd stumbled into. He took a deep breath, fought back a tingling in his eyes. He looked back to the dog. "Hi, Sunny," he said.

The dog's tail thumped.

Lance understood. The dog was dead, but he'd not left his human. How long had this spirit friend of this down-on-his-luck man remained by his side? How long had the man worn the reminder of his lost companion around his neck?

Long enough for the dog to save him, was the answer.

Save him.

The world was alive around him again and Lance jumped up, turning and sprinting back to the restaurant. The back door had no knob or lever on the outside, locking him out, so Lance pounded on the door with both his fists.

"Somebody call an ambulance!"

The door exploded open, but it wasn't a restaurant employee who met Lance across the threshold. It was the Surfer, his eyes narrowed to slits. Lance didn't care—he pushed past the creature, feeling a wave of revulsion as their skin connected, like he'd just caught a whiff of something spoiled, and yelled again for somebody to call for help. The kitchen staff, startled, gathered around him, eyes wide while Lance quickly explained. Then they moved in a rush. One went toward a phone on the wall by what looked like a small office, and another bounded out the back door to take a look for himself. He came back a few seconds later, out of breath.

"It's Jerry!" he called to the man who'd gone to the phone.

"You know him?" Lance asked, watching from the corner of his eye as the Surfer leaned against the wall by a walk-in cooler, arms crossed, waiting.

"Drifter," the cook said. "Comes by once in a while. We give him left-overs." Then the man lowered his head, rubbed at his eyes. "Christ, Mary and Joseph ... poor bastard. He was ... shit, he was a nice enough guy." The man looked at Lance, and Lance saw there was genuine concern in his eyes, empathy. "Do you think ... ah hell ... we should have tried to do more for him."

Lance wanted to say something but couldn't find any words.

"He used to always have a dog with him," the cook said, looking up suddenly and heading toward the door. "I wonder where he is."

Lance never got to see what happened once the paramedics arrived, because as soon as the cook headed out the kitchen's back door, the Surfer was moving toward Lance, his arms flexed at his sides, and Lance knew he'd done all he was going to be allowed to. He held up a hand, signaling for the Surfer to stop. "It's fine," Lance said, "I'm going." Then he flipped the Surfer the bird, just for good measure. Like before, why not have some fun, right?

The Surfer didn't care, just nodded toward the door.

Back in the parking lot, the four of them moved across the hardpacked dirt toward the Plymouth. Lance was just reaching for his door handle when Patrick Cain grabbed his wrist, hard and fast, like a snake striking from the grass.

"You don't seem to understand how this works, Lance," Patrick hissed, his dark eyes practically on fire. "You're ours now. The old you, all the things you used to do ... dead. It stops today." He gripped Lance's wrist tighter. "This is your final warning."

Lance felt the pain in his wrist and he heard the words Patrick was saying, but at the same time, he felt nothing, heard nothing. He stared blankly into Patrick's eyes, getting lost in them, hearing something else. Then he was back, and he gave Patrick a small grin.

Patrick looked down, saw his hand gripped to Lance's wrist, and then quickly pulled his hand away. But Lance could tell that the boy knew that it was too late.

"Final warning," Patrick said again, but his voice had lost some of its gusto. He walked around the front of the car and got in.

Lance slid into the back seat and the Surfer cranked the engine and they were off again. As they pulled onto the road, Patrick Cain gave Lance a glance over his shoulder. Lance stared back, that small grin still on his face.

You messed up, Lance hoped the grin said. *You messed up, and now I know.*

[8]

MAYA WENT to the fridge and opened it, and Leah watched as the woman grabbed one of the wine coolers, held it in her hand for a second, and then must have thought better of it and put it back on the shelf, grabbing another root beer instead. She asked if Leah needed anything else, and Leah politely declined, still hanging on to what Maya had said just before, about Leah being there to help her find her son.

Maya twisted off the top of the root beer and tossed it into the garbage. She didn't join Leah at the table, instead leaning against the counter and crossing her arms, the root beer bottle clutched to her chest. She took a sip, then looked at Leah quizzically. "You know Noah is missing, don't you? I mean, why else would you be here?"

Leah didn't know how to respond. Part of her, based on the way Maya had unquestionably welcomed her—a complete stranger—into her home like they were old friends, like she'd been *expecting* Leah based on some ... well, *premonition* was the word Leah settled on, made Leah think that if she did nothing except explain that, after she'd met the ghost of her kidnapped boyfriend's mother, the Universe had simply guided her here over a nearly three-day journey, with no predetermined reason other than to just *arrive*, Maya would nod and accept this as gospel.

But another part of Leah, that part of her that was so strong at reading people, judging their character and motivations, thought that there was a good possibility that much of Maya's life had been supported by some sort of belief in ... well, *something*. Whether it was religion or simply an acceptance of a higher power, a guiding force, a great shoulder in the sky to lean on when times were tough, Leah suspected that Maya had relied greatly on it over the years, and somehow Leah was a part of it.

Again, she thought it would be better for the situation if she simply played the role she'd been assigned. She could lie by omission. Fake it till she made it. Leah knew she *was* here for a reason, and if that reason turned out to be finding Maya's son, Noah, so be it.

She just didn't understand how this little boy in this nowhere town fit into the big picture of finding Lance.

Maybe it doesn't, she thought with dismay. *Maybe he's gone for good and this is what I do now. I'm taking his place in the Universe. Helping people, fighting the darkness one road trip at a time.*

Lance had always told her that he never really understood what he was doing. Boy, did she understand that now.

The idea of Lance being gone for good was too much to dwell on, so Leah brought herself back to the kitchen, back to the woman standing with the root beer bottle dangling by its neck at her side, watching her, waiting.

"Tell me what happened," Leah said. "When was the last time you saw Noah?"

Maya, her shoulders settling with the relief that Leah was on board, or maybe it was the weight of grief pressing down, sighed and shook her head. "He's done this before, you know. It's all my fault. I know that. I should have never said what I said about his uncle."

"He's gone missing before?" Leah asked.

"Yes. Well, no. He's run off two or three times, but he always comes back. Each time on his own, like he doesn't see what the big deal is, doesn't understand why I'm so upset."

"He runs away?"

"No," Maya shook her head. "He goes off on '*adventures*.'" She laughed, but the sound was sad. "Like I said, that's my fault."

Leah understood none of this but decided to tread softly. "Why is it your fault? What did you say about Noah's uncle that"—she shrugged—"caused Noah to leave home?"

Maya left the counter and slid back into her chair at the table. Set the bottle down and gripped it with both hands. Looked at Leah and asked, "You really don't know about this?"

Leah, feeling ridiculous, decided to act omnipotent, thinking it was the best way to keep Maya talking, to get the information she needed. "It doesn't matter what I know or don't know, I want to hear the story from you, Noah's mother. I want to hear your version of things. We can decide the truth together."

Maya closed her eyes and smiled, nodding her head like Leah had just delivered a moving sermon. "Yes," she said. "Of course." She cleared her throat and took another sip of root beer. "So you know—" She caught herself. "I mean, my brother and I were orphans. Our parents were killed in a car accident when we were just two and four. I was the baby. Anyway, we went into the system. Spent our entire youth in a big stone building two towns over from where we were born. The Stonebridge Home for Children, that was its name. It was this tall tower of dark gray rock with iron accents. It looked like an asylum, honestly, like something they'd use for a horror movie. But inside it was fine. We had beds and food and friends, and the staff were mostly friendly. I don't have a tragic sob story about growing up, not really, other than, you know, my parents dying."

Maya shrugged. "Things were pretty normal all in all. But then my freshman year of high school, my brother ran off and I've never seen or heard from him since."

Maya had said this last part flatly, no hint of emotion in her voice, like she was simply stating the time. But Leah suspected this was a practiced response, one Maya had worked over the years to control, and that inside, deep down, the woman still missed her brother badly, or maybe was just really, really angry at him.

Sure enough, Maya sighed and continued. "I've never understood why, that's the thing. Like I said, we lived a pretty normal life. He had friends, even a couple short-lived girlfriends. Grades were okay. He never gave any indication that something was bothering him, or that he was planning on leaving. If he had any reason to run ... I just ... well, he would have told me."

"You two were close," Leah said. It wasn't a question. She thought of her own brother, Samuel, and how close they'd been before he'd also disappeared in high school. Only now Leah knew the truth about her brother—how he'd died at the hands of Evil—and Maya, all these years later, seemed to be just as confused by her brother's disappearance as she'd been the day he'd left.

"Very close," Maya said, nodding. "I guess that's what happens when you grow up being the only family each other have. We looked out for each other, told each other everything. I mean, sure, once we got to be teenagers, things changed a little. We were living in slightly different worlds at that point." She nodded toward Leah. "You know how it is, guys and girls in high school. Each group a mystery to the other. But still ... he was ... I could just tell, you know? He was happy. He was ... normal."

"And he just left?" Leah asked.

Maya nodded. "Yep. It was a Saturday morning. I went to find him at breakfast and he wasn't there. Nobody had seen him all morning. As far as I know, nobody has since."

"Do you...?" Leah contemplated whether she would finish the question, and Maya beat her to the punch.

"Do I think my brother's dead?"

Leah nodded.

Maya studied her across the table, looked down at the root beer bottle and then back up to Leah. *She thinks I know the answer*, Leah realized. *She thinks I know whether her brother is dead or not, but she won't ask. She wants to, but she won't. She wants her son back right now. That's what's most important to her.*

"I have to accept the idea that he might be," Maya finally said. "It's the only explanation as to why he's never tried to find me, to reach out and reconnect."

Leah knew better than most that there were a lot of explanations for things happening that most people would never even be able to conceptualize, because the reasons went so far beyond their basic understanding of what it was to live on this earth.

Lance had taught her that.

The story of Maya's brother's disappearance felt like it could grow roots, take hold and become something bigger entirely, but Leah had to let it go, had to remember why Maya was telling her the story in the first place. Leah wasn't here to find the missing brother, she was here to find the missing son.

"So what does this have to do with Noah being missing?"

Maya was quiet for a minute, her eyes focused on something over Leah's shoulder, thinking. "I guess a part of it was me wanting to give Noah a better idea of who his uncle was. To say that my brother had just up and left one day felt ... wrong. Hard to explain to a kid, you know? And to say that he might be dead, well, nobody wants to dump that sort of story on a child. So I embellished a bit." Maya's cheeks turned red. "I told Noah that my brother was very strong and very brave, and that he ran away to have grand adventures all over the world." She laughed. "I had been reading him *The Lion, the Witch and the Wardrobe* at the time, and when I told him this, Noah nodded his head like he understood completely, and he said, 'Like the kids in Narnia?' And all I could do was nod my head and tell him yes, exactly like the kids in Narnia."

Leah understood why Maya was blaming herself, even though it wasn't the woman's fault. She'd been trying to be a good mother, and a good sister.

"So you see, all I managed to do was instill in my son's young mind that it was perfectly okay to run off from home to have adventures, and that the things of fantasy stories were actually real, just waiting for somebody to go find them." Maya nodded toward the refrigerator, where Noah's artwork was hanging. "That comic book idea he had ... he can't draw, but the kid has got a great imagination. Always has. So, of course he'd want to chase that. To go find his own Narnia, tell his own stories."

Leah thought about all this. "The other times that Noah left, did you ever call the police?"

Maya nodded. "Every time, of course. The first time, I thought the worst. When I called him down for breakfast and he didn't answer and then I went up to his room and found it empty, I had a panic attack. The whole room started spinning and I ... I couldn't breathe. It took all I had to get back downstairs, to check the front yard and the back, just to make sure I wasn't overreacting and that he'd just somehow slipped out to play without me noticing. I was practically in hysterics when I called 911."

"You said that Noah always comes home on his own," Leah said. "So does that mean the police were never able to actually find him?"

"Correct." Then Maya's eyes got wide and she held up her hands. "Oh, but don't think I blame them, or that they weren't doing their best. Because they were. They went all out, sending cars all around town, checking the parks, the school ... Noah's favorite restaurants. They canvased the neighborhood and the ones close by. But"—she smirked—"he's a little boy. And I guess he's good at hiding.

"That first time, he walked right through the front door at a little past eight. He had his little backpack on and he looked completely ... normal. Like nothing had happened at all. He almost seemed confused when I broke down crying and rushed to him. I picked him up and squeezed him tight and thought I might never let him go again."

"Where did he go?" Leah asked.

Maya shook her head. "I have no idea."

"He didn't tell you?"

"No. Well..." Maya smiled. "He says he goes to his wardrobe. That's all he'll tell me."

"Like the kids from Narnia," Leah said.

Maya nodded. "See? I did that. I put that in his head."

"What's in the backpack?" Leah asked and felt a quick punch of sadness at the image of Lance's backpack currently sitting on the floorboard of her Beetle, missing its owner. "You say he always comes back on his own, so what is he taking the time to pack and take with him?"

Maya made a face like she thought the question was irrelevant. "Normal stuff a kid might have. A flashlight, some of his favorite books, a few small toys. Usually a couple snacks and juice boxes. Nothing that would tell you where he was going."

Leah nodded. "Does he always carry a flashlight in his backpack? Like, when he goes to school?"

Maya thought about this. "No, I guess not. It's a little plastic Iron Man flashlight he usually keeps on his nightstand. I see it there every night when I tuck him in bed. I guess he takes it with him to find his way home in the dark."

The idea of a little boy walking alone at night, walking purposely through the streets of the quiet, empty town, gave Leah a chill. It was how a lot of unhappy movies started—the night the kid went missing. Sometimes never to be seen again.

Like Maya's brother.

Like Leah's.

"You keep calling the police," Leah said. "Every time."

"Absolutely. You see the news these days, hear the horror stories. I'd never be able to look at myself in the mirror again if something had actually happened to him and I'd just sat back and assumed my little boy had just gone off to play on one of his adventures again.

"The officers are very understanding," Maya said. "Better safe than sorry, they agree."

"But you didn't call them this time," Leah said.

Maya shook her head. "No. I didn't. This time was different."

"Because he's been gone longer?" Leah asked. "Wouldn't that make you more inclined to call them than not?"

Maya looked across the table at Leah for a long time then, like she was trying to read something behind Leah's eyes. She picked up her root beer and finished off the bottle, leaned back in the chair and rested her hands in her lap. "No. It wasn't that. I got ... I got a feeling. Stronger than maybe anything I've felt before. A feeling that today was finally the day for..." She nodded toward Leah.

"The day for what?" Leah asked.

Maya was quiet for several seconds, a momentary blip of confusion, and maybe concern, flashing across her face. Then, she slowly smiled. "You *are* testing me," she finally said.

"I'm sorry?"

"That's why you're asking the things you're asking, why you're digging. You're testing me, waiting for me to prove it to you."

Leah was now even more lost than she was before.

"Prove what to me?"

Maya smiled. "My faith."

The woman pushed her chair back from the table and stood. "Come on," she said. "Let me show you something. Then you'll see."

Leah wasn't really given a choice. Maya was out of the

kitchen and climbing the stairs. Leah stood and hurried after the woman, the blur of colors from the paintings in the hallway streaking by as she went, the large canvases on the wall heading up the stairs looming and imposing, like they were keeping an eye on her as she went. She ignored them, looking down at each step in front of her as she climbed up.

At the top of the stairs, Leah stood and found Maya standing in a doorway at the far right end of the hallway. The room was bursting with bright white light. Leah walked slowly toward it, like a moth drawn to flame, and when she got close, Maya stepped inside and pointed to the wall to her right.

Leah crossed the threshold, followed Maya's finger to where it was pointing, and then gasped.

[9]

Considering that Leah had recently discovered her own ability to see and speak with lingering souls, and had garnered firsthand experience in dealing with the forces of Evil, the idea that what she now saw on the wall in Maya's upstairs room would give her such a shock, cause all the hairs on her arms and the back of her neck to prickle and send a wave of complete disbelief and incomprehension to temporally block out all other thoughts, was nearly comical.

They were only paintings, after all.

The room Leah and Maya were standing in was a bedroom that Maya had converted into a studio. There was a daybed against one wall, just beneath the window, but otherwise the room was filled with nothing but paint supplies stuffed into shelving and overflowing from boxes lining the floor. In one corner, a large drop cloth spread out like a white pond on the carpeted floor, an easel and stool and small table sitting atop it. Leah imagined Maya perched on that stool in the corner, her back to the rest of the world, and thought if the scene itself had been a painting it might have been called "Artist in Time-Out."

And the lights. Bright white lights burned everywhere. High-wattage bulbs in the overhead fixture and tall lamps without shades glowing all around. Leah felt like she might need sunglasses if she stayed there much longer.

As if sensing this, Maya said, "Sorry about the lights—I don't usually have them all on, unless I'm working at night. There's not a lot of natural light in this room, so I have to make my own." She smiled, and Leah didn't understand how the woman could be acting so normal right now, acting like what was happening in this room made any sense at all.

"How?" was all Leah finally managed to say, her eyes once again glued to the paintings on the wall.

She didn't try to count them, was in fact scared that the more she counted, and the higher the number got, the more surreal and terrifying the whole experience would become. Like the living room walls below, the wall at the far side of Maya's bedroom studio was covered in paintings of all sizes, full of colors and depicting a young woman in various scenes: sitting on a park bench with a mirror-perfect lake reflecting the landscape; walking down a city street in the winter with her jacket pulled up to her neck and her eyes piercing through the gray from just below her stocking cap; lying on a beach with her blond hair blowing sideways and one hand frozen as it reached up to pull it from her face; and portraits ... so many portraits. Big and small and all sizes in between. Some startlingly realistic, some in more of a cartoon fashion, some done in a Picasso style that Leah found both disturbing and oddly mesmerizing.

There was no mistaking the identity of the young woman in Maya's paintings.

It was Leah.

"I told you I could prove it to you," Maya said. She stood to the side and just in front of Leah, watching Leah's every reaction. She looked proud, accomplished.

"I...," Leah started. She took a breath and cleared her throat. Tried again, but still never took her eyes off the paintings, like the art itself had latched onto her thoughts and refused to let go. "Those are me," she said.

"Well, yeah, of course that's you. I told you, my faith is strong. You've helped me through a lot over the years. I paint these both as a reminder to be thankful and as a token of my appreciation. I've taken them to a few shows, a handful of galleries here and there, and people *love* them. I had one gentleman online offer me ten grand for this one." Maya walked to the wall and pointed to one of the Picasso-style portraits.

"You sell them?" Leah asked, suddenly even more distraught at the idea that somewhere her face or likeness was hanging in some stranger's living room or hallway. *Another* stranger, that was.

"Oh no," Maya said. "I could never. These are mine. Always. I'm not out to profit off you. That would be..." She thought for a moment, her face screwing up like she'd experienced a pain. "*Blasphemous.*"

It was a big word, *blasphemous*, and the way Maya had said it Leah knew the woman had meant it. But Leah was struggling to understand, to put the pictures on the wall together with the words Maya was speaking to her. There was a story here, one that fit together perfectly inside Maya's own imagination but to Leah was nothing more than a jigsaw puzzle missing its box, an ugly pile of cardboard pieces that could end up being anything.

(*Prove my faith. Blasphemous. You've helped me through a lot over the years.*)

All of Maya's words ran together in Leah's head, repeating

themselves over and over while Leah stared at the many renditions of herself hanging from the wall. The words grew louder and louder until they were deafening. Finally, Leah closed her eyes, shushed the voices, counted to five. When she opened her eyes, Maya was looking at her, patiently. And in that moment, Leah realized that despite Maya's apparent recognition of her and the fact that the woman had been expecting her to show up at her door, she'd never once called Leah by her name, and Leah had never formally introduced herself.

"Who is it that you think I am?" Leah asked.

As though she could read Leah's thoughts once again, Maya said, "I've never known your name. Your *real* name." She shrugged, then looked away, a sheepish grin on her face, like maybe she was embarrassed. "In my mind, I've always called you my guardian angel."

Her eyes darted back to Leah, the grin still there. "I know it sounds a little cheesy, but hey, if the shoe fits, right?"

Leah was starting to feel like she needed to sit down. It sounded completely bonkers, to think that this woman, who looked as though she was nearly twenty years older than her, considered Leah to be her guardian angel. Even *with* Leah's newfound abilities, she was having difficulty not considering the woman a little off her rocker, a few slices short of a loaf.

But...

But the damned paintings.

Maya was right. They proved a whole hell of a lot.

Leah tried to focus, tried to find the right path to go down from here. Tried to think about what Lance would do.

Confident, she told herself. *Be confident.* Then, that now-familiar adage from the Universe that, as unhelpful as it was, was also undeniable. *You're here for a reason.*

Leah collected all her thoughts, looked to the wall of paintings where the most obvious and unsettling question was made clear. "How long have you been painting me?" she asked.

Maya crossed her arms and cocked her head while she thought about it. Stared at the paintings, letting her gaze drift across them, piecing together a timeline.

"Well, of course, the earliest work isn't on the wall." She turned and gave Leah a knowing look. "The first time I sketched you, I wasn't quite the artist I am today. It was nothing but a doodle, really. I did it on the back of a napkin in the cafeteria at lunch one day."

The word *cafeteria* jumped at Leah like it might bite her, and with it, the enormity of Maya's story grew.

"I had dreamed about you," Maya continued. "Two days after my brother went missing and I thought all I'd ever do again was cry for the rest of my life, you were there. We were in the cafeteria, actually. In the dream, I mean. There were people all around, but they were frozen," Maya said. "It was like ... like the world was standing still but forgot to include me. It was a weird feeling, really. Because even though I was able to move and think, even though I appeared to be the only person left that was really alive, I felt terribly alone." Maya shrugged. "Does that make sense? I felt left out. Like everyone was in on a big joke at my expense."

Maya's face went blank for a moment, as if the memory was threatening to pull her back down into that dark place, that scary moment of her dreams where she thought the world had forgotten her.

She shook her head and smiled. "Anyway. I was just about to get up from my chair and run out of the cafeteria, but then you were there. Right next to me. You reached out and took my hand and ... I just knew."

When Maya stopped there, Leah asked, "You just knew what?"

"That everything was going to be alright."

Leah said nothing.

"You didn't even speak," Maya said. "But when our hands touched, I *felt* it. I felt this great warmth and this surge of happiness, like you'd reignited a flame inside me that had been snuffed out when my brother left. You smiled at me and that flame burned and when I woke up it was still there. I carried it with me after that, and every time it started to burn down, when the heat would start to fade—times when I was feeling low, bad times during my life, like when Noah's father left us—I'd look for you in my dreams, and you'd be there. You were always there when I needed you. Always there to take my hand and get the flame burning again."

Maya's eyes were wet with tears now, and Leah was surprised to feel the own warmth of tears on her cheeks. "So, no, I don't know *who* you are," Maya said. "I only know *what* you are to me. You're the reason I've gotten this far. You're my guardian angel, and other than my love for Noah, that's the one thing I know to be an absolute truth in this world."

The room was silent for a beat, just the hum of all the lights burning the room with its bright white light. But Leah knew she had to ask the question, even though the answer was going to be impossible.

But what is *impossible?* she thought. *What do we really understand about anything in this life?*

"What year was that?" she asked. "What year was it when your brother disappeared, and you saw me in your dream?"

Maya didn't hesitate to think. "Ninety," she said. "Nineteen ninety. I'll never forget."

Leah felt another chill rush through her, and it took all her strength not to simply sit down on the floor, her legs weak. The first time Maya had seen Leah in her dreams, Leah hadn't even been born yet.

Searching for anything to say, to be able to give herself something to do to keep her mind from drowning in recent revelations, Leah said, "Leah. My name is Leah."

Maya laughed, a mixture of surprise and elation. "Well, then, *Leah*, did I pass your test?"

Leah nodded, could think of nothing else to say except, "You sure did."

Maya clapped her hands and laughed again, looking as thrilled as somebody who'd just won the grand prize. "Okay, great! So now it's my turn."

"Your turn?" Leah asked.

"Yes. Now I have a question for you."

Leah slowly nodded. "Okay ... sure."

Maya walked to the corner of the room across from her easel and stool, shuffled around some canvases that were sitting stacked on the floor, tossing a few aside as if they were insignificant before she finally said, "Ah, here it is!" and stood. She brought the painting over to Leah and held it out. "I know this might be a long shot because of the lack of detail, but do you know who this might be?"

Maya was right, there was a lack of detail. In fact, the painting was nothing but a black silhouette on a solid white background. It was a sloppy job, looked as though done in a rush. But to Leah, the image was unmistakable.

The shape was a man who was all long legs and arms, the

bulk of a backpack on his shoulders, the hood of a sweatshirt pulled over his head. He was walking away but turned back just slightly, looking back over his shoulder. Looking at Leah.

"Lance," Leah said. "His name is Lance."

[10]

TEXAS WAS big and flat and for the most part boring.

This was Lance's assessment of the state, after the Surfer had driven for what had felt like endless hours of deserted highways and rural two-lanes where the speed limits were high and the traffic was light. Lance surveyed the landscape from his spot inside the Plymouth and grew increasingly disgusted with the burnt and faded colors of everything, the lack of the smallest of hills or valleys. He missed the greens of a Virginia spring and summer, the kaleidoscope of oranges and reds of fall foliage, the pristine white of a fresh snowfall in his own backyard. He missed the looming peaks of mountains that seemed to guard the cities and towns, always lurking on the horizon.

He missed home. He missed his mother. He missed Leah.

He missed everything he loved.

He was self-aware enough to understand that his current mood and unfortunate predicament were likely infringing on his true feelings about the great state he was being ushered across. Texas, he was sure, had plenty of redeeming qualities. If nothing else, it had the Alamo. Lance had always liked the story of the Alamo. As a child, he had checked out the library's VHS copy of the old Disney movie about Davy Crockett so many times that his mother had finally bought him his own copy. He could watch it on repeat, letting his imagination take hold of him and transform him from a child in his living room into the King of the Wild Frontier. The film and the fantasy always ended the same way, with the on-screen hero fighting in his last moments from atop the Alamo as the Mexican Army overtook him, and with young Lance standing atop the couch cushions, swinging his imaginary rifle at unseen soldiers climbing up at him from the floor until the credits started to roll.

Lance doubted very much that his trio of captors would entertain a detour and pit stop for him to see in-person an icon from his childhood, he could tell that the thing called Patrick, currently slumped down in the passenger seat with his shoes on the dash and the collar of his leather jacket popped up around his neck like some sort of extra from a high school drama club's rendition of *Grease*, was still upset about what Lance had done back at the barbecue restaurant. Not the situation with the collapsed man behind the dumpster, but what had happened after, in the parking lot as the four of them were getting ready to depart. When Patrick, in a fit of anger, had made his mistake and grabbed Lance's wrist.

Lance didn't know exactly what the thing wearing the young boy's body had sensed, whether Patrick knew the full scope of what Lance had been able to do, but he'd felt enough. The boy—who wasn't *really* a boy—was powerful, more powerful than any person Lance had ever encountered before. That much had been evident from those first couple days in Travelers Rest when Lance had felt the Universe attempting to hide him from the creature that was hunting him, and how the creature had somehow still managed to track him down—*after* he'd somehow managed to also resurrect the Reverend and the Surfer. Yes, Patrick was the leader, the boss man, if you will, and Lance could be honest enough with himself to know that there was a big part of him that feared Patrick.

But he's not infallible, Lance thought, thinking of what he'd seen in the restaurant's parking lot again. And then he smiled once more at the thought of how quickly Patrick had angered when Leah had reached out to Lance in the car a couple days ago. *Whatever he is, he can feel fear just like the rest of us.*

But whatever pleasure this thought brought Lance was short-lived, because as the Surfer slowed for a stop sign and then turned left, another barren two-lane stretching ahead of them in an eternal straight path, Lance's thoughts went back to the Alamo and his childhood hero.

Will that be me? he wondered. *Am I the hero that will go down swinging against insurmountable odds, fighting a battle that's impossible to win?*

The idea that his childhood fascination with that old Disney movie and its protagonist might have somehow been the Universe preconditioning Lance to understand and accept his own destiny caused such a feeling of melancholy to wash over him that for a brief moment he felt he might get sick, heart-broken at the thought that such a pleasant fixture of his youth might have been nothing more than a tool used to prepare him for his own death.

This is what they want. His mother's voice again, loud and present in his mind. *Don't let them tear you down. You are stronger than them. You've kept them out of your mind, don't let them into your heart.*

Lance closed his eyes and took a deep breath, filling his

lungs until he felt they might burst, then breathed out, trying to heed his mother's words, reach into the darkness and take hold of them, never wanting to lose her voice.

He opened his eyes, felt calmer. He stared out the window as the sun began to set. Far off on the horizon, a line of oil rigs moved in a slow, synchronous rhythm. At this distance, they looked like nothing more than a line of farmers, working the fields and picking their harvest by hand. Half an hour later, the horizon was dotted with industrial windmills, spinning lazy and proud, like a window box of daisies dancing in the wind. The two scenes were a striking contrast to each other. Different methods to achieve a similar result: to produce energy. Some would say one method was from the past, the other the way of the future. Others, those who were more cynical (or perhaps had more of their personal wealth tied up in one industry or the other), might even say it could boil down to destruction versus sustainability or...

Yes, Good versus Evil.

Lance sighed. He needed to get out of the car. It wasn't a good sign when he found himself falling into a philosophical pit comparing the different sectors powering the world's energy initiatives to a large-scale war of the cosmos.

"Finally," the thing called Patrick said from the passenger seat, pulling his feet down from the dash and sitting up. "*Finally.*"

Feeling a sudden chill of anticipation mixed with dread, Lance turned away from the window and angled himself to look ahead through the windshield. The first thing he saw was the Ferris wheel, looming tall against the rapidly darkening sky.

"Oh boy," Patrick said excitedly, turning around to face Lance. "Can you feel it?"

Lance said nothing.

"It can feel you," Patrick said, closing his eyes and throwing his head back like he was suddenly riding a wave of ecstasy. He breathed in deep, his body shuddering with a chill. "It can feel you."

Lance looked past the boy, kept his eyes glued to the Ferris wheel as the Surfer drove right up to a tall chain-link gate that blocked off entry to the theme park beyond. Much like everything around it and before it that Lance had seen, the grounds of the park were abandoned and looked to be long forgotten.

It was a ghost town.

A ghost park, rather.

And yes, Lance realized. He *could* feel it.

One of the many veils of uncertainty that had clouded his vision of the future over the last few days had been suddenly ripped away and he could see so clearly now. His moment was coming, and it was coming fast. Lance bent down and craned his neck and continued to stare up at the Ferris wheel reaching into the sky, and he knew...

He'd arrived at his Alamo.

[11]

Lance had explained to Leah how he had spent his life being very cautious about who he let know about his abilities, who he shared his secret with. In fact, before the night his mother had died and Lance had been forced to leave Hillston, the number of people inside his inner circle of trust was essentially only his mother and Marcus Johnston, the once-police now mayor and longtime family friend. Leah had been welcomed into that circle shortly after, and, as Lance told it, as his travels and adventures had continued over the next couple months, he'd found himself telling more and more people who he really was.

"They deserved to know," he had told her. "They *needed* to know, because of what was at stake, or because of their own history. Funny thing was, almost all of them accepted what I told them as if they'd known all along, like they'd been waiting for that moment, for the truth of the world to finally be confirmed to them." He'd thought for a moment then, turning something over in his mind, testing it. He said, "Sometimes I wonder if maybe the Universe somehow manages to have me only tell the people who are worthy of the knowledge—for one reason or another."

His explanation had made sense to Leah at the time, but now she found herself presented with the same scenario. Not only did she carry Lance's secrets, but she had her own. So, the question now: In the current situation, did Maya deserve or need to know the truth? Was she worthy?

The paintings on the wall and the story of Maya having had visions of Leah before Leah had even been born, plus the silhouette image of Lance, all would have been enough in Leah's mind to make the answer to the question a resounding yes. Because there was obviously something big at work here, something that *already* knew the truth and had only been waiting for it.

But if there had been any doubt about those things being reason enough, Leah could not deny the basic fact that when she'd reached out with her mind and allowed the Universe to point her in the right direction to get Lance back, she'd followed her instinct and that beating-drum heart for two days without question or compromise and had ended up right here in this woman's home with no understanding of why.

Like Lance had said time and time again, Leah shouldn't question it but should only accept that she was exactly where she was supposed to be.

There had to be a good reason.

Which was why, when Maya had accepted Leah's answer about the name of the person in the silhouette painting being Lance, and had then asked how Leah knew him, Leah had said, "You know, why don't we go back downstairs? You've told me your story, so now I'll tell you mine."

So they were back at the kitchen table, seated across from

each other again. Maya had made a pot of coffee and Leah had politely declined any, again opting for water and imagining the look of shock and dismay on Lance's face if he'd witnessed her turning down free coffee. The thought of his smiling face, the idea of being able to share those small jokes with him again, warmed her belly more than any coffee could have.

The coffee in Maya's mug was nearly white after she'd dumped what looked like a cup of creamer into it, and Leah found herself staring into the swirls of the drink as she talked, somehow finding comfort in it. She told Maya the quickest version of the truth that she could, starting with a brief history of her own life, and then telling the story of the day that Lance had wandered into the lobby of her family's motel and the crazy, life-turned-upside-down battle of Good versus Evil journey that Leah had become a part of. She ended with what had happened in Travelers Rest, with the forces of Evil using Leah to finally track down and get their hands on Lance, and how Leah had emerged from the horrific night more powerful than before.

"And this is where it brought me," Leah said. "Right here to your doorstep." Leah shrugged but then regretted it, hoping that Maya wouldn't find the gesture dismissive or uncaring. "I have to be honest, though, I have no idea how you and your son's story fit into everything, but it's undeniable to me that the Universe wants me here for a reason. So"—and this next part was hard to admit, because Leah wanted nothing more than to get back on the road and to try and find Lance—"I'm not leaving until I find Noah and we figure this all out. Because you're a part of this too, Maya. On some scale, large or small, you and me, we're supposed to be sharing this moment together."

When Leah looked up from the mug of coffee that Maya had hardly touched the entire time Leah had been talking, she saw that the woman's face was ghostly pale. Her eyes were wide and they glistened with tears. Her mouth was frozen in a half-oval shape, like she'd tried to look shocked but hadn't quite made it, had run out of energy.

"Maya? Maya, what's wrong?"

Leah suddenly had a horrible sinking feeling in her stomach, the idea that she'd been wrong about the whole thing. Maya hadn't been ready for the truth, not *this* truth.

She thinks I'm crazy, Leah thought. *She can't accept what I've told her. Despite her own past, she can't accept mine, can't fathom my reality. It's not what she wanted from me. She didn't want to hear about ghosts and demons and the things beyond our world. All she wanted to know was how her guardian angel was going to get her son back.*

"Maya, I—"

But Leah didn't get to finish, because the tears that had been filling Maya's eyes suddenly exploded down her cheeks like a dam had burst and Maya buried her face in her hands to muffle the gut-wrenching sob that accompanied the tears.

Leah stood, unsure what to do, unsure what was happening. She had taken one small step around the table toward Maya when the woman pulled her hands from her face and cried, "He's dead! Oh... my son is dead!"

Leah froze, her mind electric with thought, trying to piece together what was happening in front of her, and what had driven Maya to this sudden conclusion.

"He's not."

Leah blurted the words without any realization she was going to speak, like they'd simply been forced from her mouth. "He's not dead, Maya."

And in a way that she couldn't explain, Leah knew this was

the truth. She felt it deep in her marrow, in her soul, the truth from the Universe. Noah was not dead. He was alive and Leah was going to find him.

"He is!" Maya said into her hands, the words muffled. "That's why you're here! I was wrong. You aren't here to find him, you're here to help me through my loss, to hold my hand again. You're here to help me mourn my son!"

"*He's not dead!*" Leah spoke the words with a hot authority, the equivalent of a slap across the woman's face, needing to sober her up.

Maya's head shot up from her hands, and she managed to choke off her sobs. Her eyes were red and watery, but also suddenly filled with hope ... and maybe a little skepticism. She studied Leah's face for a long time. "You promise? You swear to me Noah's not dead?"

Leah took another small step forward and gently laid a hand on Maya's shoulder. Spoke the truth as she knew it. "I promise. He's alive."

Maya reached up one of her own hands and squeezed Leah's, held on to it like she was adrift in the ocean and Leah's hand was a life jacket, the only thing keeping her from sinking down into the depths, into the darkness. The two of them stayed this way for a full two minutes more while Maya recomposed herself, apologizing for her outburst. Leah slowly extracted her hand from Maya's and went back to her seat at the table.

"Why did you think that?" she asked. "Why, all of a sudden, did you think Noah was dead?"

Maya lifted her coffee mug to her lips and took a small sip. Leah thought the stuff had to be cold by now, and with as much creamer as Maya had added it would have been like sipping melted ice cream. Maya set the mug down and then looked at Leah. "Because of Lance," she said.

Leah, again, was nothing but confused. "I don't understand."

"You said that Lance can see the dead. See and talk to them, right?"

Leah nodded.

"Do you think...?" Maya looked away, flicked her eyes to the refrigerator. "I don't know. Do you think, maybe, sometimes he reaches out and visits people who are *about* to die? Like, in a dream. You know, like the way you visited me in mine. Like maybe he comes to let them know that everything's going to be alright. Tells them about all the wonderful things that might be waiting for them in the next life, when they pass on."

On one level, Leah understood exactly what Maya was asking, and how the woman might have arrived at that conclusion. It wasn't a crazy notion, and to be honest, Leah *could* see Lance doing something exactly like Maya had described. He'd told her before how often the spirits he saw couldn't pass on to what waited beyond this world until he'd finished helping them. But on another level, she wasn't sure what events in Maya's own experience had so quickly made her think that the image of Lance that had come to her had anything to do with Noah.

A question that Leah should have thought to ask earlier popped into her mind, one she *would* have asked if the completely unexpected sight of Lance's image hadn't derailed what little grasp she had on the moment. "When did you see Lance?" Leah asked. "Did he come to you in a dream, like I did? Did you paint him recently?"

Maya looked at Leah, and Leah could see that Maya too realized something she should have said before. Like the two women had been dancing around a locked-away clue that each held half the key to.

"Oh," Maya said. "I didn't paint Lance."

This answer was a curveball to Leah. She cocked her head to the side, confused. "What? Then who did?"

Maya smiled. "Noah."

[12]

It made sense, after hearing it, that Noah had been the one to paint the silhouette of Lance. Leah had thought the image looked a little less professional than the other works of Maya's she'd seen, a little less polished. It looked like it had been done in a hurry ... or by a less-steady hand. Now she understood why. It had been done by Noah, the same artist responsible for the unremarkable pictures hanging on the refrigerator just behind her.

Unfortunately, it looks like he did not inherit my artistic ability—Maya's honest words about her son's interest, or lack thereof, in drawing and painting.

But she said he had a great imagination, Leah thought. *So could he have...*

No, there was absolutely no way he would have just accidentally made up the image that was, despite the lack of detail, to Leah, so clearly Lance Brody.

It's not a coincidence, Leah thought, and then she had to suppress a small grin at the thought of Pamela Brody sitting out in the Beetle's passenger seat, rolling her eyes as Leah even allowed the word *coincidence* to cross her mind.

"Noah painted the picture of Lance," Leah said, turning the thought over in her mind, working out what it meant.

It hadn't been a question, but Maya nodded her head and said, "Yes."

Then a question did appear: "You said Noah doesn't really like to draw or paint, so why did he paint that picture of Lance? Did he decide to do it on his own, or did you...?" Leah shrugged.

"Did I ask him to come paint with me? Spend some quality time with Mom?"

Leah nodded. "Yes. Anything like that?"

Maya shook her head. "No, nothing like that at all. I've accepted he's not an artist—at least not in that way. Like I said before, I'm of the mindset that kids will find what it is they love to do without their parents' help. I'm not going to force him into anything."

"Okay, sure. So, what happened? Did he just wake up one morning and walk into your studio and start painting?"

"Basically. But..."

"But what?"

Maya looked away, and Leah saw the woman's face fall a little once again, like she was ashamed of what she had to say next. "Just like with my telling him that my brother was off on adventures, I think it's probably my fault that he painted that picture. I think ... oh, I don't know." Maya sighed, looked back to Leah with eyes that were almost apologetic. "See, I've told him all about *you*. I had to, right? I mean, he's seen the paintings of you his entire life, literally, so naturally he was going to ask who the woman his mother is always painting is, right? And, well, I was honest. He knows that I believe you've been by my side all these years. The way I explained it to him, well, it's basically spiritual."

Leah nodded slowly, still uncomfortable at the idea that Maya believed her to be a sort of—"Guardian angel," Leah said, to drive home Maya's point.

"Yes," Maya said. "We aren't really religious people, not in a true Christian sense. I've never taken him to church—though he has been a few Sundays with some of his little friends, if he spends the night on a Saturday. I don't mind. It's good for him to experience other people's beliefs and cultures. But as for us ... well, I *do* believe there's a higher power." Maya grinned, pointed to Leah. "And things we can't explain and have no control over. A guiding force."

Leah nodded. *You got that right.* "Okay, so what does all that mean in terms of Noah deciding to paint Lance?"

Leah heard the impatience in her own voice, and Maya must have too, because the woman held up her hands and made a slow-down gesture, pumping imaginary brakes. "Children are very impressionable," Maya said. "Especially by their own parents. A lot of times, especially when kids are young, what their mom and dad say is gospel. Indisputable truth, right?"

"Sure."

"Well, there was the story of my brother, and then there's, well ... I think that Noah's been waiting for his own guardian angel to show up, too. Like it was only a matter of time before he would see his own protector in his dreams. Like it was"—Maya shrugged again—"just something that everyone eventually experiences. Like when you get your first loose tooth, or, I don't know, hitting puberty." She grinned, but the image was sad, like the woman really did blame herself for everything that might have led to her son being missing. "So, when he saw Lance, he did exactly what he thought he was supposed to do ... because of me."

"He painted him," Leah said, understanding.

Maya nodded, and Leah saw the threat of tears in the woman's eyes again. "In Noah's mind, I think he believed by painting Lance he was accepting him, the same way I had accepted you." Maya looked away, over to the fridge, studied the artwork on the door. "It's like he thinks we have our own religion, isn't it? That we've put our faith in these protectors that visit us in our dreams."

Leah didn't know what to say to that, because it did seem that way, but she didn't want Maya to think that the idea was a bad one, or accidentally cast any blame on the woman for her son's disappearance. And to be honest, while the idea of it being considered a religion was a bit too much for Leah to swallow, the concept of people believing in Lance and her as ... well, protectors seemed like a bit much, too ... but believing them to be a force of good, a light shining in the darkness, that was truer than Maya and Noah even knew.

"But we're not crazy, are we?" Maya said. She was looking at Leah again, and her eyes were now clear and focused. "It all sounds ridiculous, but we're not crazy, because you're here. You're *real*. And Lance is, too. And the both of you are a part of something ... something bigger than..." She trailed off, and Leah couldn't blame her. It was a hard thing to articulate.

"Yes," Leah said. "We're real, and I'm here." She reached out a hand across the table, and Maya took it and squeezed it gently. Despite everything that had been said already, Leah felt as though there was still so much more she needed to know, needed to understand. She had more questions, but she didn't know if she'd get the answers she needed. At least not from Maya. She asked, "Maya, Noah saw Lance in a dream of his, right?"

Maya took another sip of the cold coffee. Grimaced this time and set it down and scooted it to the side, away from her. "Yes."

"Did he tell you about the dream? Did he tell you why Lance was there?"

Maya looked down at the table and sighed. "He did, but I'm afraid it won't help explain much."

"I'd still like to hear about it."

Maya nodded. Leaned back in her chair and folded her hands in her lap, like she was about to recite a poem. "Of course. He said that—and this is what I mean when I say this won't be very helpful—he said that in his dream he was having one of his adventures in his wardrobe, just like usual, but then everything got really dark, and he heard a scary noise, like something scratching on the outside of the door, trying to get inside. After a while, the noise got louder and then it sounded like something was growling and snapping its teeth. He said he didn't know what he was going to do because the only way out of the wardrobe was through the one door and he was too afraid to even try to open it and peek out because whatever was outside might eat him." Maya paused, then smiled. "But then, he said the noise stopped." She snapped her fingers. "Just like that. After it stopped, he said it was quiet for a minute, and he was just about to push open the door but then it started to open on its own. He said that for a second, he got scared again, because he thought the monster had just been fooling him, and now it was coming in to get him, but then when the door was pulled all the way open, he saw ... well, he saw Lance. He said that Lance held out his hand and helped him out of the wardrobe, but he never said a word. Then ... and this is the image Noah must have painted—he said Lance just turned and walked away, into the shadows."

Leah realized she was smiling. The story sounded just like something Lance would do, if not an extremely simplified version. He'd faced down devils and survived, so of course he could rescue a little boy from the monster in his dream.

But ... Lance wasn't just a dream. He was a real person, the same way Leah was a real person. The Universe had been preparing Maya for Leah's arrival ever since the woman had been just a teenager, preparing her for this moment right here, right now, and had shown the woman's son the vision of Lance.

Why?

What was so important about any of this?

Leah sat in the kitchen chair and said nothing, her mind wandering off and wading into a deep pool of thought. Maya sat patiently, watching, waiting.

I wanted to find Lance, Leah thought. *That's what I thought I was headed to do. But instead, I've ended up here, with a woman who has been having visions of me for nearly her entire life. It's not an accident. I didn't just make a wrong turn and end up in this kitchen. No, I asked the Universe to take me to Lance and this is where it brought me. This is part of it, has to be. I'm missing something. There's another piece of this puzzle I don't...*

Leah snapped out of her thoughts and shook her head. She was doing nothing except wasting time. Of course she was missing something.

So was Maya.

They were missing Noah.

Noah, who had seen Lance in his dream.

The boy, Leah thought. *This is all about the boy. I don't know why, but he's the key to finding Lance.*

"Maya," Leah said, standing from the table. "Let's go find your son."

[13]

The chain-link fence that surrounded the amusement park had a gate that swung out in a big, wide arc, and when the Surfer pushed it all the way open, hinges squeaking and metal rattling and dirt kicking up from where the bottom scraped the ground, it left behind an opening that looked big enough to drive two semitrucks through side by side. With his job complete, the Surfer strolled slowly back toward the Plymouth, swiveling his head from side to side, looking up and down and all around, like he was doing nothing more than taking in the sights on a Sunday-afternoon walk through the park.

"That fucker is never in a hurry, is he?" the thing called Patrick Cain said from the front passenger seat.

"He can move fast when he needs to," the Reverend said from next to Lance, where he was sitting with his hands clasped in his lap, his index fingers pressed together and pointed outward, forming a sharp triangle.

Here's the church, here's the steeple, Lance thought absurdly, when he looked down at the Reverend's hands. *Open the doors and see all the people.* He waited a beat, half-expecting the

Reverend to have read his mind and to flip open his palms and wiggle his fingers. Instead, Lance looked up and saw the Reverend staring at him with apprehension. "What?" the man asked.

Lance said nothing. Looked away. The Surfer opened the driver's door and slid back into the seat, running both hands through his hair and tucking it behind his ears. Patrick made an exaggerated show of raising his arm and reaching out to point through the windshield, and in a deep voice he exclaimed, "*Onward!*"

The Surfer didn't so much as glance toward Patrick, he just put the car into gear and drove forward through the wide-open mouth in the fence. Drove onward.

Beyond the fence there was a vast sea of cracked asphalt to the right that must have once served as the main parking lot. Tall light poles formed a neat grid through the lot, some of them still hanging tight to the big signs advertising locations such as B3 and G11, like finding your vehicle was akin to playing a giant game of bingo. Several of the poles had the bulky corpses of their light fixtures discarded on the ground at their bases, as if without proper care they'd eventually wilted and died on the vine before falling.

The road they were driving on snaked away to the left and ran parallel to the park's front entryway, which consisted of a tall brick facade with several turrets positioned all along its wide footprint. It made the whole front of the park look like you were about to walk into a medieval castle. There was a trio of flag-poles atop the center turret, which was just above the main entry gate, but the poles were bare, as if the park and its land were claimed by no one, up for grabs.

The Surfer flicked on the headlights as the sun all but gave up the ghost, and drove the Plymouth along the road and then turned right at the front gate, the tires bumping up and onto the raised edge of the sidewalk and walkway, the old car jarring painfully, shaking and rattling all four of its passengers as if they'd already boarded a ride inside the park's walls. The hum of the tires changed when they met the concrete, going from the dull drone of asphalt to a higher-pitched whine. Lance looked through the windshield as the car headed straight for the entry gate, and as the headlights splashed across one of the ticket windows he saw the remains of a sun-bleached and faded sign just above one of the booths that welcomed guests to Arthur's Adventureland. The lettering had a medieval look, and was bracketed by two silhouettes of a king's crown.

Here's the church, Lance thought again. *Here's* my *church.*

Here he was, a man whose first name was Lancelot—as in *Sir Lancelot*—potentially about to meet his demise in an amusement park whose theme was based on the very lore Lance's name was derived from.

Sometimes Lance couldn't tell when the Universe stopped being funny and ironic and started being downright cruel.

Or maybe it just had a very dark sense of humor.

Or maybe it's all just part of the plan, he thought to himself. But the thought was riddled with sarcasm, because as the Surfer drove through a part of the entry gate where it looked like several turnstiles had been removed, leaving behind a space just large enough for a car to squeeze through, and drove inside the park, Lance suddenly felt like the high walls were falling inward, about to crash down onto him. And in that moment, he wondered if the Universe had a plan at all, found himself questioning all the truths he'd learned to carry with him.

Here's the church, he thought again, trying to calm his mind.

Here's the church.

The Surfer drove the car another twenty yards, driving out from under the large overhang that had covered the ticket windows and entry gates and revealing the nearly full-dark sky and the horizon. The Ferris wheel loomed larger than before, rising high above the rest of the park, like a giant sentinel.

Here's the steeple.

Here's the church. Here's the steeple.

Something didn't feel right. *Nothing* felt right. That small thread of a feeling he'd had before when they'd arrived at the chain-link fence surrounding the park, that feeling of dread and sorrow and despair, now not only seemed to be floating all around them but felt *alive*, like it was moving with a purpose, dancing with the breeze and looping around lampposts and slinking under doors. The feeling was heavy, suffocating. And Lance thought of Patrick's words—*It can feel you*—and realized that the boy was only half right. Whatever was here *could* feel Lance, the same way Lance could feel it, but it wasn't just that.

It was *reaching* for him.

Lance kept his eyes locked on the Ferris wheel, tried to control his breathing.

Here's the church. Here's the steeple. Here's the church. Here's the steeple.

He felt very alone. Isolated. Once they'd crossed through the park's gates and had been swallowed by the abandonment within, Lance felt as though suddenly he was the only person left alive on earth. Everything outside the park might as well have been a different planet, a different *Universe*.

But...

Another feeling reached him, this one weaker. Faint, as if

clinging on to its own dying breaths, using the little strength it had left to find him, to reach out and shake Lance's hand and...

It was a *good* feeling, the feeling of Light shining into the Dark. A feeling of hope. Of ... redemption? But there was pain, too, in that feeling, mixed in like medicine stirred into a child's glass of Kool-Aid. A bitter, foreign taste beneath the sweetness.

Fear, Lance thought. *It tastes like fear, too.*

The Surfer stopped the Plymouth just past the entry gate and parked. He killed the headlights and shut off the engine and the world fell silent. That feeling of loneliness crept in fast again, surrounding the car, banging on the windows, trying to break in. Lance looked out his window and saw they'd parked next to a short and long building that shared the same stone facade as the park's entrance, with a drooping red awning hanging down in ripped tatters from above the door, making the entrance look it was decorated with party streamers. A placard with the same medieval lettering as the ticket booth told Lance the building was Guest Services.

"Are we stopping to get a map?" Lance asked, needing to say anything to break the silence, slice the tension he could feel building inside him as the feelings—the good feeling *and* the bad one, the one reaching out for him with grasping fingers—battled for his attention. "Also, I could really go for a funnel cake right about now. Anybody else hungry?"

The other three passengers all ignored him. Instead, the Reverend was looking out his own window. He shook his head. "Been a long time," he said. "I wasn't sure I'd ever come back here again."

Patrick scoffed. "You wouldn't have, if I hadn't saved your ass."

The Surfer grunted.

"Yeah, you're right," Patrick said. "I know. You did a lot to save him, too. But don't forget who brought *you* back, either."

The Surfer said nothing and made no more sounds. Just reached for his door handle and pulled it. Stepped outside. The Reverend did the same.

Lance reached for his door but Patrick said, "*Wait.*" His voice leaving no room for compromise. Lance waited but felt the anger inside him spark to life. He hated taking orders from this kid, this *thing*.

Here's the church. Here's the steeple.

Lance watched as Patrick stepped out of the Plymouth and then nodded to the Surfer. The Surfer moved forward and opened Lance's door. Lance looked up and met the Surfer's eyes, and the meaning in them was as clear as if the thing had spoken. *Don't do anything stupid.*

Lance Brody has spent his life doing what others would likely consider stupid, but he was smart enough to realize that right now was not going to be one of those moments. Back in Paul and Breanne Michie's living room, the Surfer had done nothing more than tap his finger to the side of Lance's head, just above the temple, and had sent Lance into a deep and infinitely dark hole from which there was no escape. He'd felt as though he were falling, spiraling with his arms and legs pinwheeling and his mind lost in an eternal emptiness. Until it had all stopped and Lance had opened his eyes again and he was in the back of the Plymouth with no memory as to how he'd gotten there, as if it had all been a bad dream.

But Lance knew it had been no dream at all, and it was not something he was ready to experience again.

So, he held up his hands in an *I surrender* gesture and slowly stood from the car. The air felt cool but was somehow sticky, an unpleasant feeling crawling along his skin. A flock of birds flew by overhead, the blossoming moonlight causing their winged shadows to sail across the ground, warped and distorted like something out of a monster flick.

But they aren't the monsters, Lance thought, watching as his trio of captors gathered in front of him. *They are.*

The thing called Patrick Cain moved toward the entrance to the Guest Services building and turned the knob and pushed open the door. Lance was surprised to see the warm glow of light spill from the right side of the doorway, a sign of life in an otherwise dead place. "Honey, I'm home!" Patrick called out.

The Reverend followed Patrick inside, and the Surfer pointed for Lance to do the same, taking up the rear as Lance walked toward the opened door. Lance stepped across the threshold and was hit with a wave of body odor and mold and something sickeningly greasy, like when you leave a fast-food bag in your car too long on a hot summer day. The front-facing area of Guest Services was empty except for a long counter whose top was littered with dust-covered stacks of brochures and flyers and three long-out-of-date computer terminals. On the wall behind the counter were posters advertising park features and packages and deals, along with safety information and obscure awards that Arthur's Adventureland had garnered over the years. The most recent award Lance could see was from 1991.

But this area of the building was not what Patrick had come for. There was a large door to the right with the words STAFF ONLY stenciled across it, and this was where the light was coming from. Patrick stood just inside this room and was looking around. "Now where in the hell did Karina run off to? She's—"

Before Patrick could finish his next sentence, a dark figure dropped from the ceiling above him, just a flash of black and white that materialized and came into focus and Lance saw to actually be a woman. She hit the ground and stayed crouched down and then shot out one of her legs in a sweeping motion, knocking Patrick's legs out from under him. The boy went down fast, but even faster the woman sprang up and her arms shot out and she wrapped them around Patrick's torso and pulled him back upright.

"All that power, still slow as fuck," she said and laughed. Her voice was throaty and deep, and to Lance her laughter sounded like those annoying mufflers street racers put on their flashy cars to try and sound cool.

Patrick pushed her away. "Fuck you." But then, to Lance's surprise, he laughed too and stepped aside, letting the woman see Lance for the first time.

"That him?" Karina asked. "He's the one?"

"The one and only," Patrick said. "Wasn't that hard to track him down, really."

Lance shot a glance at the kid. "You sure about that?"

Patrick looked like he was about to respond, but Karina moved past him, walking toward Lance. She was very tall, at least six feet, and wore black pants with a black trench coat that made Lance think she looked like she could have walked right out of one of the *Matrix* films. Her hair was such a bright light blond that it appeared white. Then, when she was directly in front of Lance, he saw that her hair *was* white. White as snow. Her eyes were green and sparkled like gems, but the rest of her face was plain and forgettable, a lost face in the crowd. That face could be anyone's.

She studied Lance up and down for a few seconds then shrugged. "Hmm. I guess I was expecting more."

Lance didn't know what to say to that. Couldn't seem to pull his gaze away from the woman's hair, and he also couldn't fully wrap his head around what he'd seen happen in the STAFF ONLY room.

Was she hanging onto the ceiling?

He felt himself beginning to panic, everything suddenly becoming too much to take in and understand. He took a deep breath. *Get it together, Lance. What is wrong with you? You've been dealing with this stuff your whole life. You were* born *for this.*

So why did this feel so different?

Here's the church. Here's the steeple. Here's the church. Here's the steeple.

Once again using the rhyme as a sort of mantra, he worked to get his mind back under control. Then, something else happened that left him so surprised he actually felt his jaw drop open.

Karina looked away from Lance and over to the side, where the Reverend and the Surfer were standing by like guard dogs. "There's my big boy!" Karina said, that deep voice sounding downright sultry. In a blurry flash of speed she covered the space and wrapped her arms around the Surfer's neck, entwining her fingers into his long blond hair and pulling his face toward hers. She kissed him, hard and furiously, and to Lance's amazement, the Surfer kissed her back with just as much vigor, their two tongues darting around like dueling snakes fighting for the same prey. Then, as quickly as she'd started it all, Karina pulled away and pushed the Surfer back, his body slamming against the wall hard enough to make a sound like thunder.

"Enough!" she said. "Later." She gave him a wink. Then she

turned back to Patrick, who'd been watching everything apathetically from the STAFF ONLY door with his arms crossed. Karina nodded toward Lance. "He going in?"

Patrick nodded. "For now. It's been a long few days." Then he nodded to the Surfer.

The Surfer moved forward and grabbed Lance just above the elbow. Lance's body went hot with electricity. It wasn't painful, but it was unpleasant enough that Lance thought it if lasted much longer he might get sick.

Here's the ... church. Here's ... the steeple.

The Surfer walked toward a hallway leading away from the STAFF ONLY room, pulling Lance along. Lance allowed it, focusing on moving his legs one at a time as the current surged through him, his limbs buzzing. As they passed the STAFF ONLY room, Lance looked inside and saw it was actually a large office with a single desk and a bunch of old filing cabinets, most of their drawers opened and empty. There were two chairs in front of the desk, and despite the buzzing in his head and his vision that was beginning to grow fuzzy, Lance did a double take when he saw a horse's head sitting in one of them.

It wasn't a real horse, he realized, but part of a costume. Something a long-ago employee of Arthur's Adventureland had probably dressed up in for minimum wage and sweated his balls off as he danced around the park trying to make a few kids smile and keep a few more from pulling his tail or throwing their snow cones at him.

There was a big metal door with a plexiglass window in its center at the end of the short hallway. Karina was at it, a key in her hand that she shoved into the lock.

Here's the church. Here's the steeple.

The Surfer moved behind Lance and placed a hand in the

center of Lance's back, just as Karina pulled the door open. Lance caught a glimpse of the words stenciled on the door as it swung by.

GUEST HOLDING AREA.

It was a theme park jail.

Here's the church. Here's the steeple.

Karina pulled the door all the way open and

Open the door and see all the people

the Surfer shoved Lance inside and the door slammed closed behind him. Lance looked around the small space he was now a prisoner in.

He was not alone.

[14]

Maya's mood had shifted.

Since Leah had arrived, Maya had managed to mostly keep herself together, aside from the small outburst she'd had after Leah had told the woman about Lance, which Maya had wrongly (Leah *hoped*) interpreted to mean that Noah was dead. But there had still been an underlying sense of apprehension, a buzzing of concern beneath all the calm pleasantness Maya had been putting forward. And Leah couldn't blame her; her son was missing, after all. It was the fact that Leah herself was there, Leah realized (and perhaps earlier, even just the thought that Leah would be arriving to help), that had kept Maya this way. Because even though Noah had run off before, and had returned home unscathed each time, Maya was a mother and Noah was her little boy and it was a big and dangerous and cruel world out there and of course Maya would worry. Worry like hell.

But now, while there was still a bit of that worry inside her—worry Leah found that she could actually *feel* coming from somewhere deep down in Maya's heart, like the small pulses of a headache coming on—it was fainter than earlier, and Maya's mood had shifted into something more ... *excited*? Yes, that was the word Leah liked best. There was a giddiness now to Maya's actions, and she was talking a lot, rambling as she went about hastily making them a couple of peanut butter and jelly sandwiches each ("In case we get hungry," she'd told Leah. "And I'll brew a thermos of coffee, too.") at the small kitchen island.

"Are we taking your car or mine?" Maya asked as she slid the sandwiches into plastic baggies and sealed them up with practiced hands. *Like she does every morning for Noah*, Leah thought. *When she packs his lunch.*

"Is it better if I drive, since I know the area? Or should you? Does it matter? I guess we don't know how long this could take, do we? I mean, I guess if you knew *exactly* where Noah was, we wouldn't even be doing this, would we? I'm sure you would have just brought him to me ... or, I don't know, phoned me up and just told me and I could go get him." Maya put the knife she'd used to make the sandwiches in the sink, where it clattered loudly onto the plates from dinner. She went over to the coffeemaker and emptied out the rest of the pot she'd made earlier and started a fresh brew, pulling down a thermos from one of the cabinets and setting it aside to fill later.

Leah never got a chance to answer Maya's question. In fact, she'd honestly lost track of whether there had been a real question in all that to begin with. Maya spun around from the coffeemaker and blew a strand of hair out of her face, but it didn't move, was stuck to the sheen of sweat that had formed on the woman's brow. "Okay," she said. "I should go change. I need to put on something, I don't know..." She shrugged, looking for words. "More comfortable, I guess." Then she laughed and waved a hand at Leah. "You know what I mean."

Leah looked at the stack of sandwiches on the counter, safely tucked away in their plastic bags, watched the coffee drip into the pot. She looked at the thermos next to the coffeemaker. A tall metal thing that looked like something you'd expect a construction foreman to walk onto the site with, dangling from one hand with a hardhat tucked under his arm.

She acts like this is a stakeout, Leah thought. *Like we're a couple of buddy cops going out to spy on the bad guys.*

And then, a thought that raised the hairs on Leah's arms: *Will there be bad guys? Did somebody* take *Noah this time? Is that why he didn't come home like usual?*

This thought spun in Leah's mind and began to take a more solid shape. It would explain a lot more about why she was here in the first place. Maybe Noah had been kidnapped and if Maya had called the police they would have taken too long to find him on their own, but Leah, with her newfound special gifts, might be able to track down the kidnappers more quickly, find the boy and rescue him before anything *really* bad could happen.

Yeah, Leah thought. *You and what army?*

Which was true. Lance, being tall and athletic and having enough muscle to get by, could at least hold his own for a while in a physical altercation with another human being, but that wasn't where his true strength lay. For most of Leah's time with him, Lance had flexed his other muscles, the ones nobody else could see. He used those muscles to fight off monsters and demons and devils and whatever else you wanted to call the things that poked through the veil and slithered over to the other side.

Can I do that? Leah wondered. *Can I fight a devil with my mind ... my soul?*

Maybe. But that didn't do much good against human

kidnappers. People who might be armed with knives and guns and anything else that could easily draw blood and puncture organs to end a life.

If there are *kidnappers, I find Noah and then I call the cops. Let them send in the cavalry.* Though, Leah supposed if she had a shotgun right now—*any* gun, really—she could make use of some of the things her daddy had taught her. She'd probably spent more time at the local shooting range growing up than any other little girl in Westhaven. She smiled briefly at the fleeting memory of her daddy standing behind her, his strong hand pressed against the flat of her back for support as little Leah took aim and fired at the target downrange. Those were good times. Times before her mother had gotten sick and before her brother had been killed. A different life.

No, Leah didn't think this was a kidnapping. It just didn't feel right. But how could she ever be sure?

Spin the wheel, round and round it goes. Are there kidnappers or not, nobody knows.

"Did you hear me?" Maya asked.

Leah stopped watching through her mind's eye and focused on the world in front of her again. "What's that?"

Maya was standing in the hallway, almost into the living room. "I said you can come sit on the couch for a bit while I go up and change. Shouldn't be but a couple minutes. I want to write a note to leave, too. For Noah. Just in case he manages to come back on his own while we're out."

"Oh," Leah said, standing from the kitchen table, the table she felt like she'd been sitting at for hours and hours, when in reality it had only been a few minutes longer than one. "Okay, sure. Thanks."

Maya waited at the foot of the stairs until Leah made her

way quickly down the hall of paintings (trying not to look at any of them while also trying not to make it look like she was avoiding them) and into the living room. Once Leah had taken a seat on the sofa, Maya smiled and nodded, as if pleased by her own hospitality, and said, "Okay, back in just a few." She was halfway up the stairs before Leah heard the footsteps stop and then start to retreat. She saw Maya lean down, just her head and shoulders visible from the nook where the stairway disappeared up above the ceiling. "Leah, I just want to say thank you again. Thank you, *thank you*."

Leah forced on a smile. "We'll find him," she made herself say. But she was thinking: *Don't thank me yet.*

Maya smiled back, hers big and genuine. Then she was gone, footfalls fading up the stairs and heading down the hallway to a bedroom.

Leah let out a breath, relishing the quiet. Happy to have a moment to herself to think. She laid her head back against the couch, which wrapped her in a loving embrace. The room started to fade away as she realized how tired she was, her eyelids becoming heavy and uncooperative. Her mind drifted, and again she thought about people who might have taken Noah. She'd decided (sort of) that this wasn't a kidnapping (she hoped), and that was mostly because she didn't know what the *why* would be. Why kidnap Noah? Ransom, maybe? No, that didn't feel right. While there was nothing particularly low-class about Maya and Noah's home, it didn't exactly scream anything that would imply there was lots of cash somewhere.

The paintings, maybe? Could they be worth a lot? Is Maya a bigger deal than she's letting on?

Again, it seemed unlikely.

Leah was once again about to completely dismiss the idea

that Noah's disappearance involved a kidnapping when another scenario flashed hot like oil in a pan. In the moments before sleep was going to grab hold of her, she found herself thinking of Lance, which in turn led to the image of the last time she'd seen him, standing in the Michies' living room while the Reverend and the Surfer and the young guy named Patrick played their hand.

The Reverend and Surfer and Patrick, oh my.

The Reverend and Surfer and Patrick, oh ... MY!

What if this whole thing was a trap? What if when Leah had reached out to the Universe and asked for help finding Lance, it hadn't been the Universe that had answered her call? What if it had been the *other* side? What if there *were* people who had taken Noah, people like the Reverend and the Surfer and Patrick (people who maybe weren't really *people* at all), and just like Lance had been hunted by Evil his whole life, maybe now Leah was big-time on Evil's radar, too, and they were drawing her in. Maybe Noah was nothing but bait.

Another thought, this one so dark it was blinding: What if Maya was in on it?

No ... NO. Leah, her toes just touching sleep's tide as it rushed at her, pushed these bad thoughts away. None of that made sense.

Because Maya had her story, Leah thought. *Maya's been waiting for me since she was just a teenager. She's been painting me for years.* And...

And Noah saw Lance. For some reason, it was this fact that finally settled Leah's mind. *Noah saw Lance. I have to find that boy.*

She had to find them both.

Leah's last moments of consciousness began to fade

completely as sleep floated her out to sea, and she let it take her, the same way she'd let those waters take her mind away in the convenience store parking lot nearly three days ago. It felt good, to just float for a minute. The water was warm, like a bath, and she could smell something sweet ... chocolate and...

Peppermint?

And then the water suddenly went ice-cold, cold enough for Leah to gasp at the shock of it and open her eyes and...

"Is that good?" Lance asked from beside her.

Gone was the living room with the walls covered in paintings. Gone were the sofa and the still-lingering smell of burgers mixed with coffee.

But no, that wasn't quite right. There *was* the smell of coffee, coffee to go along with the chocolate and peppermint. Leah found herself standing on a sidewalk, bundled up in a big puffy coat and with a stocking cap on her head and a scarf around her neck. Snow flurries swirled on a gentle breeze in the night sky, a breeze that threw more of that sweet and rich aroma at her. She looked down at her gloved hand holding a cardboard to-go cup, steam snaking from the cutout in the lid. She looked up, saw Lance standing on the sidewalk next to her, just outside the bright windows of what looked like a café and bakery. Big stenciled lettering told her the place was called Downtown Joe. Lance was looking at her with a small grin and expectant eyes, waiting for an answer.

Leah sipped the beverage and shivered at the goodness. "Very good," she said. "Want to try it?"

Lance shook his head and held up his own to-go cup. A large, of course. "No, thanks. Too sweet for me. I'll stick with the black stuff." He reached for her free hand with his and she took it instinctively, a perfect fit.

"Not even a splash of cream? Man, I bet you scrape the frosting off your cake, too."

Leah turned and saw a black man dressed in blue jeans and a heavy sweater with an unzipped coat over it standing next to one of the wrought-iron tables outside Downtown Joe. He was holding beverages in each hand, and the three of them were all sharing a laugh at his joke when the bell above the café's door jingled as Pamela Brody stepped outside, calling over her shoulder, "We'll get together soon, Mary! Have a merry Christmas!"

The black man held out one of the cups for her and Pamela took it, asking, "What are we all laughing about?"

"Marcus was just telling me how boring I am," Lance said.

"He's not wrong," Leah added, giving Marcus a wink.

Marcus held up his cup to point at Leah, nodded his head as if to say, *See?*

"He's not boring," Pamela said, joining in on the fun. "He's just ... particular."

Lance rolled his eyes and groaned. "Oh, that sounds *way* better. Thanks, Mother."

They laughed some more and then they were walking down the block, the Christmas lights strung around the lampposts and across storefronts twinkling against the black sky, heliographing off windows and the chrome accents of cars parked along the street. As they reached the end of a street, where the old brick buildings of downtown began to fade away, Leah began to see more people walking together in groups, moving across the large parking lot and a quarter acre or so of grass next to it that surrounded a small white church that sat back from the street. The church's parking area was well lit, and a bright spotlight illuminated the tall cross that punctuated the house of God's roof.

Lance stepped off the sidewalk and pulled them in the direction of the church, falling in with the other people as they all began to form a line to enter the church's opened doors.

Leah glanced up at the lit-up cross as they moved across the grass, watched as the snow flurries were caught in the spotlight before dancing away.

Here's the church, here's the steeple.

Lance's voice.

"What?" she asked, turning to look up at him.

He shook his head. "Didn't say anything."

"Oh, I thought..." Leah didn't finish, because her eyes went to the brick marquee sign positioned at the parking lot's entrance. The sign, like the steeple, was also lit by a spotlight from each side, these smaller and mounted on the ground to shine up at the words. Aside from the regular schedule of worship services and Sunday school, the sign advertised that on December twenty-third at seven p.m., the church would be hosting A CHRISTMAS CELEBRATION IN MUSIC performed by the Hillston City Choir.

"My mom loves this," Lance said as he and Leah made their way slowly up the steps to enter the church behind the line of people. "We come every year."

"I know," Leah said. "You already told me that when she asked if we wanted to come."

Lance nodded. "Oh, yeah."

"Hey, what's wrong?"

Lance looked down at her. For a moment, his eyes were serious, the warm light spilling from inside the church's opened doors glowing like small fires in them. "It's strange, but ... churches sort of make me nervous."

"Have ever since he was a baby," Pamela said from behind them.

Leah turned and saw Marcus and Pamela holding hands on the step just below her and Lance. "Really?"

Pamela shrugged. "I can't explain it. And neither can he."

Lance wrapped an arm around Leah as they moved forward and stepped inside the church. "And I don't plan on trying to explain it tonight, either. I'm just here for good music."

The church was warm inside—too warm, maybe—but it was cozy and smelled of pine and old paper. The four of them walked to the front of the sanctuary, where the second-row pew had a sheet of paper taped to it with RESERVED printed on it. Lance stopped and stepped aside and let Marcus slide in first. A man from the third-row pew said, "Perks of the job, eh, Mr. Mayor?"

Marcus laughed and reached over the pew and shook the man's hand. "One of the very few, I must say." This got a chuckle out of the rest of the row as Pamela slid into the pew next, followed by Leah and then Lance.

When they were all seated and had unspooled themselves from their coats and scarves and gloves—except for Lance, who only had on his hoodie. Leah *had* insisted that he at least wear long pants if they were going to a church—Pamela Brody reached out a hand and laid it on Leah's knee. She leaned over and whispered, "He's not here for the music, dear. He's here for me. He knows I love it, and I love that he comes with me." She patted Leah's knee two, three times. "And I'm very glad you're here, too. I'm glad you two found each other."

Leah smiled and felt a great warmth spread through her. "Me too," she said.

Pamela winked at her and patted Leah's knee one more

time, and then the lights in the church dimmed and a woman wearing a sensible red dress stepped up to a microphone and said, "Are we ready?"

Only ... her voice was familiar.

The church was gone in a flash, like somebody had simply flipped a switch and shut off the whole world. Leah shot her eyes open and was back in Maya's living room. Maya was standing in front of her, just next to the coffee table.

"Um, I ... sorry, what?" Leah stammered.

"'Are we ready?' I asked." Maya took a step back, like maybe she could sense Leah was a bit disoriented. "Are you okay?"

Leah looked around the room once, swallowed down the mixture of emotions that were inside her, felt the happiness of the moment she'd just witnessed begin to drain like somebody had just pulled the stopper in a bathtub. Her reality crashed into her, but she took it on the chin, head up. She took a deep breath.

"Yes, I'm fine," Leah said. She stood from the sofa. "Ready when you are."

But she wasn't fine. Not at all.

[15]

Leah had taken a step toward the front door, but then stopped.

"Actually, do you mind if I use your restroom before we leave?"

Maya nodded. "Of course, of course," she said. "Please, my house is your house. You should know that, you have been living in my head for twenty years, after all." She winked and laughed, and Leah was too preoccupied with her own thoughts to dwell on how damn giddy Maya was still acting. *Nervous*, she thought. *She's just nervous and I'm leaving it at that.*

Maya pointed down the hall leading back to the kitchen. "That door on the left."

Leah groaned on the inside at having to walk down the tunnel of paintings again. She kept her head down and saw for the first time the brass doorknob on her left, midway down the hall. She let her eyes drift upward, seeing the thin cutout for the door frame. That and the brass knob were the only signs a door actually existed here. The rest of the surface was covered with various-sized canvases, almost completely hiding the door away like it was some sort of secret passageway.

Which it wasn't, thankfully. Leah pulled the door open and reached inside for the light switch, happy to see nothing more than a small half-bath that smelled as though it had been recently cleaned (*Because she was expecting me...*) and that had blessedly blank walls that were painted a light purple. Nothing hanging except a silver ring for the hand towel and the mirror above the sink.

Leah went to the sink and turned on the cold tap. Let it run for a few seconds before cupping her hands under the faucet and splashing her face. The splash of cold water felt good, and worked to clear her mind—but it also brought back the memory of the cold night air and the snow flurries and everything she'd just seen when she'd drifted off to sleep.

"What *did* I just see?" Leah asked herself, her quiet voice whispering around her as it echoed off the small room's purple walls.

A dream.

That was her first thought, but the more she tried it on, the more it didn't seem to fit. It felt too real, for starters. It wasn't like other dreams she'd had in her life, where they might seem real enough at first glance, but after you were in them for a few seconds, your mind began to realize that something was off. That you weren't so much participating in the actions of the dream as witnessing them. There was usually that light feeling, too, like gravity didn't quite work right in dreamland, and your mind wasn't as clear as normal. There could be a fuzziness to your thoughts, a haze you couldn't quite see through.

There was none of that with what Leah had just experienced in Maya's living room. Sure, she had laid her head back and closed her eyes and had felt herself beginning to slip away to sleep, but then...

She remembered the way the warm waters that had been floating her had snapped to an icy cold and the world had flashed black, and in that split second there was nothing.

But then there had been everything.

Everything. That was the word that made it real, that made it a dream that wasn't really a dream. Leah hadn't just witnessed the things from that nondream, she'd fully experienced every detail of them. She'd felt the bite of the winter air and the wetness of snow flurries on her cheeks, the scratchiness of her scarf around her neck. She'd tasted the peppermint and chocolate of her beverage, and felt the coating on her tongue that it left behind. And when she'd looked into Lance's eyes in those brief moments of conversation outside the café and again, in a longer, more intimate gaze on the steps of the church, what she'd seen was no simple best-effort recreation that her subconscious had made for her based on her own memory but instead was a perfect one-to-one match of the eyes that she had so grown to love.

The body was easy to build in her dreams. You get the basic height and shape and facial features right and your mind will fill in the rest as needed. But the eyes ... eyes were where the emotion and the intelligence lived, the windows into a person's soul.

The eyes Leah had looked into had been Lance's real eyes. If she understood nothing else, she understood that.

It had been real. All of it. She had not dreamed. She'd closed her eyes and opened them somewhere else.

No ... that's impossible.

Because how could it have been real? In what Leah had

experienced, Pamela Brody had been alive and well, walking hand in hand with Marcus Johnston and telling Mary from Downtown Joe to have a merry Christmas. But in reality, Pamela Brody was dead. In fact, her spirit had occasionally been riding shotgun as Leah had made her way here from Travelers Rest. And sadly, Leah had never had the pleasure of meeting Lance's mother when she'd been alive.

She'd never met Marcus Johnston, either, and had never even seen a picture of the man. Had only learned of him through Lance's stories. Yet ... Leah knew that if she were to go on the Internet right now and do a search for Marcus Johnston, the pictures she'd find would undoubtedly show her the man from her dream that wasn't a dream.

And they were a couple, Leah thought. Marcus and Pamela had been holding hands and he was holding her drink for her and ... Lance had never said anything about his mother and Marcus being an item. Lance said his mother never dated, and that he thought a big reason for that was because of him. *He* blamed *himself for it.*

It was real, but it couldn't be. Pamela Brody was dead and she had never dated Marcus Johnston and Leah had never been to Hillston and—

I've never been to Hillston.

This thought froze her, the cold water tap still running into the sink. Leah stared at her reflection in the mirror, her features locked into in a half-confused, half-shocked look, eyes squinted, mouth open. Her lips were wet from where she'd splashed her face, and a few droplets dripped down her chin.

Because she'd never been to Hillston but she'd known exactly where she was. When Leah had been living through that dream that wasn't a dream, she'd not been experiencing

Downtown Joe for the first time, she'd been there several times before. She'd not been seeing Marcus Johnston for the first time but had been introduced to him several weeks earlier. Leah had recognized everything around her and had known the people she'd been with as though she'd not been *this* Leah at all, but a different Leah altogether. One that had been preloaded with a full working knowledge of a completely different reality.

And then there had been Lance, and his nervousness about churches. But more than that, there had been a complete lack of any sort of knowledge or understanding that the Lance Brody that Leah had walked down the downtown Hillston blocks with and had stood on that church's steps with had been anything more than just a regular, normal guy that Leah was deeply in love with. *That* Lance didn't fight devils and demons and had never glimpsed a spirit. To that Lance, the Universe was nothing more than the vastness of outer space—planets and stars and black holes and other things that scientists could see and name and measure with data and explain to the world.

And the Leah that she'd been in that time didn't even know that the Lance in front of her was different, because there was no other Lance. There was no other Leah. There had only been—

Out in the hall, Maya knocked twice on the door and called, "Leah?"

Leah quickly shut off the tap and dried her hands and took a breath. Whatever had happened, it felt important, but she didn't have time to think about it anymore. There was a little boy that needed to be found, and Leah still thought he would be able to somehow give her more answers. Answers to questions she didn't even know how to ask yet.

Leah opened the door and found Maya standing back, her

arms crossed. "Sorry," Leah said. "I..." She didn't even know how to finish the thought.

Maya eyed her. "Are you sure you're okay?" she asked. "You look ... well, you sort of look like you've seen a ghost."

Leah couldn't help it. She laughed and shook her head. "No," she said. "Not this time."

She made her way down the hall and to the front door, once again doing her best not to look at any of the paintings.

[16]

The GUEST HOLDING AREA was bigger than Lance would have guessed. A perfect square that measured maybe twelve by twelve feet, it was certainly no solitary confinement. In fact, Lance had to wonder if the engineers who had designed the building had worked off an assumption that Arthur's Adventureland was going to see its fair share and then some of unruly patrons. The walls were the color of pencil lead and the floor and ceiling were a dirty white, cobwebs floating in the corners and streaking the walls with ghostly tendrils. Two rows of fluorescents ran the length of the room in long tracks, but only one was working, casting one side of the room in a hazy gloom. Three metal benches formed a U shape at the far end opposite the door, and to Lance's right he found another door that he could just spy through to find the dull metal toilet and sink basin, which *did* look like something from a prison. At least what he'd seen of prison from movies and television. Aside from the air vents built into the ceiling, there was nothing else to see. The air smelled of mildew and strongly of body odor, bringing to mind the high school locker rooms he'd frequented during his basketball-playing days.

Lance took in all these details in a flash, just a quick glance around the room, before his focus settled back on the man who had just stood from the metal bench against the far wall and was now walking toward him.

"Well, shit," the man said. "I gotta say, seeing you gives me the chills, man."

He was a tall guy, just an inch or so shorter than Lance, wearing tight-fitting blue jeans and a sleeveless red T-shirt beneath a black leather vest with shiny silver zippers on the pockets. The jacket, just like the skin on the man's face and arms, looked as though it had weathered ten thousand days of beating sunshine and sand and grit and gravel and pavement. The man, who was close now, just a few feet away, and outstretching his hand toward Lance, wore his thinning gray hair pulled back in a short ponytail, and the crow's-feet around his eyes were so deep they looked more like ocean trenches.

"Emmett Emmanuel Dean," he introduced himself.

Lance never let his eyes leave the man's own gaze, but he shook hands. Emmett's palm was like sandpaper, and his grip was strong. When he squeezed Lance's hand and then released it, his arm swinging back down to his side, Lance saw the cords of muscles jump and flex in the man's neck and shoulder. The guy might be thin, but he was strong. *And in more ways than one*, Lance thought. Along with the handshake, the man had given Lance a faint trickle of energy. He wasn't sure what it was exactly, but it had told him enough. Emmett Emmanuel Dean was friend, not foe. They were on the same side.

"Nice to meet you, Emmett," Lance said, amazed at how

polite social protocol refused to take a back seat in his mind, even while he was being held captive. "I'm Lance Brody."

Emmett took one step backward, his black boots thudding loudly in the empty room. "Lance Brody," he said. He looked Lance up and down, shook his head and gave a small smile. "Nice to finally put a name to the face. Oh, you can call me Ed, by the way. All my friends do."

"Are we friends?" Lance asked.

Emmett—Ed—took another step back and crossed his arms, and Lance saw more ropy muscle pop and lock beneath the guy's heavily tattooed arms, making the long-faded inky shapes ripple and dance as if they were alive. His face was half-hidden in the shadow of the unlit side of the room as the light spilled across him, and when he grinned Lance was reminded of Two-Face from the Batman movies.

"Boy, I'd say at this point we're more than friends. We might be all each other has left."

Lance said nothing. Because what was there to say to that?

"So yeah," Emmett said. "Call me Ed, friend."

When Lance continued to say nothing, his tired mind trying to make any sense of what was happening here, Emmett pointed to one of the benches and said, "Here, sit down."

Lance remained where he was at first, but when Emmett moved and sat down on the bench at the back of the room, Lance eventually followed suit and sat on the bench on the left. It was hard and too short. Lance leaned back against the wall and stretched his legs out in front of him, crossing his ankles.

To his credit, Emmett stayed silent. He seemed to be able to sense that Lance was playing it all through, working it out. Trying to formulate ... *something*. Anything.

"You've seen me," Lance finally said. "Before today. You said it was nice to put a name to the face."

Emmett nodded. "Just once. But I've never forgotten it. You've been burned into my memory."

"Where?" Lance asked.

Emmett looked at Lance like he should already know the answer to this. He held out his hands, palms up, gesturing around the room. "Right here."

"Here?"

"Yep."

"You saw me here? In this room?"

Emmett nodded. "Bingo."

"Impossible. I've never been here in my life, Ed. I can promise you that."

But as soon as the words left Lance's mouth, he remembered the trickle of electricity he'd felt as he'd shaken Emmett's hand. Considered that the man, as far as Lance knew, was also being held prisoner by the thing named Patrick and his merry band of goons. "Wait...," Lance said. "You saw me here in, what, some sort of vision?"

Emmett nodded again and flashed a big smile full of crooked yellow teeth. "In one of my bubblies."

"Bubblies? I don't ... *what*?"

Emmett turned himself sideways and scooted himself into the corner of the room, with his back against the wall opposite Lance and his legs stretched out on the bench. The bottom of his boots told a lifetime of stories.

"I don't know if I was born with them," Emmett said. "But my earliest memory of one was when I was just a tyke. Maybe three or four years old. I saw my daddy on his bike—he had this big old Harley that didn't run half the time, but he loved that damn thing—and he was just ridin' home from work, comin' down our street when the truck he'd been following slammed on its brakes for a dog that had chased a squirrel into the road. Daddy hadn't really been paying close enough attention, and by the time he noticed, it was almost too late. He skidded to a stop just in time to avoid rear-ending the pickup, but he had to swerve and he lost his balance and the bike went over. His right leg got pinned against the sidewalk. He fractured his ankle.

"I didn't see any of this happen in real life, you understand? And nobody ever told me the whole story. All my mother ever said to me was that Daddy had been in a little accident and hurt himself but he was going to be fine. And all Daddy ever told me was he'd let his head get too high in the fuckin' clouds and he'd paid the price. But I knew it all, every detail, because I saw it in my head before it had happened, earlier that day while I'd been sitting in front of our shitty little television with the big-ass rabbit ears on top, eating a cheese sandwich and watching fuzzy cartoons. I'll never forget that moment, that first time."

Emmett paused and then looked at Lance as if checking to see if he thought he was crazy. Lance didn't think Emmett was crazy at all, so all he did was nod once. "I call them bubblies because I always get the hiccups right after," Emmett said. "I did that first day when I was three or four and I've gotten the damn things every single time since. It's annoying as hell, but hey, I guess it's a small price to pay." He shrugged.

Emmett's story had been short, but the impact of his words had rocked Lance backward. Because despite Lance's ever-present gifts and abilities, and his seemingly increasing strength to use these abilities—plus discover a few new ones along the way—there was one thing that he'd never been able to do.

"You can ... see the future," Lance said. He hadn't been able to conceal the awe in his voice.

"I can," Emmett said.

Lance looked across the room, eyed the third bench. He looked back to Emmett, waited a beat before asking, "What else?"

Emmett laughed, a single bark that sounded more like a cough. "What else? Shit, son, that ain't enough for you? What the hell do *you* do?"

Lance felt the smile spread across his face and then couldn't help but laugh himself. It felt good to laugh. After all the hell he'd been through the last few days, after all the ugly feelings that had repeatedly tried to creep in and bring him down, after all the anticipation of some great and unknown ending that he appeared to be speeding toward, damn it felt good to laugh.

"Well," Lance said, "since you asked ... I can see the dead. I can talk to them too. I can also see other things. Bad things. Things that don't belong in this world. I fight them, when I have to. Oh, and my entire life seems to have been dictated by these" —he shrugged—"feelings I get. Like premonitions or instinct, or whatever you want to call them." Here, he felt the weight of everything begin to crush him down, his questioning of everything starting to rise up again. "I've been a puppet for the Universe. That's my only purpose, I know that now. They"—he pointed out the door—"have been hunting me for a long time. And now they have me."

Because I let them take me, Lance thought.

"Whatever happens here, it's going to be big. Final, maybe. I don't know. All I know is I can't run from it, not this time."

Emmett was quiet for a long time. He uncrossed and crossed his arms, like he was trying to get comfortable. He didn't question anything Lance said. Instead, he asked, "That instinct you talk about, is it sorta like, when you meet a person sometimes you just get this little tingle inside, and that tingle tells you right off everything you need to know about that person, without really telling you anything? Like, hey, this person is a really nice guy, or this dude is a fuckin' asshole that needs to be dealt with?"

Lance nodded. "It can be. More or less."

"It's like an energy, isn't it? Like you've walked into a cloud of static electricity, and it sorta makes your fillings buzz?"

Lance nodded again. "I guess that's one way to describe it. I've also heard people say it's like they're picking up a radio transmission in their head that's being broadcast from a big tower."

Emmett smirked. "Yeah, I've experienced that too."

Lance was trying to keep himself from getting too excited at having found somebody else who at least shared some of his own abilities, somebody else who was fighting the same fight with some of the same weapons. His fascination and own curiosity prompted the question: "And you've had those feelings since you were a kid too?"

This time, Emmett shook his head. "Nope. Experienced them for the very first time the moment that *Baywatch* motherfucker shoved you in here."

Lance said nothing.

"You talk about a broadcast tower. Kid, I think you're it."

Lance fought down the sadness that stirred in his gut. His friend Bernie, who he'd only known for way too short a time, had said the exact same thing to him. That conversation hadn't taken place that long ago, but like everything else that had happened before Lance had awakened in the back seat of the

Plymouth Horizon with the Surfer behind the wheel, it felt like ages ago.

Lance sighed. "If you're here, they must think you're some sort of threat to whatever they're planning to do."

Emmett must have already considered his own reasons for being there, because he quickly replied, "Or they think I'm an asset."

Lance ran with the idea. "Good point. If you can really see the future, they might think you can show them all the possibilities of how this will shake out. Or ... I don't know, act as some sort of, what, psychic weatherman? Predict the day where the conditions will be just right?"

"Conditions for what?"

Lance had no idea. Shrugged.

"Well, the joke's on them," Emmett said. "If they think I can control my bubblies, they aren't as smart as they think they are." He paused, eyed Lance suspiciously. "Unless..."

"Unless what?"

"Unless they think *you* have the ability to control me. Can somehow, I don't fucking know, tap into my mind, flip the switch. I can feel how damn strong you are, kid. Honest. It's like nothing I've ever felt before. Who's to say what you can really do?"

Lance was about to say that was a ridiculous thought, but then he was horrified to realize the man might be right. Lance's powers had increased greatly over the last few months, and for him to say anything was impossible would be ignorant. Because he *didn't* fully know his own strength and was constantly surprising himself. His mind flashed to the character of Lennie from Steinbeck's *Of Mice and Men*.

What would happen if they somehow made me? he

wondered. *If I got inside Emmett's head and flipped the switch, would I break him like Lennie broke the rabbits?*

He had to push the thought away. It wouldn't do any good to ponder such things. He needed to focus on the present.

The endgame for all he and the Universe had been working toward was fast approaching and it could only end in one of two ways: victory or defeat. Lance looked over to the locked door and then once more to the bench across the room. Finally, he looked back to Emmett. It didn't look like either of them were going anywhere, so Lance might as well try and learn as much as he could and figure out just what Emmett's role in all this was.

Because, Lance thought, *if I'm here for a reason, so is he.*

"Ed," Lance said. "Tell me about your bubbly. The one where you saw me."

Emmett swallowed, his Adam's apple bobbing behind the leatherlike skin of his neck. He uncrossed his arms and laced his hands behind his head, then looked up at the ceiling, his eyes going distant, like he was trying to bring forward the memory.

"You know how people talk about having their *Come to Jesus* moment?" he said. "Well, seeing you ... I guess that was mine."

[17]

THEY DECIDED to take Maya's minivan. After covering so many states in so few days, Leah was tired of driving. Plus, Maya knew her own town and would be able to more easily navigate its streets herself instead of constantly giving Leah directions. Leah jumped into the passenger seat, trying her best to shake off any of the lingering feelings of unsettling confusion left behind from the vision she'd had. The inside of the minivan smelled of air freshener and turpentine, but it was clean and tidy and much newer than Leah's Beetle, and Leah nearly moaned in appreciation of the comfortable captain's chair. Maya fastened her seat belt and pushed the button to start the engine. The headlights bloomed to life and Leah glanced at the blue numbers of the clock on the center screen, saw how late it was getting.

Where does a little boy go and stay with it being so late, so dark?

Leah had chosen to operate on the assumption that Noah was in fact out and about of his own free will and not being held captive. And even if she had decided otherwise, she would not betray these thoughts to Maya. She didn't want to scare the woman or put upon her any stress and worry beyond what Maya must already be feeling (and doing well to hide) until the situation absolutely called for it.

In Maya's eyes, Leah was her and her son's savior, and Leah intended to act as such. Even if she had no idea what she was doing. *Because that's what Lance would do.*

You're stronger than you think. His voice in her head.

Leah nodded to herself as Maya backed the minivan around Leah's Beetle and out of the driveway, headlights painting the other houses in the cul-de-sac. When they were headed down the street, Maya finally asked the question that Leah had no real answer for. "So where are we headed?"

There were no streetlamps here, just the dots of porch lights marking the houses as they passed like twinkling stars. Quiet suburban life, still and tranquil. It reminded Leah of home, of her life before. She thought briefly of her daddy, wondered what he was doing right now. She saw him, in her mind, sitting alone in the living room of what had once been their family home but was now vacant except for one. She saw him on the old sofa with the sagging cushions, the flickering light of the television screen reflected on his face. One of his hands held the remote, the other held ... what? A cup of coffee, or something stronger? Something in a bottle?

No, Leah thought. *He's been better. A lot better.*

And it was true. Leah knew that there would have been no way she could have brought herself to leave him behind—leave him *alone*—if he hadn't been capable of handling it.

I was ready and so was he.

Leah thought of all that had followed in the short amount of time that had passed since she'd packed up her car and said goodbye to her daddy and driven out of town, off to join Lance. She thought of the good they'd done together. She thought of how good they *were* together. She thought about her own gifts, her own strengths that she'd come into. She thought about the moment right now, sitting in Maya's minivan and heading off to help the woman find her missing son. A woman who had been seeing Leah in her dreams for years, and a little boy who had seen Lance.

It was all part of the plan. *Leah* was part of the plan. And despite the tragedy she'd recently witnessed, despite Lance being taken from her, despite all the Evil she knew to exist in the world around every corner, Leah did not believe the Universe would sacrifice her father in order to bring her into the fold.

We had our closure, Leah thought. *Lance gave us that. It was time for both Daddy and me to move on.*

Leah wasn't sure if she'd ever be able to completely swallow the pill of guilt that tasted bitter on her tongue, but she'd learn to live with it. While she was thinking of him, and to make herself feel a little better, she quickly pulled out her cell phone and fired off a quick text.

Goodnight, Daddy. I love you!

She put the phone back into her pocket and looked up to see that Maya had stopped the minivan at the stop sign at the end of the street and was looking at her patiently, waiting for an answer to her question.

Leah tried to clear her mind, pushed away all thoughts that did not include Maya and Noah. She closed her eyes and breathed in deep, tried to find those waters that would float her toward her unknown destination. The current found her, and

Leah let herself go. She opened her eyes and said, "Left. Head back into town."

In the glow from the dash, Maya's face lit up with a big smile. She nodded once, as if Leah had correctly guessed an answer that the woman had known all along. "Makes sense," Maya said. She nodded down the road to the right. "Nothing out that way except farmland and the road that will take you back to the highway. It's one of the reasons my ex-husband and I chose this neighborhood. It's right on the edge of town. As far away as we could get from everything without *really* being away from everything, you know?"

Leah nodded but said nothing.

Maya flicked on the minivan's turn signal even though there was no car behind her and checked the street for oncoming traffic in both directions even though the road was clearly empty.

I make her nervous, Leah realized. *She trusts me, but I still make her nervous.*

Which was understandable, Leah reasoned. Hell, she made herself nervous, if she was being honest.

Maya made the turn and drove toward town. They had only gone about a quarter of a mile before there was a great swelling of anxiousness inside Leah's belly and the gentle current that she'd been riding in her mind suddenly became a rough sea, a massive wave growing from the depths and towering above her, ready to crash and toss her away as if she weighed less than nothing at all. It was suffocating, that feeling. Leah's breath caught in her chest and her heart began to beat a staccato rhythm as her head buzzed with dizziness. The hair along her arms and on the back of her neck prickled and her stomach lurched and—

Maya slammed a foot onto the minivan's brake pedal, and even though they hadn't been traveling fast, the tires skidded briefly before the vehicle came to an abrupt stop. Leah's seat belt locked and the fabric bit into her collarbone.

"Oh my stars!" Maya looked at Leah and touched her gently on the shoulder. "Are you alright?"

Leah took a quick inventory of herself and nodded. "Yes, I'm fine," she said through a panicked breath.

And she found that she was in fact fine. The rough sea in her mind had settled and the anxiety had faded. Her breath and heart rate were returning to normal.

"I'm so sorry," Maya said. "He came out of nowhere. It's a miracle I didn't hit him." Maya laughed, a nervous sound that let loose some of the woman's own anxiety she'd been working to keep hidden away. "But you know what they say about 'em. Nine lives and all that."

Bathed in the glow of the headlights, the large gray cat sat directly in the middle of the road, its eyes radiant like cosmic orbs. The sign for Fuller's Funeral Home and Crematorium was to the cat's left, the darkened building sitting back from the road and in the shadows as if tucked away for the night's sleep.

"That's Genesis," Maya said. "He lives at the funeral home." She shrugged. "I guess death doesn't bother cats the way it does most people, huh?"

Leah stared at the cat, remembered the feeling she'd had as she'd driven into town hours earlier, that feeling as if she had been being pulled toward the funeral home instead of Maya's house before it had quickly passed. But not before...

But not before I had to take one last look, Leah thought. *Not before I saw this cat in the rearview mirror.*

Maya tooted the horn twice, just a soft and quick *bip-bip*. The cat didn't move, only stared directly at them.

No. It stared directly at Leah.

Leah felt the hairs on her arms and on the back of her neck prickle again, and the gentle pull of her mind's current began to drift her.

I see you, she said to the cat. *I see you*.

The cat bounded to its right, and made its way past the Fuller's Funeral Home and Crematorium sign and into the parking lot.

Maya had just set her foot on the accelerator, the van creeping forward, when Leah reached out and grabbed the woman's hand. "Wait," she said. And then, knowing how ridiculous it sounded but knowing deep down that it was only what was right, she added, "Follow the cat."

[18]

If Maya thought the instruction to follow the cat was odd, she made no indication of it. Instead, she flicked on her turn signal again (the ever-cautious driver) and made the left turn into Fuller's Funeral Home and Crematorium's empty parking lot.

The minivan's headlights cut cones of light over the blacktop and peeled across the front of the darkened building like a pair of ghosts trying to outrun being seen. Leah sat up in the passenger seat and leaned forward to see over the dash. The gray cat—and my, he *was* big—was sauntering across the lot without looking back, his tail straight up in the air like a flag they were meant to track and follow.

"Are you...," Maya started. She seemed unsure what words to use next. "Are you, I don't know, *sensing* something?"

"Yes," Leah said. But she left it at that. How could she ever explain exactly what she was feeling—the way her mind floated through the everchanging current of an imaginary ocean where the Universe controlled the tide; the way her body's respiratory and circulatory systems reacted in tandem with this mind's-eye environment; how her hair would prickle and her skin would tingle and how it never quite made any sense, except ... except it did? It did make sense, but only to Leah, and only in these moments.

She heard Lance's voice again, another thing he'd said to her once: *Often I just know things in the way only I can know them.*

Leah understood now.

Maya didn't question her or ask for more details, but she too sat up straighter in her seat, and Leah could hear the leather creaking as the woman's fingers gripped the steering wheel tighter. Her eyes were wide and the rest of her body appeared so tense that Leah thought the thermos of coffee that they'd brought along with them wouldn't be needed because Maya was wired with adrenaline.

Or maybe she senses something too, Leah thought. She remembered what Pamela Brody had said to her in the car on that first day she'd appeared: *There's a piece of every mother's soul inside their children.*

Maybe it was that connection now that was sparking to life. Maybe the bit of Maya that lived inside little Noah was reaching out for her now, telling her he was close, ready to go home.

The cat paused at the corner of the building and now it did look back at them, headlights electrifying its eyes in a brief flash of brilliance before, apparently satisfied that they were still following, it disappeared around the side of the building. Maya followed. There was a wide paved path along the side that led around to the back, and when they were halfway down it, Maya pointed and said, "That door there at the end, that's where they bring out the casket and load it into the hearse. Then the driver heads back to the main parking area and leads the procession out onto the street. Most folks here are buried in Mormont's Park—which I've always thought was a lovely name for a cemetery, even if it does cause some confusion for the odd tourist who shows up expecting an actual park where they can have a barbecue or throw a frisbee—but a few now and then choose to be placed in Red Knoll Cemetery, which is the next town over. I think it's mostly a family thing, the ones that go there..."

Leah looked ahead and saw the dark fabric awning that protected the top of the door Maya had pointed out, the place where folks got loaded up for their final ride. There was no need for Maya to have told her anything about the cemeteries (*God, please don't let us end up in one of those tonight*), and Leah took the woman's rambling as another sign of her nervousness. Leah could understand. After all, when you were trusting your guardian angel to show you the way to find your missing son and the first place you ended up was the local funeral home, it didn't exactly paint happy pictures in your head.

The cat was nowhere to be seen as they approached the end of the building. In front, the headlights illuminated a row of dense trees that lined the rear of the funeral home's lot. Their mostly bare branches waved lazily in a quickening breeze, and dead leaves swirled at the base of their trunks as if trying to leap back into their parents' arms. Maya drove forward and when the nose of the minivan was past the building's side wall, a droplet of gray fell into Leah's peripheral.

The rear lot was not as well kept as the funeral home's front. Back here, the asphalt was cracking and needed to be resealed, stray weeds squirting through in some places. Two hearses were parked one behind the other parallel to the back of the building, and a much older one, with flat tires and a rusted front fender, was backed into the back right corner of the lot, as if it too were waiting to be loaded up for its own final ride, off to the great junkyard in the sky. The cat was sitting patiently three-quarters of the way across the asphalt lot, and when Maya steered the minivan toward it, it moved again, making a diagonal back toward the building, stopping just in front of a door all the way at the far end. There was another awning over this door, but just like the rest of the funeral home's rear lot, it too was in slight disrepair, its fabric torn in spots, tattered strips hanging down from one side.

"Ever been back here?" Leah asked as Maya slowed the van and then put it into park once they'd reached the back door.

Maya shook her head and then shivered, whether because of the cold or because of the ominous vibe that suddenly seemed to have filled the van, Leah wasn't sure. "No. Never. Only inside and around the front. Last time was this past spring. Jessica Jenson passed away. Breast cancer. Terrible. They caught it too late. She owned a fabric store that was just lovely. She bought two of my paintings and hung them there. They're ... well, I suppose they're still hanging there."

Leah glanced in the sideview mirror, saw the blackened rear window of one of the hearses. She made herself look away before her imagination conjured the image of a body suddenly sitting up inside, turning to look at her with eyes that were no longer human.

It was silly, really. To have the ability to see the dead and still get creeped out by nightmarish images you might see in horror films.

The cat meowed. Just once, barely audible over the minivan's idling engine, but once was enough to snap Leah back to attention. She leaned forward and studied the animal. *I see you*, she said to it again, reaching out with her mind. *I see you.*

The cat turned and walked casually toward the funeral home's back door and then slipped easily through a cat door that was cut into the bottom third of it. But wait...

"That's a really big cat door," Leah said, squinting, trying to make sure her mind wasn't playing tricks on her.

Maya shook her head. "Must have been for Winter."

Leah didn't look away from the large pet door, but she crinkled her brow and shook her head. "Why would ... do they change the size of the door for each season?"

Maya was quiet for a beat, then tried to stifle a laugh which made it sound like a small cough. Now Leah did turn to look at the woman.

"Sorry," Maya said, waving her hand in an apology. "Nathan—that's Mr. Fuller—had a dog named Winter. It was a husky, and the sweetest thing you'd ever meet. Nathan used to walk him through the neighborhood. In the summer, if I saw them coming in time, I'd bring Nathan out some iced tea and a small dish of water for Winter. We'd chat for a bit and then they'd be on their way. Winter passed away, gosh, I guess it's been about two years ago now." Maya paused and looked out the windshield, staring at nothing in particular, as if reliving those warm summer days full of friendly chitchat and cold drinks. "Sweetest thing."

She's a good person, Leah thought. *I can feel it the way I can feel my own beating heart.*

And for some reason this revelation felt bigger than it should have, as if Maya's pure soul had been waiting all this time for recognition, longing for somebody—somebody like Leah—to come along and say...

I see you.

I see who you are.

Leah looked at the pet door again, a door big enough for a husky to easily glide in and out from. "Maya," she said. "You said Noah was a little small for his age, right?"

Maya nodded. "Yes. But the doctors expect he'll hit a growth spurt soon enough. His father was over six feet."

Leah didn't care about how big Noah was going to get, she only cared about how big he was right now, and if when off on one of his adventures he somehow found himself in this back lot of the funeral home, how easily he could have slipped himself through the same door the cat just had. She looked to her left, out the other side of the van and toward the row of trees and the woods beyond. Tried to imagine a path, as the crow flies, from here to Maya's home at the end of the cul-de-sac on a street less than a quarter mile away. It would be an easy walk, she figured, if you were willing to make your way through the woods.

Leah got out of the minivan and walked to the funeral home's back door, hearing Maya kill the engine and then step out to follow. The two women stood in front of the door, the tattered strips of the awning overhead slapping each other playfully in the breeze, and Leah reached out and tried the doorknob. It was locked, of course. A deadbolt just above the doorknob didn't give at all.

Leah thought that there must certainly be an alarm system installed, but when she looked down at the pet door again, she considered the idea that maybe the alarm was only wired to open/close sensors on the doors and windows, possibly glass-breaker sensors, too. But maybe there weren't any motion sensors inside. Maybe if a person managed to get in without smashing a window or picking a lock or kicking in a door, they'd have full run of the place.

But why? Why would somebody break into a funeral home?

But the answer was obvious.

Because he's a little kid with a big imagination and an appetite for exploring.

Leah pointed down to the pet door. "Think we can fit through that?"

Maya's face was stone serious. "He's in there, isn't he? My little Noah is ... *in there.*"

"But he's *alive,*" Leah quickly affirmed. She had no physical evidence of this fact, but she remembered the pull she'd felt as they'd been driving along the street, hell, the pull she'd felt for the last two days as she'd let her mind's current drift her across the country. The boy was important, somehow, and Leah had been brought here to find him alive. She knew

(*Often I just know things in the way only I can know them.*)

this was the truth, even if she didn't understand the full implication of it all.

"You, maybe," Maya said. "Skinny little thing. But me"—she patted her hips—"I don't know."

Leah looked from the door to Maya and then back to the door. "I'll go first and then, if I make it in, I want you to try. When I find Noah, I want you there with me. I don't want him to only see a stranger. I don't want to frighten him any more than he might already be."

Is *he frightened?* The kid, if Leah had it right, had managed to hike through the woods on his own and climb through a pet door and into what he must clearly understand to be a funeral home ... a place where there were sure to be dead bodies.

"You're not a stranger," Maya said. "He's seen your face his entire life. In my paintings."

Leah said nothing. Just nodded once and then squatted down and carefully worked her way headfirst through the pet door's heavy plastic flap. It was a little tight around her shoulders, but once she found the right angle she was able to slide right in, pulling her knees and feet through and then pushing up from the floor fast, as if there might be an attacker waiting that she needed to fend off. She did a quick spin around and saw nothing but a small darkened kitchen that smelled faintly of cleaning chemicals and ... other chemicals, things she suspected had nothing to do with causing a stainless-steel sink to shine or scrubbing caked-on grease from a casserole dish. The appliances were beige and looked decades old. The refrigerator hummed and rattled like something was trying to escape from inside. A square Formica-topped tabled sat in the middle of the room, surrounded by four metal folding chairs. Two of the chairs were pulled away, scooted back after their occupants had left, and Leah shivered a chill as she imagined two corpses lumbering up from somewhere down below and making their slow and uncoordinated trek down the hallway and into the kitchen, maybe to share a beer with each other one last time, commiserating the end of their stories.

Maya's head popped through the pet door. Leah stepped back and watched as the woman wiggled to get her shoulders through and, as Maya had predicted, struggled to find an angle where her hips would be able to free themselves. With a few grunts and a single mumbled curse word, Maya eventually popped through the door and Leah reached down and helped her up.

The two women stood in silence, the fridge humming and rattling. "I guess we didn't trigger an alarm," Leah said. "Unless it's silent."

Maya nodded. Opened her mouth to say something, but just then Genesis the cat leapt up onto the table in the middle of the kitchen, causing both women to jump back and let out surprised gasps, grabbing onto each other and then quickly laughing at their foolishness. The cat watched them apathetically. His eyes seemed to glow in the dark, and Leah watched as the cat's gaze drifted from one woman to the other before it turned and jumped back to the floor and padded through a doorway into the hall.

Leah pulled her cell phone from her pocket and turned on the flashlight, shining the light ahead and moving to follow the cat. The hallway was very wide and ended abruptly to her left, where a large landscape photograph of a mountain range full of fall foliage was framed and hung. Down the hallway to the right, the cat sat outside a set of closed double doors. Leah walked toward it and shined her light up at the small sign affixed to one of the doors. It read: STAFF ONLY.

She reached for the brass knob, expecting it to be locked, but was surprised to feel it turn easily in her grip. With Maya so close behind her that Leah could feel the woman's breath on the back of her neck, she pushed the door open slowly. The hinges made no sound. As soon as the door was halfway opened, the cat shot away, bounding back into the kitchen. The sound of the plastic flap on the pet door followed soon after.

"My stars...," Maya whispered. "It's like he got spooked."

But Leah barely heard her. She was shining her light into the vast space, which turned out to be a storage room of sorts. The entire left and far walls were fully lined with caskets. But the caskets weren't laid out lengthwise, like you'd normally expect to see them when attending a funeral or watching one get lowered into the earth. Here, to maximize the storage room's space, the caskets were set on their ends, standing tall like a row of soldiers shoulder to shoulder, awaiting orders. Upright like this, they almost looked like they could be elegant closet doors, or...

Maya's words from earlier slapped Leah in the face.

He says he goes to his wardrobe. That's all he'll tell me.

Leah took a step into the room. "Noah?" she called.

Silence.

She turned and looked at Maya, who was just coming inside the room. When she crossed the threshold and let the door go, it swung shut behind her with a soft thud and click. "You try," Leah said.

Maya nodded. Stood tall and cleared her throat. "Noah, honey. Noah, are you here?"

For just a second, there was again just silence. But then, a voice. Small, but not afraid. "Mom? Is that you?"

Maya instantly burst into tears, letting out a rush of air as they fell quickly down her cheeks. She laughed and shook her head, wiped the tears away. "I'm here, honey. I'm here. Where are you? Are you stuck?"

Two things happened then. One, the hair on the back of Leah's neck didn't just prickle but practically vibrated, and an icy hand gripped her heart. The ocean in her mind darkened with storm clouds and the water began to churn and a great clap of thunder seemed to shake her vision. Two, Noah's voice came again. "Careful, Mom. It's out there."

Leah understood.

The three of them were not alone in the room of coffins.

[19]

"You KNOW how people talk about having their *Come to Jesus* moment?" Emmett had said. "Well, seeing you ... I guess that was mine."

The words hung in the air between the two men in the GUEST HOLDING AREA, got tangled in the cobwebs and stuck there for all to see and examine. Whether he liked to admit it or not, Lance understood that throughout his life he had essentially played the role of savior for several people, in several towns, all with different problems. The word *savior* could mean different things to different people, could carry great weight or be so light that a small gust of wind could send it sailing away, forgotten as quickly as it had been formed. It wasn't a title Lance would ever give himself; he was only a young man who had tried to do good for people, tried to fight back against the demons that plagued the earth—both metaphorically and literally.

But whatever he was about to hear told from Emmett Emmanuel Dean's lips would be something different, something beyond anything Lance had ever experienced. Because with all those other people Lance had helped, his time of saving, in all its many forms, had only come after he'd arrived, after he'd met them and heard their stories and done what he could to set things right.

He'd never met Emmett before, never seen him, never spoken to him, and never heard of him. Lance had known the man less than an hour, but it seemed Emmett had known him a lot longer than that.

"I'm not saying that to try and be damn dramatic either," Emmett added. "I mean what I said, Lance. Seeing you changed my life. I don't know what all this is"—he gestured around the room—"but I know it's important, and we're both supposed to be here."

Lance nodded, just once. "Tell me."

Emmett uncrossed and crossed his arms, the ropy muscle of his forearms making the faded tattoos wiggle like serpents. "I will," he said, "but first I want to ask you a question, if that's alright."

"Sure," Lance said, smiling. "Anything. That's what friends do, right, Ed?"

Emmett smiled, but it was weak, almost pained. "That's right." He cleared his throat. "Earlier, you talked about your purpose. Said something about how you were a puppet for the Universe, how your whole life had been sort of guided to this moment."

"Correct."

"When did you know?" Emmett asked. "When, with all your powers, did you realize that you were being driven toward something big, something *important*? And when you realized it, did it change you at all? Did it change your life?"

For such a big question, Lance was surprised at how easily

the answer came to him. "I think I've always known, at least on some level," he said. "When I was younger, I think I tried to ignore it, tried to push away the potential grand scope of what I was and what I could do, but it was always there. Just this nagging sense that, whatever I had planned for myself in life, the Universe was going to intervene and make sure that at the end of the day I did what was required of me. It made sure I never strayed too far from the path it had set out for me."

Emmett shook his head, and this time the smile was one of sympathy. "Ever since you were a kid?"

Lance nodded. "Since the day I was born."

"*Damn.* How did you deal with that? I mean, young boys, and certainly teenagers, are fucked up enough most of the time without all the *Sixth Sense* bullshit you carried around with you."

Again, the first part of the answer came easily enough. "My mother," Lance said. "She was always there to hold my hand. To boost me up or talk me off the ledge. She was the biggest reason. Her, and the fact that I've tried to never take myself too seriously." Lance felt a grin creep across his face. "But if I'm being honest, I probably got that from her too. Though I don't think she always appreciated my brand of humor." He stopped himself before he fell any further down his own well of memories. Brought himself back to the moment, Emmett's moment. He sighed. "So yeah, I tried to ignore it for as long as I could ... but then, well, my mother was killed and my life got upended and I couldn't pretend any longer."

Emmett studied Lance's face, and Lance let him. He held the man's stare and waited for him to work out whatever it was he was trying for. Finally, Emmett pointed to the door that led back to the office area. "They killed her, didn't they?"

This answer was more complicated, and Lance didn't feel like getting into it. Instead, he crossed his arms and asked, "Did you see it? In one of your bubblies?"

Emmett shook his head. "No. It was just a feeling. I'm sorry for your loss."

"Thank you."

"What was her name?"

"Pamela."

Emmett smiled. "Pretty name."

Lance nodded, felt a lump in his throat threaten to block his words. "She was beautiful."

A quietness fell over the room, a small moment of silence held in honor of Lance's mother.

"My dad died ten years ago," Emmett said. He was looking up toward the ceiling again, ready to continue his story. "Heart attack. Old bastard loved his fried foods and cigarettes, and the only exercise he ever got was hauling around bike parts or lugging the cooler of beer out to the backyard when we'd have a barbecue and he'd invite over all his buddies. He was tough, my daddy. The heart attack that finally got him was his third. Three strikes, you're out, right? He was tough, but he was ... good, I guess. I mean, he was definitely rough around the edges—sometimes too rough—but he wasn't bad, not really. He wasn't a perfect father, but shit, who is, right? He was enough of a father for me. I saw and heard about a lot worse things other kids' dads did when I was growing up. And those were just the ones that stuck around."

Emmett's words struck a surprising sting of envy into Lance's soul. He had never known his own father.

"He loved me and my mom," Emmett said. "We knew that.

Even though he had his fair share of slipups, we knew. Overall, we were a happy family."

"Slipups?" Lance asked.

Emmett nodded, smiled while still staring up at the dirty white ceiling. "That's when I started using the bubblies to my advantage. Looking back, I suppose it's possible that the Universe was trying to show me that I didn't need to be scared of my bubblies, that they could be used for good. They could be used to help people, starting with my mom and me.

"See, my daddy liked to drink. I don't know that I'd go so far to say he was an alcoholic, but on the weekends, and sometimes even midweek if the right team was playing and he and a few of his buds would go watch down at the bar, he'd knock back his full share of cold ones. He wasn't an overly pleasant man to begin with." Emmett looked at Lance and pointed a finger at him. "Not *mean*, mind you, but just"—he shrugged—"gruff."

Lance nodded. "Rough around the edges. Like you said."

Emmett snapped his fingers. "Bingo." He looked back to the ceiling. "So, when he had too many beers, that gruffness would turn into a sort of ... blind rage. It was like all of a sudden all the little things that might have ordinarily just caused him to mutter a cuss word under his breath now resulted in full-on meltdowns. And, well, my daddy was a big man."

Lance felt a sinking feeling in his gut. "He got physical?"

Emmett nodded. "Yep. But not in the way you're thinking. My mom was too damn smart to have stuck around or have kept me there in the house if he had beat us. No, when he got drunk he tended to take his anger out on the house, thankfully. He'd come home and be like a fucking bull in a china shop. I'll spare you all the details, but let's just say he ended up patching more than one hole in the walls of the living room and hallway, replaced a couple windows, a few doorknobs, a microwave ... oh, hell, he wrecked a bunch of shit.

"He was always somber and sobered up the next morning. Always apologizing and hugging us and telling us he was going to fix everything. And he did. If he couldn't do it himself, he had a buddy who could. He always cleaned things up and made them right. But that didn't change the fact that when the tornado was actually coming through, it was scary as hell to watch, and you were always afraid of what *might* happen if you eventually ended up in its path.

"So one day, maybe two years or so after that first bubbly I got when my daddy wrecked his bike, I was riding the bus home from school and when it pulled up to the stop in our neighborhood I saw my mom standing there on the sidewalk with a few of the other parents, and it happened. The whole bus and the other kids just vanished, and I saw in my head—like I was watching a movie—my daddy kicking in the back door of our house, the one off the kitchen in what my mom always called the mudroom, because he was swaying so much he couldn't get the key in the lock. My mom had been in the mudroom, straightening a few things, and when the door exploded open a chunk of wood splintered from the frame and caught her in the eye. She screamed. It was an awful sound. A sound I'd never heard her make before.

"Then the whole image snapped away and I was back on the bus, just as it was coming to a complete stop and the kids were starting to stand up to get off. I started hiccuping as I made my way down the aisle to the front. It was a Friday, which meant Daddy would more than likely be heading out with his buds after dinner. I was smart enough to put the pieces together to at least test my theory."

Lance nodded. "You told your mom?"

"Not exactly. What I really did was bug the ever-loving shit out of her, begged her to take me one town over to the movie theater to see some stupid fucking Disney film that had just come out. We didn't go to the movies a lot, mostly because of the drive, plus the expense, I'm sure. We usually waited and rented our movies on VHS once they got them in down at Hi-Tech Video in town. Daddy knew a guy there that would always put his name at the top of the reservation list when he asked." Emmett smirked and shook his head. "Daddy always knew a guy, always had a buddy somewhere. I think that was maybe his own gift. I think I got a part of that, too, honestly. I've always been able to talk to people easily, make them feel at ease. Make them feel like I'm their bud."

"So did she take you?" Lance asked. "Did your mom take you to the movie?"

"Sure did. She asked me if I wanted to take my pal Robbie with us, and I think she felt happy when I told her no, that I wanted it to be just the two of us. I think she must have thought that it wouldn't be forever that her little boy would be little and want to spend time with her, so she might as well take advantage of it while she could. I felt a little guilty about that. Because of course I wanted to take my friend to the movies. But I knew we'd be getting back late and Robbie would end up spending the night, and I was pretty sure I knew what we'd all be coming home to.

"And sure enough, I was right. We stopped for ice cream on the way home, and there was an accident on the highway that stopped us for what felt like forever, so we didn't pull into the driveway until quarter till midnight. Daddy's bike wasn't there, which didn't mean he wasn't home. Like I said, Daddy was rough, but he wasn't bad, and he certainly wasn't dumb. He'd usually find a ride home if he'd had too much, even if he ended up burning through more of his paycheck for cab fare. Sure enough, when we went through the front door, the place smelled like burnt popcorn and the microwave door was open and the water from the kitchen faucet was running even though the kitchen was empty. Mom told me stay put, and she walked into the kitchen, calling my daddy's name. He didn't answer, but I saw her go around the corner toward the mudroom and heard her cuss. Then she came back and smiled at me and said everything was alright and to go ahead and go off to bed, and to make sure I brushed my teeth extra good, because of the ice cream.

"The next morning I got up and went to make myself a Pop-Tart and peeked into the mudroom and saw that the door frame was broken and there was a piece of duct tape keeping the door closed. Daddy's keys were sticking out from under the little shelf where we were supposed to put our shoes."

On the whole, Emmett's story was that of a small victory against an unnecessary accident that might have cost his mother an eye, but Lance marveled at the implications. Emmett had been just a boy at the time of this particular bubbly, but as the man had grown into the person he was now, had the stakes of his bubblies grown with him? Had his visions allowed him to graduate from saving an eye to saving a life ... or *lives*?

"This happened a handful of other times," Emmett said. "Over the next couple years I managed to find ways to get myself and my mom out of the house on nights when I saw that Daddy was going to do some damage."

"Did you ever tell her?" Lance asked. "Did you ever tell either one of them what you could do?"

Emmett shook his head. "Nope. I was afraid they'd take me to the doctor, or worse, cart me off and lock me up in the loony bin." He eyed Lance, cocked his head to the side. "Did you ever worry about that sort of thing?"

Lance nodded. "Sure. Mom and I only trusted one other person in town with my secret. A police officer that eventually became the mayor and a great friend." Another pang of sadness hit Lance in the gut as he realized that he might never get to speak to or see Marcus Johnston again. He wished he could have gotten to give the man a proper goodbye and thank him for everything he'd done for the Brody family over the years.

"Turns out I didn't have to worry about my mom finally catching on to my not-so-subtle warnings that dad was about to have an episode. Aside from the fact that she was getting more attuned to the pattern herself, she eventually had enough and put her foot down. And let me tell you, when my mother put her foot down, she slammed it down hard and didn't let up. She sat my daddy down at the kitchen table one Wednesday night—I remember it was Wednesday because the Schwan's truck had just left and I was happy because Mom bought me some of their mac and cheese—and she gave him his ultimatum. I was in the living room watching the television, eating my microwaved mac and cheese, but I turned the volume down a bit so I could hear them. She told Daddy that he had two choices. He could either stop drinking so much and coming home acting like a complete embarrassment to our family, or she was going to pack her and my suitcases and leave him, plain and simple. One more night of drunken destruction and he could say goodbye to both of us forever."

Emmet was smiling at the memory. "She kept her voice so calm, and you could tell she had practiced her little speech. She told Daddy he was too good a man and had too many important things in his life to keep acting like a child. And you know what he said?"

"What?"

"Nothing. The kitchen got real quiet and then I heard Daddy go out the back and soon after the sound of his Harley starting up. He drove off and didn't come back till after my bedtime. That night when I was lying in bed, I was sure I was going to get a bubbly. Was *hoping* for one, because I thought it would show me whether or not I was going to have a daddy anymore. I didn't think I'd ever fall asleep, but I did. The sound of his bike's engine woke me up when he got home. I don't know what time it was, but the house was dark and silent and it didn't matter. He was home."

"Did she keep her word?" Lance asked. "Your mother?"

Emmett shrugged. "She would have, trust me. But she didn't have to worry about it. I never saw Daddy have more than a single beer or two at a time for the rest of the time I lived at home. I started seeing a lot more soda pop and glasses of iced tea. *God*, the sweet tea he'd make. So much sugar it was like syrup. But anyway, I never had any more bubblies about my own family after that time. Like I said, he was rough around the edges, but my daddy loved us. He made his choice."

"How long after this did you see me?" Lance asked, unable to contain his own curiosity.

Emmett adjusted himself on the bench. Cracked his neck and popped his knuckles. Looked at Lance and said, "I'm getting there. I want you to hear all of this. I need to ... well, I guess it just feels good to finally tell somebody."

[20]

Lance had been trying to keep himself patient, because he wanted—no, *needed*—to hear Emmett's story. But when the man fell quiet for almost two full minutes after telling Lance it felt good to finally tell somebody whatever it was he was about to tell, Lance felt the irritation begin to stir inside him. He glanced at the door that sealed him and Emmett off from the rest of the empty park and the rest of the world, then gave another quick glance to the bench opposite him before finally looking back to Emmett.

"Ed," Lance said, "I'm not trying to be rude, but I don't exactly know how much time we have before they come back for us, and the more I know before that happens, the more we know about each other, I think that's for the better. So, unless you've had one of your bubblies that's told you we have another couple hours of free time to kill..."

Emmett understood. He looked away from the ceiling and nodded. "You're right. I'm sorry. I guess I was just caught up in my own mind, reliving it all." He laughed and then rubbed his face with his hands. "It was sort of like my life flashing before my eyes." He looked at Lance, his eyes now serious and red from where he'd rubbed at them. "Do you think we're going to die here?"

Lance shrugged. He had asked himself a version of this question at every town where he'd stopped since he'd left his hometown. That feeling that everything had been building to this, the taste of finality that had seemed to accompany his every breath since the Reverend and the Surfer and Patrick had taken him, had only grown stronger. "I think there's going to be death, yes," Lance said. "I'd like to say that it won't be us."

"But you can't." Emmett nodded. "I wish I could say for certain. I wish I could see it. I wish I could see a way out of this for us, Lance."

Lance shook his head. "I don't think that's the point, Ed. I don't think we're supposed to *get out* of this. I think we're going to have to survive whatever it is that's coming. Stand our ground and hope that we're strong enough."

Emmett thought about this. "Do you think we are? Strong enough?"

"I don't think we'd be here if there wasn't a chance we were."

For a moment, Emmett seemed to like this answer, but then his face fell and his lips pursed and he shook his head. "Maybe you are, Lance. In fact, I'd bet you're more than strong enough to take on these monsters *and* the horses they rode in on. But me..." He looked up to the ceiling again, his head resting against the wall. "This is my punishment. The Universe is giving me my chance for atonement." He sighed, long and heavy, and then closed his eyes and continued his story.

"You know how in that *Back to the Future* movie, I think it was the second one, the bad guy gets his hands on the sports almanac from the future and then goes back in time and makes a bunch of money by betting? See, my bubblies were never anything like that. I could see the future, sure, I'd confirmed that well and good when I was just a tyke. But for a long time, the things I was seeing were little things, and things close to home—like my daddy's accident, and knowing when he was going to drink too much and come home to cause a scene. In high school they got more frequent, but again, it was smaller stuff at first. Like knowing we were going to have a snow day because a blizzard was gonna come dump fourteen inches, or deciding to take rural routes instead of the highway heading out on a date because there was going to be a traffic accident that would slow things down." He laughed. "Hell, Lance, I was so dumb and ignorant when I was a teenager—you know how they all are, think they're immortal and impervious to any harm—I didn't even stop to think that the reason I might have foreseen the traffic accident wasn't just to get me and my date to the movies on time, but to make sure we weren't part of the accident itself. My point is, it's no wonder the Universe—it feels good to have a name for it, by the way—didn't trust me with anything more important than that sort of thing.

"But then I graduated and got older. No college for me, just started out by helping my dad in the shop. I'd been learning all about bikes my whole life, whether I wanted to or not, so it just seemed like the natural order of things. Eventually got the itch to get out of town, which was understandable, considering what a tiny place I'd spent my whole life in. It's weird, you know, spending all your time helping people fix the things that take them places but never going anywhere yourself. Anyway, I found a job at a garage in a bigger town the next state over and have bounced around from shop to shop ever since. I'd work and save up enough cash to hit the road for a while, finally getting to see this great big beautiful country of ours, and then when funds got tight I'd stop and work some more. Some places I liked a lot and would stay for a year or so, sometimes two, others I was in and out as fast as I could, once my wallet was fat enough.

"Joined a few gangs—and I'm not talking *Sons of Anarchy* shit here, either. Just good guys and gals who love to ride. There's a culture and a comradery you build out there, just you and your crew and a rumbling engine between your legs and miles of blacktop in front of you."

That smile was back on Emmett's face, the good ole days apparently rolling by in his mind the way the landscape must have rolled by during all those miles.

"I've been back and forth across the country more times than I can count," Emmett said. "I've seen it all, Lance. All the good, all the bad, and all things that fall through the cracks." He cleared his throat, cracked his knuckles again. "The bubblies followed me the whole time, and they started getting darker, you know? They got..." He searched for a word. "Heavy. I had visions that would tell me that the roadside joint in New Mexico we were thinking of stopping at for lunch the next day was going to get raided by the ATF and four people would get shot and killed before it was all over, or one time, I saw that there were going to be dirty cops working security at a bike festival we were going to, planting narcotics in peoples' bikes and then making bogus arrests unless they'd pony up some cash to make it go away. I saw a lot of the bad in people, Lance, saw a lot of it before they had a chance to show it.

"I did my best to steer myself and any group I was with clear of the bad stuff, but it could be hard to do, you know, without ever really being able to explain why. I met some superstitious guys on the road, a lot of very spiritual ones, too, and I suppose that if I had explained my bubblies to some of them they might have accepted it, or at least not laughed in my face. But I was too scared. It was a secret I'd had my entire life ... why change things? What good would it do? At the end of the day I could only control my own actions. I couldn't always save everyone."

This was something Lance himself had struggled with over the years. It didn't seem to matter how many times he did good, how many bad things he helped keep from happening, there were always others. There was always going to be pain and suffering and loss in the world, and he couldn't cure them all. He could only take one day, one moment at a time, and do everything he could to make them count.

"There were still the little things, too," Emmett said. He laughed again. "Like the time I told Pete Harbinger not to order the fish tacos from that food truck or he'd spend the next thirty-six hours shitting himself. Now *there's* a vision I could have done without."

Lance chuckled and could sense that Emmett had reached the part of his story he'd been building toward.

Sure enough, the man's face grew solemn again, and after maybe thirty seconds of silence, Emmett looked at Lance with guilty eyes. "I let her die, Lance. I was selfish and I let her die."

Lance said nothing.

"Melody Rhodes," Emmett said. "I'll never forget the name. The newspaper said she had been twenty-three years old and originally from Birmingham but had moved away after college to put her engineering degree to use for one of the big oil companies. The newspaper also said that after going out with some friends to a honky-tonk called Fritters, she'd ended up raped and murdered. Her body was found in a dumpster behind a strip mall less than a mile away.

"I saw her that night, Lance. I was at Fritters the night she was raped and killed. I was there with one of the other guys I was working with at the time—a big fucking guy named Joe who I swear to you could bench-press a Harley in his sleep but was one of the most laid-back and gentle dudes I'd ever met. We called him Sleepy, because his eyes always looked half-closed and he never hurried." Emmett shook his head. "I don't know why I'm telling you all that, it's not like the details matter, but I guess it just helps me tell it all, you know?"

"Sure," Lance said.

"Sleepy and I are there at the bar, just watching the game and relaxing a bit—it had been a *hell* of a week, twice as busy as usual at the garage, and we were both beat—and I saw her and some of her friends walk in shortly after we got there. Sleepy actually saw them all first, because I heard him whistle under his breath and say 'My *goodness*' and when I followed his stare, I saw them. Three girls and two guys, all young and perfectly beautiful, you know? The way all young people are to old guys like me. The girls were all wearing tight jeans, and yeah, they had nice asses. That's what got Sleepy whistling. I was about to clap him on the shoulder and say something dumb, like tell him to pick his jaw up off the floor, or ask him how many pills he'd have to pop just to get hard enough to do anything about it, but then it hit me. A bubbly."

Emmett swallowed and his eyes narrowed to slits, like he was trying hard to see something far away.

"It was quick, Lance. Like the snap of your fingers. But in

that snap, all of Fritters blinked away and I wasn't sitting on a barstool anymore. Instead, I was standing on the side of the road in the pitch black of night. Off in the distance, maybe a mile or so away, I could see the lights of some buildings, but in front of me was nothing except a small sedan on the gravel shoulder of the road with steam hissing out of the hood, and a big silver pickup truck idling beside it. Melody Rhodes was up on her tiptoes, and she said into the passenger-side window of the truck, 'Yeah, I'm not far. Thank you so much!' and pulled the door open and climbed in. The truck drove off, and then everything snapped back into place and I was back on the barstool and Sleepy was asking the bartender for another round of beers. I started hiccuping and Sleepy looked at me with those half-closed eyes and said, 'Another beer will cure those right up.' I forced on the best smile I could muster and picked up the bottle the bartender had just set in front of me and clinked it against Sleepy's and said I look forward to finding out.

"And the hiccups did stop. After a few sips they stopped, and even though Sleepy laughed and was proud of his own medicinal advice, it wasn't the beer. The hiccups never lasted long after a bubbly. Usually only a minute or two, like my body was physically trying to cleanse itself of some toxin, whatever remnants the bubbly had left behind inside me. So yeah, the hiccups stopped, but the cold feeling didn't."

"Cold feeling?" Lance asked. He sat up straighter on the bench and crossed his arms, mimicking Emmett.

Emmett thought for a moment and then nodded. "That's the best way I can describe it. But it wasn't like a cold on the outside—this feeling was on the inside. Like ... like I had ice in my veins. But no, that's not really it either. It was like I had sadness in my veins. Sadness and worry and heartbreak. It was like I'd just experienced a great loss.

"I hadn't had that feeling until the bubbly. Until I'd seen Melody Rhodes climb into that pickup truck. It had seeped into me then, and followed me back to Fritters."

Lance nodded. "You knew something bad was going to happen if Melody got into that truck. That's what the Universe was telling you."

"I did. I didn't know what, but the whole thing was making me sick. It was this clinging sense of dread that I couldn't shake. But you know what I did, Lance? You know what Emmett Emmanuel Dean, certified piece of shit, did? I fucking ignored it, Lance. I did *nothing*."

Lance felt something rise in his throat, and he was surprised to see it was anger.

You don't get a choice, he thought to himself. *That's not the way it works.*

"At first I thought I might do something," Emmett said. "At first, when that cold feeling was strongest and it was still early enough, I figured I'd wait till the girl left and I'd maybe tell her to call a cab instead, or get a friend to take her home. Hell, I even thought maybe I'd follow her on my bike, and when her car broke down it could be me that got to her first instead of whoever was driving that silver pickup. You know, I could be a regular old Prince Charming riding up on a hog instead of a steed. That was my plan. I was going to make sure she was alright."

Emmett sighed big and rubbed at his face again, leaving red marks on his stubbled cheeks. "But then it got later and later, Lance. The game Sleepy and I were watching went into extra innings and we kept drinking and ... I was so damn tired, Lance.

Like I said, it had been a long fucking week and the A/C in the shop wasn't working right and, hell, I was getting *old*. Sometime around midnight, I found my eyes closing as I sat there on that barstool, doing my best Sleepy impersonation. He clapped me on the back with one of those big strong hands of his and jolted me awake, nearly knocking me to the floor. He said he was heading out, asked if I was alright. I told him I was. Said I was going to hit the head and then probably head home myself.

"And that's all I really wanted to do. I was buzzed to shit—okay, I was probably drunk—and exhausted and in that moment all I wanted to do was go home and go to bed. That cold feeling was still there, Lance, but I was pushing it down, trying to fight it off. I felt sick to my stomach, but I told myself it was the nachos and wings Sleepy and I had shared. I tried convincing myself that the bubbly I'd had didn't mean anything. That all it was really saying to me was that the young lady was going to have car trouble, but not to fret, a good Samaritan in a silver pickup was going to save the day. *He'd* be her Prince Charming, not me. Hell, maybe she even knew the guy, right? I mean, she'd sounded happy and relieved when I'd watched her bounce up on her tiptoes and say, 'Yeah, I'm not far. Thank you so much!' Because aren't women these days smart enough not to get into the truck of a complete stranger in the middle of the night? Haven't they seen enough horror stories on the news and don't they take all these self-defense classes? And this girl had a fucking *engineering* degree, Lance." Emmett shook his head, sighed again. "Or course, I didn't know that at the time. That's just something else I told myself after, to try and make myself feel better.

"I toughed it out another twenty minutes, and when Melody Rhodes and her young and beautiful friends showed no signs of leaving, had in fact just put more money into the jukebox over in the corner by the pool tables, I knew I had to go. I wasn't going to make it much longer. Between the alcohol and the exhaustion and the sick feeling inside me, I was done. So you know what I did? You know what big and righteous act I offered before leaving, just something to try and fool myself into thinking that I tried to do the right thing?"

Lance shook his head.

"I walked over to their group—they were all singing and laughing and having the greatest time of their fucking lives—and when they noticed me I did my best to smile and I told them all to please be careful driving home. They all stared at me, like who is this old creepy dude and why is he talking to us? But then..." Emmett's voice broke, and he swallowed and cleared his throat again. "It was Melody who actually spoke. She smiled at me, and Lance, I swear when she did, that sick feeling inside me flashed away for just a second, just a snap of the fingers like when I'd had the bubbly. She said thank you, and that they would be careful."

Lance watched Emmett's face as the man fought back the tears.

"And then I left," Emmett said. "I turned and walked away and rode my bike back to this tiny apartment I was renting above a family's garage and I collapsed onto the bed and was out. I slept till damn near noon the next day, and when I woke up the story was already on the news, about how a young woman's body had been found in the dumpster behind the strip mall. I knew instantly that when they identified the body it was going to be Melody. I knew it with every fiber of my being. And along with that knowledge I knew I had failed. I had failed the test of whoever or whatever was in control, whatever was giving me my bubblies—failed the Universe—and, more devastating than that, I had failed at being an honest and decent human being. I knew something bad was going to happen to that girl, and I chose to look the other way. Why? Because I was *tired.*" He shook his head. "What a piece of shit I am. I talked myself into letting a young woman die just so I could get a few hours' sleep."

"Ed—"

Emmett held up a hand. "No. Don't try and make me feel better. I'm almost finished anyway."

Lance said nothing.

"I tried to kill myself a week later," Emmett said. "I couldn't live with the guilt. I know they say two wrongs don't make a right, or some bullshit like that, but in my mind, me killing myself *would* make things right. I needed to balance out the order of things. Because it just didn't make any sense that I was alive and Melody Rhodes wasn't. I felt like I'd stolen a life, and now I had to repay one.

"There was this stretch of highway about thirty miles out of town that had a real sharp bend to it that overlooked a canyon. It was the first place that popped into my head when I knew I was ready to die. I hopped on the bike and drove out there and when the bend was up ahead I cranked the throttle and had that engine roaring with everything it had to give. The plan was to hit the guardrail going every bit of a hundred or more and then get shot through the air and plummet to the bottom of that canyon and splatter like one of those fucking *Looney Tunes* episodes. If there was any mercy to be had for me, maybe I'd die of a heart attack on the way down. I was pretty sure I wasn't as tough as my daddy, and the first one would do the trick.

Emmett shook his head. Looked at Lance. "But then you showed up."

"Me?"

"Yep. I was about a hundred yards from the bend and then" —Emmett snapped his fingers—"I wasn't on the bike anymore but sitting right here in this room, watching that door open and you be pushed inside. They brought you in and the door closed behind you and then you and I just stared at each other and for that second or two, Lance, I swear it was like I had been filled with helium. I was the lightest and happiest and most at peace I had ever felt in my life. It was like you were a beacon of hope personified. You *radiated*, Lance.

"You looked at me and your lips didn't move but you spoke to me. In my head, you spoke to me. Just a single word. 'Stop.' And then I snapped back to real life and the bend was even closer than I had expected and there was still enough of that helium feeling inside me and I jammed on the brakes hard. I mean, I was grabbing everything, downshifting as fast as I could. Ended up laying the bike down on its side and slid the last thirty or forty yards until I slammed into the guardrail.

"I was still hiccuping when the paramedics and police arrived. And while they were checking me over and patching me up and asking all their questions, all I could see was your face in my mind, and all I could hear was your voice telling me to stop.

"It was all clear to me then, like some great understanding had been slotted into my memory with no real reasoning to support it. It was just a fact, plain and simple and unquestionable. The Universe was giving me a second chance. I didn't know who you were or what this room was, but I remembered that feeling you brought into the room with you and how it filled me up with such hope and happiness and I knew that my only goal left on earth was to live long enough to see this scene play out.

"That was three years ago."

Lance shook his head. "But ... I don't..."

"The Universe used you to save my life, Lance." Emmett said. "So maybe now I'm here to save yours. Maybe that's my penance. Maybe I go down so you can rise up."

[21]

Leah and Maya stood completely still, just inside the door of the coffin room. The door that had gently closed and clicked shut behind them, sealing them in. As Leah felt the hair on the back of her neck continue to stand up and the flesh on her arms prickle in alarm, she had to fight away the idea that the door hadn't closed of its own accord but had instead been purposely shut by whatever else had been waiting in the room.

Maya moved to take a step forward, but Leah caught her arm and stopped her. Maya gave Leah a quizzical look, her face pale and mostly hidden in the shadows as Leah's phone's flash-light struggled to light the pitch-black room. Leah said nothing, just shook her head. Maya, again, didn't question her. Simply nodded and then faced forward again, calling out, "Noah, sweetie, what's out here? We don't see anything. Why don't you just come out or tell me where you are and we'll come get you and then we can all go home and have a big bowl of ice cream? How's that sound?"

Noah's voice reached out from somewhere ahead of them,

from somewhere along the far wall. His voice was muffled and sounded far away, the quiet echo in the open space making it nearly impossible to tell exactly where it was coming from. "Something *is* there, Mom. I hear it sometimes. It sounds like wind. Like angry wind, in a big storm. And when I hear it, sometimes things shake. My wardrobe shakes, Mom. And something was trying to get in, I think. Something wanted to come in and get me."

Noah had sounded very brave as he had told this part, but all at once his voice cracked and he started to cry and he blurted, "*It's like my dream, Mommy. Like my bad dream where something wanted to eat me!*" He choked back a sob, coughed, and then through his tears he asked, "Do you see the boy, Mommy? Do you see the boy I painted? He can fix it! He can make the bad thing go away!"

Lance isn't here, kid, Leah thought. *I hope you can deal with me, the sloppy seconds.*

Leah was just about to call out to Noah and let her know that she was there and she was going to help him, when the shadows in the right corner of the room shifted and one of the coffins fell over and landed with a thunderous noise that seemed to shake the entire room. Maya and Leah both screamed and Leah jumped back and swung the hand holding the cell phone flashlight up and toward the fallen coffin and just caught the blur of shadow that was now shooting toward her like a bolt of lightning across the night sky.

Leah dropped the phone, and it landed on the floor with its light shining up, casting an orb or light into the room like a lantern. She threw up her hands to protect herself, braced her body for the impact that was sure to follow.

But no impact came.

Instead, she heard a man scream. A loud, ear-piercing scream that seemed to reach all the way to Leah's bones. A scream filled with such anger and sadness and confusion and ... pain. It was the sound of a soul suffering.

"There it is!" Noah yelled from his hiding place. "There's the angry wind!"

"That was just a coffin falling over, honey," Maya said. Her voice was panicked, but her words made Leah realize it was still only the fallen coffin that had caused Maya's spike in adrenaline.

Did she not hear the—

Leah lowered her hands and then screamed herself. She couldn't help it. The shadow that had shot across the room at her had stopped directly in front of her and had taken the shape of a middle-aged man. He was tall and loomed over her like a tree, bending at the waist to peer down at her with eyes that were hot with rage. His entire image seemed to be shimmering, vibrating with aggression like a plucked guitar string. He was thin, almost gaunt, and when he opened his mouth, it was like looking into a cave in which no light had ever reached. An eternal blackness filled the man, and his face contorted into a snarl and he screamed again, leaning closer to Leah as the noise threatened to shatter her eardrums.

"See!" Noah screamed. "There! Did you hear the wind, Mommy!"

Leah forced herself to remain calm. Stared into the spirit's angry eyes, and when the man screamed again, the piercing sound eventually grew softer and the noise became coherent. A single word spoken, drawn out in a cry. "Whhhhhhyyyy?"

"Honey, I don't hear anything," Maya said. "I think maybe your imagination—"

"Shhh," Leah said, cutting her off. She kept her eyes on the man in front of her but asked Maya, "You really can't hear anything?"

"No," Maya said, suddenly concerned. "Should I? Why can't I? What's wrong?"

Leah looked from the man in front of her and then over to the coffin that had fallen on the floor. Thought about Noah saying that the room had shaken before, and that something might have been trying to get into his wardrobe to get him.

The spirit in front of her was angry. Very angry.

Poltergeist, Leah thought. Lance had told her about these situations. A human spirit that was so angry they were able to manifest that anger into an energy that could actually affect the physical world. They were rare, he had said. *Just my luck*, Leah thought. *It's only, what, my third day on the job?*

Another scream caused goose bumps across all of Leah's body. *"Whhhhhhhyyyyyyyy?"*

The man shot across the room again, back to the fallen coffin. He leaned down and reached out with his enormous hands and Leah heard the quick zap of static electricity as he made contact with the coffin. He lifted the lid and then slammed it down hard. Maya yipped a yell and Leah heard her feet shuffling as the woman headed back to the door.

"What's that?" Noah cried from his hiding place. "What was that, Mommy? Are you okay? Did it hurt you?"

The man slammed the coffin lid again and again and again, each time the room boomed with the explosion, and each time the man cried his question. "Whhhy?" Slam. "Whhhy?" Slam. "Whhhy?"

"Leah? Leah, what's happening? What do we do?" Maya called from behind her.

Leah gave the woman credit for sticking around, for not bolting through the door and out to the car and peeling rubber as she sped away from this place.

She won't leave her son, Leah realized. *That coffin could come and swallow her whole and she wouldn't run. Not if it meant she could keep her son safe.*

Leah had no reason not to tell Maya the truth. They were well beyond the point of Leah trying to keep her gifts a secret. "There's an angry spirit here with us," Leah said. "A very tall man. He looks like he might be in his late thirties, maybe early forties. He's ... well, he's causing a scene."

There was another zap of electricity, this one stronger than before. The entire room seemed to spark with a blue light and then the man gave off a noise that sounded like a grunt mixed with the roar of a tornado and he lifted the coffin and threw it across the room. It slammed into the row of caskets on the left wall. Two of them rocked back and forth for a couple seconds before one settled in place and the other fell forward and crashed to the ground atop the one that had been thrown, forming a makeshift cross. The noise was like that of a house collapsing. It seemed like all Leah's senses were intensified, as if the energy that was radiating from the spirit was electrifying her, too.

"Can he hurt us?" Maya asked. Leah turned and saw the woman's back was flat against the door. Her face was set hard like stone, determined. "Can he hurt Noah?"

Probably, Leah thought but did not say. Instead she said, "No. I won't let that happen."

Because this is why I'm here. This is what Lance does every day, and this is what I do now.

But what *could* she do?

She rifled through her memory as she took a tentative step toward the spirit. The man was standing tall again, and his gaze was shifting all around, his eyes darting around and following things Leah could not see.

What would Lance do?

She thought back to their conversations. Conversations during which she suddenly wished she had asked more specific questions. He had told her that most of the spirits he encountered were simply stuck between the here and the there. Often, they just needed help passing over.

But how? Leah wondered, taking another cautious step, the man's gaze still not focusing on her. His image was still vibrating with energy, but he was shifting ever so slightly in and out of focus as Leah approached. Like he was...

Getting tired, Leah thought. *He's getting tired. It must take a lot of strength to be able to do what he's doing, to interact with our world with such force.*

Closer still, Leah found that rage in the man's shifting gaze, and with it, for the first time she saw the fear that was there, too.

He's trapped, she thought. *He's lost and afraid and*

(Whhhhhyyyy?)

confused. He's tired and afraid.

Leah took the last step she was willing to take, putting her just within arm's reach of the man. She took a deep breath and tried to relax her mind, tried to clear away her own fear and anxiousness and worry and confusion that had come along with the current situation. She tried to melt all that away so that there would be nothing left in the room except for her and the man who needed her help.

She heard the gentle waves of the ocean in her mind, and the light still shining from her phone's flashlight seemed to dim.

"Sir?" she said, though she knew her lips were not moving. Knew she was making no sound that could be heard by anyone living.

Like he'd been slapped, the man's face jerked in her direction, and those angry eyes fell upon her, alight with dark energy.

Leah did not flinch away, held the man's hot gaze. "I see you," she said. "I *see* you. And I'm here to tell you that it's alright. Everything is okay."

She did not know this man. Did not know his name or his profession or his story ... did not know how he had died. But in that moment, those few seconds where she held his stare and spoke to him and saw the features of his face soften just a touch, Leah knew he had been a good person. She felt it, the way the waters in her mind grew warmer to let her know. He wasn't Evil, he was just scared.

And he's tired ... he's scared and he's tired. He wants to rest.

Leah saw her mother. Not there in the room with her, not as a spirit, but as a memory. As a child, Leah had been prone to nightmares. The dark terrified her until she was nearly a teenager, and when she would wake from a scary dream and find herself alone in her darkened bedroom—the little nightlight next to her dresser was *never* bright enough to shine away the monsters—she would pull the covers over her head and call out for her mother. Over and over and over

("*Whhhy?*" Slam. "*Whhhy?*" Slam. "*Whhhy?*")

again she would call for her mother until she would hear the bedroom door click open softly and then she was there. Her mother would sit on the edge of the bed and pull the covers away from Leah's face (and the nightlight *did* seem brighter then, always brighter when her mother was there) and she would stroke Leah's head gently and tell her to close her eyes and to—

"Close your eyes and think of your favorite place," Leah said to the man. "Think of the place where you're the happiest you've ever been. Find that place in your mind and go there."

The man's image wavered, faded away for a full second before popping back into view. He looked angry again, at first, but then some of the vibration seemed to slow, his figure becoming more at rest. When he looked at her, his eyes were lighter, softer.

"Close your eyes and think of your favorite place," Leah said again, reaching out for him with her mind, wanting to take his hand in hers. "I want you to see it, and smell it, feel it. I want you to think of all the good times you've had there."

There was a brief moment where Leah thought it wasn't going to work. She felt another pulse of electricity begin to build in the air like the calm before a thunderstorm, and the hairs on her arms prickled again, but then, as quickly as the feeling had arrived, it vanished.

And the man closed his eyes.

Leah smiled. "You can see it now," she said.

And Leah saw her own favorite place, the place she'd always seen when she was a little girl and her mother would come into her bedroom after a nightmare. It was a little lake about a half hour outside of town, where sometimes her whole family would load up into her daddy's truck and drive out to spend the day. She was at that lake now. Saw her daddy with a cooler of beer, chatting with some other men as they fished from one of the small docks that jutted into the water. Saw her mother in a beach chair, shaded by the big umbrella that was duct-taped together because Daddy didn't want to buy a new one, reading a paperback novel while occasionally glancing out to the lake to make sure the kids were alright. And Leah saw herself, too. Saw her and her brother, Samuel, splashing each other in the shallow water and laughing as they floated out on the big blowup raft Daddy had bought them after they'd begged and begged.

"Are you there?" Leah asked the man. "Can you smell it?"

Leah could smell the humid summer air mixed with the aroma of burgers and hot dogs somebody was grilling near the pavilion that sat back along the tree line.

"Can you feel it?" she asked the man.

Leah could feel the sand between her toes as she ran toward the water, felt the cold splash of the first cannonball from the dock.

Could feel the love she and her brother had shared for each other. Warmer than the sun, deeper than the middle of the lake.

The man's energy pulsed.

"Good," Leah said.

This was the part, when she was a little girl, where her mother would tell her to go find that place in her dreams, because it was waiting for her. To go be happy there, because the monsters and the scary things couldn't come to her happy place. She was safe there. Which, now that Leah was older, she understood to be bullshit. Because in real life, the monsters do come to your happy place. They come in broad daylight and they rip your world to pieces. They steal your mother away by giving her cancer, and they murder your brother.

"Go there," Leah said to the man, swallowing down her own blip of anger. "It's waiting for you. Go there and be at peace. Go there and rest."

The man opened his eyes. He cocked his head to one side, hesitant.

And now Leah did reach out with her hand. "It's okay," she said. "I'll go with you."

The man looked down at her outstretched hand for a long time, uncertainty palpable in the air between them. But when Leah closed her own eyes, she felt a small tickle of electricity in her palm and she knew he had accepted her help.

She was back at the lake, walking barefoot down the dock. She reached the edge and curled her toes over the wooden planks.

"Ready?" she asked the man.

There was another buzz of static in her palm, and she heard the man's voice in her mind. For the first time it was clear and completely devoid of aggression. Instead, it was soft and sad. "I'm sorry," he said.

"It's okay," Leah said. "We all get scared."

The man said nothing.

"We jump on three," Leah said. "Ready?"

There was a long pause, and for a moment, Leah thought she had lost him. But then a warm feeling filled her veins that she quickly recognized as happiness.

"Ready," the man said.

Leah counted to three and they jumped.

When she hit the water, the lake vanished and the room full of caskets rushed back into focus, like Leah had been thrust forward into it. Her phone was still on the floor, shining its light up toward the ceiling, and Leah bent and scooped it up.

"Is he ... is he gone?" Maya's voice from behind her. "It feels different in here. I can't explain it, just ... different."

Leah didn't have to look around to know the answer. "Yes," she said. "He's gone."

"Noah!" Maya called, louder than was necessary, her adrenaline probably still spiking. "Noah, you can come out now. Leah got rid of the scary man."

He was the one who was scared, Leah thought.

Noah must have been able to sense the way the room's atmosphere had changed, too, because five seconds later the lid of one of the caskets along the rear wall popped open and a little boy stepped out. He held a small flashlight in one hand and he clicked it on, temporarily blinding them.

"Noah, honey, light down," Maya laughed as she rushed toward her son. "You're blinding us."

Noah lowered the light and Leah saw a handful of comic books and action figures at his feet that must have fallen out of the casket when he'd opened the lid. There was a child's backpack resting in the bottom of the casket as well, and an empty candy bar wrapper and juice box.

Maya scooped Noah up in her arms and hugged him fiercely, happy tears cascading down her cheeks. Then she stopped and pulled back, looking down at the boy's pants. "Uh-oh, looks like you had a bit of an accident."

In the glow of the flashlight, Leah saw Noah's face turn red. "Yeah. I was in there a really long time." Then he looked at Leah and his face changed. The red drained away and he smiled big and pointed at her. "Hey! You're the girl from the paintings!"

Maya laughed and hugged her son close again. "She is, honey! She is! She's the one who saved you."

Noah's head turned left and right, looking all around the room. "Where's the boy? The boy I saw in my dream? Is he here too?"

"No, honey," Maya said. "He's not here, but Leah knows him. He's her *boyfriend*. Isn't that funny?"

Leah laughed along with the two of them and tried to share in the joy of their reunion, but all the while she stared hard at Noah's face.

She couldn't understand how it was possible, but she would swear she had seen the boy before somewhere.

[22]

Since Maya was unable to pry herself apart from Noah—and Leah couldn't blame her—Leah rushed over to the casket in which Noah had been hiding, trying not to think how twisted the idea of hiding and playing in a casket really was, and scooped up his comic books and trash, dumping it all into his little backpack and zipping it shut. Then she ushered them all back to the outdated kitchen and they squeezed through the pet door again, little Noah squealing with delight as he watched his mother wiggle her way out.

In the minivan, Noah spied the sandwiches and said he was starving. "Well, I should think so, mister!" Maya said, handing him one and then adding, "I've got coffee, too, if you're thirsty." She held up the thermos.

Noah had already ripped the sandwich bag open and was chewing a big bite. Peanut butter now outlined both sides of his mouth. He made a disgusted sound through his mouthful and said, "Coffee is for grownups. I'll wait for home."

Maya laughed like Noah had just made the funniest joke she'd ever heard, and when she started the minivan Leah saw the light from the dash reflected in the tears in the woman's eyes. Leah reached out a hand and rested it on Maya's knee. Their eyes met, and Maya smiled and mouthed the words *Thank you*. As they drove around the side of the funeral home, Genesis the cat's eyes sparked in the headlights from where it sat just in the grass, watching them go.

The drive back to the house was silent and short, but long enough for Noah to be passed out asleep by the time they pulled into the driveway and Maya killed the engine. "Poor little guy," she whispered as she and Leah looked back at the boy from the front seats. "What a day he's had." Maya turned to Leah and asked, "Do you think he'll remember it? Do you think he'll remember what *really* happened?"

Leah thought about all that happened back in the room full of coffins, and how Noah had been able to hear...

(*It sounds like wind. Like angry wind, in a big storm.*)

Well, he'd been able to hear *something*. Not the spirit's voice full and clear the way Leah had, and if Noah had popped himself out of the casket before Leah had helped the man cross over, she was certain he would have seen the same thing that Maya had: nothing except a few flying and toppled caskets.

But he had been able to hear something and Maya hadn't. He was young, his mind still impressionable and open, not closed off like many adults'. And Maya had said that Noah had a big imagination. He was primed to accept the unexplainable. Plus...

He saw Lance in a dream and Maya has been painting me for years.

"Yeah," Leah said. "I think he will. But that's a good thing."

Maya nodded. "Because it means he'll learn his lesson not to go off on his own to play in a funeral home, or anywhere else, because bad things can happen."

"No," Leah said. "Because it means he'll understand the world is a lot bigger and stranger than most people want to believe. The supernatural is only fiction to those who haven't experienced it. Trust me," Leah said, smiling, "this will give him a leg up."

Maya looked back to her son, considered this. "He's a tough one, that's for sure."

"I agree."

The two of them stared at Noah's sleeping form in the back seat for a bit longer, Maya with admiration in her eyes, and Leah with the growing feeling that she'd seen Noah before. She knew she hadn't, the same way she knew she'd never met Maya before today, even though she'd apparently been visiting the woman's dreams since before she was born. But the nagging feeling of familiarity would not dissipate. As Maya pulled the groggy Noah from the back seat and carried him inside, Leah following them along the sidewalk, the feeling only grew stronger, pulling Leah along as if she too were being carried.

Maya carried Noah up the stairs and Leah stayed in the living room, plopping down onto the couch with a sigh. Above, she heard the sounds of footsteps and water running, a toilet flushing, mumbled conversation, and then finally, a door shutting softly before Maya headed back down the stairs to join her. The woman fell into the sofa like it was a life preserver, and she sank into the cushions with such a look of relief on her face it was as though all her cares and worries in life had been stripped away and she could breathe again. Which, Leah figured, in a way, was true. Noah was all that mattered, and Maya would have done anything to find and save him. With that mission complete, everything else was nothing but a cakewalk.

"He wants to see you," Maya said, her head leaned back and her eyes closed. "I hope you don't mind, but he said he wants to tell you goodnight. It's okay if you don't want to go up. He's probably already asleep anyway."

"Of course I'll go up," Leah said, standing from the couch. What she didn't say was that it would be a great opportunity to get a closer look at the kid, try to work out why the sight of the boy was causing such a stir of feeling inside her.

Maya found the strength to lift her head from the couch cushion and smiled and told Leah which door was Noah's. Leah crept up the stairs quietly, genuinely not wanting to wake the boy if he had fallen asleep—he *had* had a very long and unusual day. She turned the knob and then slowly pushed open the door, seeing that Noah was sitting up in bed with his little hands clasped in front of him like he was waiting for their meeting to start.

"Hey there," Leah said, stepping into the room. She sat on the edge of his bed, and she smiled as she realized she was positioned the same way her own mother always sat when she'd come into Leah's room after Leah had called for her after a nightmare.

"Hi," Noah said. "Thank you for helping me. My mom wanted me to tell you that."

Leah laughed. "You're very welcome." In the dim glow of a small night-light plugged into an outlet next to Noah's bed, the boy's features were soft, yet still familiar. But they were taking on another form too, one that Leah *did* recognize. It was in the way his nose seemed to end in a round little bulb, and the barely visible dimples on his cheeks. The small curls of hair around his ears. *He looks like his mom*, Leah thought, embarrassed it had taken her this long. *That's why I think I've seen him before.* She chastised herself for being so slow on the uptake, but it was late and she was tired and she'd spent the last few days driving across the country, so she would try and cut herself a little slack.

But...

"Is your boyfriend okay?" Noah asked. "The one that came to see me in my dream—you know, the way you come to see Mommy."

I have no idea, Leah thought. *I hope so, but probably not. He's with some very bad people and...*

"Yes," Leah said. "He'll be okay. He's just off on an adventure." She reached out and squeezed the boy's hand. "Just like you were."

Noah nodded. "Mom said I'm not allowed to go off on adventures anymore without her, unless it's just in the backyard. Which is super boring. She also said no more wardrobes. But I'm okay with that. I don't want to go into wardrobes anymore. It's not like in the books. Hey, are we going to go find my uncle now?"

The question caught Leah off guard. "What? Why would we...?"

Noah looked at her like she was five years old and he was trying to figure out how to explain something to her. "Your boyfriend, that's what he told me."

Leah felt the room closing in on her, her mind struggling to process what Noah was saying.

"I didn't tell Mommy that because she gets real sad when she talks about Uncle Patrick. She doesn't think I see, but I do. She misses him a lot. But that's what your boyfriend told me when he came to save me in my dream. He said that we'd go and find my uncle now that I was safe, but he's not here, so are you going to take us?"

With the name, the pieces clicked. Leah looked at little Noah's face and watched as his features shifted to take on an entirely different persona. It made Leah's stomach drop, and before she even realized what was happening she was bolting from the room and heading down the hallway for the stairs.

Leah had thought Noah looked like Maya, which was where that pull of familiarity was deriving from. But now she understood fully, and she feared the truth for what it was. Of course Noah looked like Maya—he was her son—but if he looked like Maya, there was also a good chance that if the dominant traits got passed down, he might look a little like Maya's brother, too. Noah's long-lost uncle.

And I've seen the uncle before, Leah thought, even though her mind was already doing the math, knowing that it made no sense.

But...

The supernatural is only fiction to those who haven't experienced it.

"Maya!" she called, bounding down the stairs two at a time.

Maya leapt from the couch, her eyes wide and her hair sticking up. "What's wrong? Is he okay? What happened?" She was already moving toward the stairs.

Leah stopped her. Grabbed the woman's shoulders and said, "I need to see a picture of your bother. Right now. Do you have one?"

Maya's face went through a full cycle of confusion and disbelief before saying, "I don't—"

"Now, Maya!" Leah felt bad for yelling, but her heart was racing and her head was spinning and...

It can't be.

But she knew it could. Somehow, it could.

Maya stared at Leah for a single second with those wide eyes looking like saucers before she nodded and then ran up the stairs. Leah waited, listened to Maya's rushed footsteps as she headed down the hall. She heard a drawer open and close, papers rustling, another drawer opened and slammed shut. Leah focused on her breathing, trying to regain control of her emotions. Closed her eyes and counted to ten.

She got to seven before Maya was back down the stairs, holding out an old Polaroid. Leah took it with a trembling hand and looked into the captured image.

It was a picture of a young Maya sitting on the bleachers in what looked like a high school auditorium. She wore jeans and a long-sleeved tie-dyed T-shirt that looked to have been decorated in school colors. Her hair was bigger and frizzier than now, but still very pretty. The other kids around her were dressed the same, packed into the bleachers tight. It must have been some sort of Spirit Day (*ha ha*). And yes, looking at young Maya in the photograph confirmed that Noah did look very much like his mother when she was younger.

And he also looked even more like Maya's brother.

Maya's brother, no more than sixteen, sat next to his sister with his arm around her and making bunny ears behind her head. He had a small, sly grin on his face.

The last time Leah had seen that face, the boy had been shoving her head into a fireplace.

Leah was staring into the face of Patrick Cain.

[23]

When Emmett had finished telling his story, he kept staring at the ceiling, his eyes flitting back and forth across the surface as if his memories were still up there, projected for all to see. Lance saw nothing but cobwebs and grime, said nothing, his own mind digesting Emmett's tale. When Emmett finally looked away from the dirty ceiling to glance at Lance, Lance realized that the man was waiting for him to speak.

Lance didn't know what to say. He was tired, and he was frustrated. Tired from the long car ride with little sleep, frustrated because he felt helpless. He was locked away in a room with no way out, and with no greater sense of what their plan of action should be after having heard Emmett's story.

Emmett ... the man who could see the future. The man who had seen Lance locked away in this very room three years before it had happened. He'd gotten the vision at a time in Lance's life when he'd still been living happily at home with his mother. A time when his mother had been alive. A time before the Reverend and the Surfer and the thing called Patrick Cain. A time before Leah had come into his life with all her brightness and love and ... God, he missed her.

But the memory of his mother and Leah helped him refocus. Because the idea that Emmett had experienced his bubbly of Lance being ushered into this room three years before it had happened—before so much had happened—helped to instill a great truth in Lance's mind. One that was now completely impossible to ignore.

I'm supposed to be here. We're *supposed to be here. This has always been the destination. This has always been the plan.*

Whether Lance had ever had any actual free will in his decisions, whether the path he'd chosen might have zigged instead of zagged, or bobbed instead of weaved, he knew now in his heart and his soul that eventually the timeline would have taken over, the Universe would have grabbed his hand, and he would have ended up right here, sitting in this room with Emmett Emmanuel Dean.

The more Lance thought about it, the more he figured that he and Emmett must be like keys to two locks on the same door, each one vital, each one required to get the door open. He thought about something he'd heard his teacher say in his high school economics class one time, about how some big companies never allow all their top executives to fly on the same plane together, because if the plane should happen to crash it would wipe out the entire senior team and the company would end up in its own death spiral.

Emmett could see the future. The one thing Lance couldn't do.

Lance could do lots of things Emmett couldn't do, it seemed. But that didn't matter. It wasn't a contest. It was a collaboration.

The feeling of dread and despair that Lance had been

working hard to keep from clouding his focus since he'd arrived at Arthur's Adventureland seemed to lessen slightly as Lance accepted a brighter version of things that came along with his new understanding.

He had known his whole life that he was a solider for the Universe. He was put on this earth to do good, to fight Evil. If Emmett had seen Lance in this room three years ago, then this fight had always been looming on the horizon. And even though Lance had never understood how the Universe worked, and would likely never fully understand, he did know this:

It would not have brought him to a fight that he didn't have a chance to win.

Emmett was a key, and Lance still needed to figure what the man was supposed to unlock.

Lance gave another glance to the bench directly across from him, nodded once, and then turned to Emmett.

"You should have helped her," he said. "But you already know that."

Emmett swallowed hard, his throat clicking. He looked at Lance with shame in his eyes. "I do. She'll haunt me until the day I die."

Which might be very soon, was what they both were probably thinking, but neither said.

"I'm not saying that the Universe has fully forgiven you," Lance said. "But I do agree with what you said about getting your second chance. Your moment for atonement. Whatever waits for you after isn't up to you or me, but we can try our best to control what happens before we get there—to the after."

Emmett nodded enthusiastically. "Right, right. We're going to fight these bastards, aren't we?"

"I just need you to do one thing for me, Ed."

More nodding. "Of course. Anything."

"If you get another bubbly while we're here, don't you dare ignore it." Lance offered a thin grin. "I don't give a damn how tired you are."

Emmett laughed, the sound not fitting with the aesthetic of the room. Lance let the man recompose himself and then asked, "How did you get here anyway? I certainly didn't see a motorcycle out front."

Emmett spun around on the bench to put his feet back on the floor. Then he stood and cracked his neck and back. He pointed to the locked door. "That twenty-first-century vampire chick picked me up at a bar outside of Flagstaff. I was there watching a game, and she came up beside me and asked if I wanted to buy her a drink. I recognized her instantly, from the bubbly where they shoved you into this room with me. How could I ever forget any of their faces? So, I knew it was time. My past had finally caught up with me.

"I told her that I didn't see that happening, and when she smiled at me and said, 'You see a lot of things, don't you?' I think I felt fear—*real* fear—for the first time in my life, Lance. I nodded and told the truth. I said that I do. Told her that I'd already seen her, and that I knew what was coming. And you know what she said?"

Lance shook his head.

"She said, 'If you really did, you'd be even more scared than you already are,' and then she took me by the hand and I followed her out of the bar and when we got to the parking lot everything went black. When I opened my eyes again, I was here."

Lance nodded. It was exactly what he'd been expecting. There was absolutely no question that Emmett Emmanuel

Dean was important to whatever was about to happen. "They tracked you down the same way they tracked me."

"But *why*, Lance? I still don't understand what I'm supposed to be doing here. I want to help, but I don't know how. Do you?"

Lance ignored the question, decided to ask the one that he'd been holding on to from the moment he had been pushed through the door. "Ed, when you got here, was there anyone else with you in the room? Was there another prisoner?"

Emmett stopped his pacing and stood up straight, looked at Lance with concern, like he might have missed something he shouldn't have. "No. Nobody but me."

"What about in your bubbly? Was there anyone else besides me and them out there?" Lance pointed to the door.

Emmett shook his head. "No. Why, was there supposed to be? Did something go wrong?"

Lance looked to the bench directly across from him, to the spirit of the man who had been sitting and waiting patiently as Lance and Emmett had swapped their stories. The man looked as though he might have just been waiting for a bus, except for the fact that half his skull was caved in.

[24]

Leah stood by the stairs, watching Maya pace up and down the hall of paintings, as if the news that after all this time somebody had finally seen her long-lost brother had rendered her incapable of holding still, years' worth of the alternating hope and fear, acceptance and denial, all flooding out of her at once.

"My stars!" Maya said, coming out of the hallway and finally managing to stay put in the living room. She looked at Leah with eyes brimming with tears. "You're sure it's him that you've seen?" She pointed at the Polaroid Leah still had pinched in her fingers. "That picture was taken a long time ago, you know? I mean, maybe it was somebody else, or..." She stopped herself, shook her head. Smiled at Leah with a face alight with happiness. "No, of course you're sure. Because you're you! Is that why you've really come? To finally tell me the truth about what happened to Patrick?"

Leah knew that the next words she spoke were going to sound like the ravings of a person fit for an asylum—but only if they fell onto the ears of nonbelievers. Maya, she knew, was a believer, had believed in Leah and Lance, had seen the casket fly through the air in Fuller's Funeral Home and Crematorium. But what Leah had to share with her now ... well, it was going to be a tough pill to swallow.

"Maya," Leah said. "I've seen Patrick, and I know it was him because he looked exactly the same as he does in this photograph. He hasn't aged a day."

Maya laughed and shook her head. "Well, he must have gotten better genes than me, because some mornings when I look in the mirror I think I look *at least* ten years older than I should." She laughed again and added, "I wish I knew his secret."

Leah stepped forward and set the Polaroid down on the coffee table and then reached out and took both Maya's hands in her own. "Maya, you trust me, right? You believe in what I am, and what I can do?"

Maya quickly nodded, and Leah watched as some of the unbridled happiness that had recently filled the woman's eyes was replaced with fear. "Of course. I ... you know I do."

Leah took a deep breath, figured it was best to just let it all out, spare no detail. "Good. That's good. Because what I'm about to tell you now is going to sound absolutely insane. Before I met Lance, I would have thought it was insane too, but—"

"The supernatural is only fiction to those who haven't experienced it," Maya said, a small grin on her face. She squeezed Leah's hands. "Whatever it is. I'll believe you. Just please tell me he's alright. That he's alive."

Leah sighed. "He's alive," she said. "But he's not the same person you knew as a kid. I don't ... I don't think he's still your brother. At least not entirely."

Maya didn't pull away, but Leah felt the woman's body

stiffen. Her face grew hard and her eyes narrowed when she asked, "What do you mean *not entirely*?"

"Do you remember the story I told you earlier, about the three people that hunted Lance and me down in Travelers Rest? How one of them, the leader who shoved my head into the fire-place, was basically a teenager?"

Maya nodded but said nothing. She wasn't getting it. Wouldn't make the leap on her own.

"That was Patrick," Leah said. "He was the boy. That's what I meant when I said he hasn't aged a day. He is *literally* the same age. At least his body is. I don't know exactly what it means or how it works, but..."

"But *what*, Leah? You can tell me. You *need* to tell me." Maya's words were like stone, hard and unquestionable. "I deserve to know."

Leah stared into the woman's eyes, gave her all the respect she deserved as the truth was delivered. "I can only guess, but whatever the Evil thing *really* is that has been hunting Lance, I think it's using your brother's body as some sort of vessel. That's what really happened to Patrick when you two were in high school. He didn't run off, he was stolen. I think this Evil took his body for its own and has been using it ever since."

Maya was quiet for a very long time. She held on to Leah's hands, even when the tears did finally fall down her cheeks. She held Leah's stare, searching it for a deeper meaning that just wasn't there. Leah had already laid it all out in its ugliest, rawest form. "But ... but why isn't he aging? How is he still a kid?"

Leah shook her head. "I don't know. But what I do know is that Lance—well, he said that this thing, the thing that's inside Patrick, was the most powerful Evil he'd ever felt." Leah shrugged. "The human body probably isn't much of a match for something like that."

Now Maya did pull her hands free. She turned and sat down on the sofa and put her face in her palms. "I think I'm going to throw up," she said. "This is..." She took several deep breaths and got her emotions under control. Slowly, she looked back up at Leah, and Leah was surprised to see the woman smiling at her. "This is not exactly what I expected," Maya said.

Leah sat on the couch next to her. "It rarely is, I'm starting to think."

Maya nodded. "I knew he was still out there. It's going to sound crazy, but—"

"Crazier than what I just told you?"

"No. No, I suppose not," Maya laughed. "It's going to sound crazy, but I swear I've always been able to feel him. Just a teeny-tiny bit of my brother, somewhere deep in my heart. Like a second pulse. It wasn't always there, and I'm sure I've just been imagining it all these years, wishful thinking or maybe just ignorance, but when I would feel it, I just knew ... I just knew it meant he was still alive, and that maybe one day he'd come and find me. I've always held on to that, even when I pretended I'd convinced myself otherwise."

Leah stood and turned and then sat on the coffee table so she could face Maya. "Well, you were right, he's still out there. And it's not crazy at all. I have a friend who once told me that there's a piece of every mother's soul in their children. A connection that's unbreakable. I think that might be true for siblings, too. I used to feel that way about my brother, before I lost him. Like there was some wavelength we shared, a secret tunnel just for us."

Maya wiped the tears from her cheeks. "So what does this all mean? Now that we know, what do we do?"

Leah stood from the coffee table. "We go find him. Right now."

"*Now?*"

"Yes," Leah said, stepping toward the hall of paintings. "Evil isn't going to wait for us to be well rested, I'm afraid. In fact, it's not going to wait at all. It's taking a lot of self-motivating to even convince myself that we're not already too late." She paused, added, "Noah helped with that, actually."

"Noah? What do you mean?"

"He didn't want to tell you about a part of his dream—his Lance dream—because he was afraid it was going to make you sad. But he told me, just a few minutes ago when I was up in his room. He told me that in his dream, Lance told him they were going to go off and find his uncle."

Maya clapped a hand over her mouth.

Leah nodded. "This was never about Noah," Leah said. "I was pulled here because of Patrick, to learn the truth about him. But the truth alone doesn't do me any good. I don't know why, but I need you with me on this, Maya. I don't know why else I'd be here. I don't know why else the Universe would have been putting me into your dreams all these years if not to let you know that when the moment arrived, that when the day came that I finally showed up at your door, it was going to be for something *big*. Something bigger than driving less than a mile away and finding your son playing hide-and-go-seek in a funeral home." Leah stopped to catch her breath, then added, "I don't think you need me at all, Maya. I think Lance and I need you."

Less than half an hour later, a red minivan merged onto the interstate that was middle-of-the-night empty. Maya drove, sipping from one of the two thermoses of coffee she'd brewed and brought along. Leah rode shotgun, a plastic shopping bag full of sandwiches and snacks at her feet. Noah slept in one of the rear captain's chairs, his head resting against the window, the breath from his open mouth fogging the glass.

Beside Noah, in the other captain's chair, was the spirit of Pamela Brody. She watched the little boy sleep with a melancholy smile on her face.

Leah had not told Maya about the fourth passenger in the van and did not turn to face Pamela as she spoke along their hidden channel, "I don't feel anything, he must still be shutting me out. Well, *something* is shutting me out. Are you sure this is the right way?"

Pamela did not take her eyes off Noah. Said, "It's the right way. It'll take more than Hell to keep me away from my son." Then, in a voice that gave Leah chills, Pamela added, "They don't have any idea what we can do."

[25]

"THERE's somebody else here with us," Lance told Emmett. "He's been on that bench across from me since I arrived."

The man on the bench, with half his head looking like a car's fender after being rear-ended, continued to stare at Lance but gave no indication he'd been mentioned or acknowledged. Emmett turned to look at the bench, but Lance knew he would see nothing.

"He's had some sort of accident," Lance said. "Or"—and he suspected this was more likely the case—"somebody killed him. His head has been beaten in."

Emmett didn't take his eyes off the bench. "By them?" he asked, nodding back to the locked door. "Is that what they're going to do to us?" He didn't sound afraid, only curious. Like a man who had already accepted his fate and was now only concerned with working out the details.

"I don't know," Lance said.

"Who was he, do you think? Was he like us? Was he"—Emmett shrugged—"valuable to them?"

"I don't know."

Emmett turned to Lance. "Well, what's he *saying*? You can talk to them, right?"

Lance stood for the first time since he'd been shoved through the door, and he shook the pins and needles out of his legs and feet. He stretched his back and headed the short distance across the room, stopping just in front of the bench.

The man, with his one good eye, looked up to Lance and nodded in greeting. His image flickered for a moment, like bad reception on a television screen, then came back into focus.

His energy is fading, Lance thought, and he found this odd. *How long has he been here?* And then another thought chilled him. He hadn't seen a spirit look this weak, look as though they were nothing more than a hologram in a bad science fiction movie, since he'd met the ghost of one Mr. Fontaine, whose body had been possessed and then forced to drive his Toyota Camry head-on into the front of a jewelry store. Lance had met the man's spirit only moments before it had been torn away and ripped to shreds by...

"Hi," Lance said. "You're going to have to forgive me for being blunt about this, but I don't exactly have a lot of time for beating around the bush and exchanging pleasantries. What is it that you want? Why are you here?"

The man's jaw was broken, and when he moved his mouth to speak, the one side hung limp and unresponsive. It reminded Lance of what you might see happen to a stroke victim.

"I ... have..."

The man's voice was like a bag of gravel and his image flickered again. He'd sat silently through all of Lance and Emmett's conversation, waiting his turn, and now Lance wondered if the man had waited too long. Wondered if now that it was the spirit's turn to speak, he wouldn't have enough energy to complete the task.

And would that be the worst thing? Lance wondered. Because, when you looked at the situation as a whole, even *if* the man with the caved-in skull needed help, what could Lance do while being trapped in a room at an abandoned theme park? Whatever was waiting for him outside the walls, whatever he'd been brought here for, Lance knew it was much bigger and more important than helping a single soul.

Lance felt a twinge of guilt at even thinking this, at being so willing to deny a spirit in need of help, and he thought about Emmett's story of ignoring his bubbly of Melody Rhodes.

No ... this isn't the same. It's...

"A...," the man continued and then popped completely out of view for half a second. When he reappeared, it looked as though some of the color had washed out of him. "A ... message," he croaked.

"You have a message? For me?" Lance asked.

The man nodded and sat back against the wall, as if relieved the job was finished.

"Okay," Lance said. "What's the message?"

The man leaned his head back, the caved-in side slumping into the wall. He looked up at Lance, and the pain and sorrow visible in the man's expression were enough to break Lance's heart.

"*Please...*," the man's gravelly voice whispered. "*Pleeeease...*"

Lance swallowed, tried to push down the sympathy building inside him. He didn't have time for this. He didn't *understand* this.

"What's the message?" he asked again. "Please tell me."

The man popped out of view again, and when he reemerged

he was nearly transparent. He held out his hand, like he wanted help getting up. "Show..."

Lance looked down at the man's hand, taking a second before he comprehended. He looked at Emmett and said, "I don't know what's about to happen—I mean, I don't know what this looks like from the other side—but don't freak out, okay? I'll be alright." Then, right before he grabbed the spirit's hand, he tossed on, "I think."

And when Lance's fingers slid through the spirit's palm, his mind slid into the ether, zapping across the wavelengths and into...

He was kneeling on the ground, the earth hard and dry beneath him. Weeds were growing tall and pricking at his bare legs and arms. It was dark, the moon half hidden and the shadows a faded metallic silver that reminded him of a saw blade.

But these were not his thoughts. Lance saw all of this through eyes that were not his, only windows for him to look from as he was thrown into the memory embedded into the dead man's spirit.

Footsteps heard through the ears that were not his.

The eyes looked up, and Lance felt the heaviness of the man's body, a sluggishness that had to be either drug- or alcohol-induced. The eyes found the base of a Ferris wheel, the rooftops of empty park buildings and long-abandoned rides beyond. A tall woman stepped forward, emerging from the shadows and blacking out everything else, her white hair radiant in the moonlight, as if it were its own source of light. Her trench coat caught a breeze and billowed behind her. She shifted to smooth the coat down and the moonlight glinted off something new. Something long and heavy in her right hand.

A metal baseball bat.

Lance felt the man's legs try to stand, felt the muscles not respond to his brain's commands, numb and weak. The man only managed to sit back on his thighs before falling onto his butt with a painful grunt. He raised a hand no higher than his waist, splaying his fingers out, a desperate attempt to fend off the inevitable.

"P-p-please." he managed to say, just as the woman with the white hair gripped the bat with both hands and lifted it high above her head, its metallic glint creating an eclectic arc in the darkness, before swinging it down with all her strength.

Lance was forced to read the man's last thought, the one spawned in the moment that he knew he was going to die. The man's consciousness flashed to the image of a pretty woman in a green dress, entwined in his arms as they danced at what appeared to be a wedding reception. The music was slow and their steps were clumsy but also perfect, and as the song neared its end and the man leaned his head against hers, breathing her in and marveling over how he'd gotten so lucky, she'd whispered in his ear *I love you*, and Lance felt the heat flush through the man's veins and—

And as the bat connected with his skull, the man said "I love you too" to the memory and there was a great flash of pain, pain beyond anything he'd known, and the dark night turned black and there was nothing.

Until there was something.

A red line sparked in the nothingness, growing in intensity before curving in an arc and then splitting, like a pair of lips parting to take a sip. Lance, still attached to the man's soul, felt the spirit begin to fall, a giant fist grabbing and ushering him toward the parted red lines at an incredible speed. Screams echoed all around, a cacophony of anguish and rage and torment, ricocheting off the emptiness and sticking like darts into the man's spirit.

A burst of spectacular red light pulsed like a strobe before winking out just as the split red lines snapped shut and the nothingness blinked and was replaced with a searing desert landscape. Charred and burnt, all blacks and ash grays, an orange-and-red haze covering everything, thickening like low-hanging clouds over a range of craggy and broken mountaintops full of jagged rocks and crumbling fissures.

The screams were deafening. The man's soul twisted in place and saw nothing but a sea of others, a great mosh pit of agonized souls, pressed together and writhing in their pain and anger like a bed of entangled snakes. They stretched on for miles.

But there were not just the souls. Enormous creatures made of the shapes of nightmares slid and slithered and stomped across and through the tormented prisoners, squashing and slicing and swallowing those in their path. Tentacles and claws and rows of razor-wire teeth, innumerable eyes of all sizes.

And on the horizon, some of the mountains began to move, to shift closer, and the man's soul had just enough time to realize that they weren't mountains at all but even greater beasts—packs of them lumbering forward slowly, leaving nothing behind but destruction and decay.

The man's soul felt the chains of fear and agony wrap around him and pull him into the pit, and he tumbled forward into it, feeling a brief sickness of disgust as he was consumed by the others, taken into their den of torture, and then all his thoughts and memories and every last trace of who he'd ever been was fed upon, devoured by the Evil that ruled this place, and he was no longer him, he was them. No longer one, but many. Doomed to suffer and be fed upon for eternity.

Lance felt himself disconnecting from the man's soul in those last agonizing moments of memory and had a brief rush of his own fear at the horrifying idea that, while tethered to the man's spirit, his own soul might become trapped along with him, the connection bound in some grotesque twist of fate. For Lance Brody had seen this place of nightmares before, but only from the outside looking in. That day in the woods outside Bernie Parsons's house when Lance had died and faced down the devil.

The devil had crawled from this place.

"*Pleeeease...*" The man's soul gave a final plea, a quickly fading whimper in Lance's mind, just before their connection was snapped and the hellish landscape rushed away as if being sucked into a vacuum, and Lance was alone with just his own mind again.

He waited in the impossible darkness, afloat in a void, feeling small and enormous at the same time as he waited for the wavelengths that connected all of the Universe to whisk him back to his body, back to the room with Emmett Emmanuel Dean.

Nothing happened.

He tried to focus on the room, rebuilt it in his imagination. Saw the cobwebs in the corners and the broken light fixture. He saw the benches and the scuffed floor and...

Maybe I need to click my heels together three times and say there's no place like—

A sound shattered the silence, the direction it was coming from indiscernible. But Lance recognized it for what it was. Somebody was slowly clapping their hands. Lance tried to move, to turn in place and search for the source of the noise, find the owner of those clapping hands, but physical movement was not an option in this place—he had no body, no form. Only thought and energy, a consciousness on steroids.

The clapping grew closer, getting louder, and then stopped with no warning.

Then a voice, clear and recognizable, invaded Lance's mind, kicking down the door.

"Impressive, isn't it, Lance?" the thing called Patrick Cain asked. "All that pain, all those souls ... it's fucking beautiful. I know that's not very poetic—maybe not up to your high-level vocabulary, Mister Smarty-Pants, but it *is* ... fucking beautiful. I'm glad you got the message ... got to see it for yourself."

If Lance had had a body with shoulders, he would have shrugged. He fired back, "Sorry, guess I wasn't that impressed. I've seen that show before. Didn't care for it much."

"What?" Patrick asked, his voice revolving through Lance's thoughts as though circling him as he spoke. "That little peek you got in the woods? No, that wasn't the same. You weren't *there* that time. This time you got to see it all, see everything we've been building, the *scale* of it."

Lance found himself struggling for words, surprised that Patrick—

"Of course I know about that," Patrick said, reading the thought. "You think I wouldn't know when one of my top soldiers is killed? And your energy, Lance ... when it shows up, boy, do we fucking feel it. It's like an earthquake. That day in the woods is when I knew the only way we'd get you here was if I took care of things myself."

Blind in the darkness, trapped in place, Lance worked to control his nerves. Patrick was toying with him, testing him, trying to push him.

And Lance suspected it was purely for the thing's own amusement.

"Who was he?" Lance asked. "The man who wanted my help? The man who showed mc that place?"

In Lance's mind, Patrick scoffed. "Wanted your help?" He laughed, the sound ugly and amplified, echoing off unseen canyons. "He's nobody. One of the countless we've consumed. We just needed to hand you a conduit, a way to show you. You wouldn't have let me in without a fight. I figured sympathy would be our best option. You have a hard time saying no to a person in need, Lance. You think it's a strength, but—"

A bright white light flashed in the distance, like a star being birthed. It sparked and arched across the void, reaching for Lance, and Lance felt its pull, felt the vacuum effect again. Then, like the drop of a roller coaster, Lance felt himself plummeting downward, the emptiness rushing by him and light filling all his thoughts and blinding his mind and—

An eruption of cheering snapped the scene into place. Lance was standing on the sidelines of the basketball court in his high school gymnasium. He paced up and down the bench, looking at the players seated there, their faces flushed and sweaty, their eyes locked onto him. Lance felt different, off. His body felt heavier, his movements slightly less fluid than normal. He felt...

I'm older, he thought. But the thought wasn't fully present. It came from the background of his mind, competing to push its way through to the front, to the Lance of this time, of this place, of this memory.

Lance looked down and saw the whiteboard in his hand, the outline of a court waiting for him to mark it up with the next play. He saw he was wearing not shorts and hoodie and sneakers, but a dark blue suit and dress shoes.

"Coach!" a kid yelled from the bench, just as the buzzer overhead sounded, rattling Lance's teeth with its blare. "What are we running?" the kid asked.

Lance glanced at the scoreboard, saw they were up two with forty seconds left. "Box and one on the Saunders kid. Don't let him get the ball, and if he does, force him left. We just need one stop." He stuck his left hand out, and the players piled their hands on top of his, but not before Lance noticed the silver wedding band he was wearing. Backseat Lance had time to think *What the...?* before the buzzer rocked the gym again and the time-out was over and Lance yelled, "Hillston on three! One, two, three—"

"*HILLSTON!*"

The huddle broke, and as the players took the court, Lance looked up and saw Leah seated in the crowd, in the place where this version of him knew she always sat for every game, Four rows up, slightly down from the center. Her eyes met his and she smiled; he smiled back. She too appeared to be older, maybe six or seven years more than the Leah etched into backseat Lance's memory, but as beautiful as ever.

Lance was just about to give her a wink and then turn around to watch his players finish the game when somebody switched off all the noise, the gym falling silent. The images faded, the gym emptying itself of everything except the two of them. And Lance felt himself change, felt the backseat version of him jump up front and take the wheel, felt himself coming back into his own. He looked down and saw that his suit and fancy shoes were gone and he was back in the shorts and hoodie.

He looked up, saw that Leah had changed too, and the look

she had on her face was one of surprise mixed with elation mixed with fear. The moment was brief, only a few ticks of the clock, and then things changed, the gym falling away completely, being erased in great strokes. Lance felt himself begin to be pulled backward again, sucked back into the ether.

Leah called out to him just as the blackness swallowed everything. "We're coming!" she said. "We're coming for you!"

And there was another great rush of speed and a flash of that blinding white light and Lance felt himself fall backward and—

He landed on his butt in the middle of the floor, hard enough that his mouth snapped shut and he bit his tongue, the coppery taste of blood bringing him fully back to the present. There was a shuffling at his side and he turned to see Emmett holding out a hand to help him up.

"Whoa," Emmett said. "You okay? What just happened?"

Before Lance could answer, the door to the room flew open and slammed into the wall. The thing called Patrick Cain stormed in, his face twisted in anger and confusion. He kicked Lance down, planting one foot into his chest. He pressed down hard, pushing the air from Lance's lungs. "*Where did you go?*" Patrick hissed. "*What happened?*"

Lance coughed and sputtered for air. "I ... don't ... know."

Patrick sneered and knelt down, clamping both of his hands on either side of Lance's head and slamming it back against the floor. Lance's vision blipped black and then swirled with stars as the room came back into focus. "*Where?*" Patrick hissed again.

Emmett jumped forward and grabbed one of Patrick's shoulders, pulled him away. Patrick's eyes burned with red rage and he leapt from the floor and shot a hand to Emmett's neck. The man screamed a single high-pitched note and then collapsed to the floor, the zippers of his vest jingling on impact like a fallen wind chime.

Lance scrambled to a sitting position and pushed himself backward until his back hit the metal bench along the wall. Patrick spun toward him, those red eyes glowing hot.

All Lance could do was tell the truth. "I went to a ... basketball game," he said, still trying to catch his breath. "I was ... I was the coach."

Patrick stopped. The anger in his eyes faded as he stared at Lance on the floor. Neither of them spoke, but Lance didn't like the way Patrick was looking at him.

He especially didn't like it when the thing's face grinned at him.

When Patrick spoke, it started out as only a whisper. "Incredible," he said. He shook his head, and that ugly grin grew larger. "You're doing it and don't even have to try."

He turned and walked out of the room, closing the door on his two prisoners.

[26]

"I SAW HIM!"

Leah woke from the dream and jumped forward in the minivan's passenger seat so fast the seat belt burned her neck. Maya gasped and the van swerved to the left, crossing the center line before she corrected the wheel and got them back in their lane and then slowed down. "My stars," she said, hand on her heart, "you scared me. Are you okay? Who'd you see?" She turned toward Leah, and in the glow from the dash, Leah saw the hope in the woman's eyes. "Was it Patrick?" Maya asked.

Leah shook her head. "No. It was Lance. I saw him ... but, like, I *really* saw him this time. And he saw me!"

The road was dark and still mostly empty. Behind them, an eighteen-wheeler's lights lit up the cabin before it roared by on their left and left them glowing red in its taillights. "What do you mean 'this time'?" Maya asked. She checked the rearview, looking back at Noah. Leah turned and saw the boy was still asleep. She was glad her shout hadn't woken him. Beside the boy, the ghost of Pamela Brody still sat. The look she gave Leah was unreadable, offered no advice.

"Did you see him too?" Leah asked the woman's spirit. "Did you feel him?"

Pamela shook her head. "No, dear. Whatever you saw, it was meant just for you. You have your own connection to him, as do I."

Leah wanted to ask more questions, tell the woman about the vision she'd had back at Maya's house where they'd all been in Hillston together, headed to the church for the choir's Christmas performance. She wanted to know what it meant, how it was possible for her to have seen those things—things that could not be possible.

Leah hadn't told Maya about the vision, so she did now, then went on to tell her how this most recent vision was different.

"It started out the same," Leah said. "I guess I dozed off and then it happened again. I felt myself floating away, toward another memory. But it's like not really a memory, right, because it didn't actually happen. But anyway, I floated away and then *poof*"—she snapped her fingers—"I was sitting in a high school gym watching Lance coach a basketball game. And it was so strange, because he looked older. Had put on a little weight." Then she laughed. "And he was wearing a *suit*! He looked so handsome.

"They were in a time-out and, this is another weird thing, I was watching the players on the bench, and I knew all their names. Every single one. Like I'd been watching them play for years. And I knew who was a good shooter and who needed to play better defense and ... it's like my head was filled with an entire existence different than my own."

Leah paused here and felt a flutter of happiness in her stomach. "And we were married. I had just noticed the ring on my finger when the time-out ended and I looked up and Lance was looking at me. And that's when it happened. It's like all the memories that weren't really memories faded away and it was just me and Lance left in the gym, all alone. And it was really us then, like, the *real* versions of us. Then I felt it, our connection surged and came to life for the first time since ... well, since he shut me out. He must have felt it too, because his face changed, like he was really seeing me for the first time.

"When that happened, I froze up. I was so shocked that he was actually there, that I was *really* with him, I didn't know what to say. And I waited too long, because then everything started to disappear, like somebody was peeling away a sticker and there was nothing underneath but black paint. I panicked, and the only thing I could think to say was to tell him we were coming for him. I shouted it as loud as I could." Leah slumped back in the seat and rested her head against the headrest, closed her eyes. "I hope he heard me. I hope he knows I haven't given up."

Maya reached a hand out and rested it on Leah's knee. "He knows," she said. "If he's half as brilliant as you make him out to be, he knows."

From the back seat, Pamela whispered in Leah's mind, "He knows. He loves you, and he's yet to realize how powerful that is. For all of us."

Leah nodded and felt a single unexpected tear slide down her cheek. She told both women thank you, squeezed Maya's hand. "I can help drive, if you're getting tired."

Maya shook her head, held up one of the thermoses of coffee. "This one's almost empty," she said. "I could probably drive to Mexico."

Half an hour later, Leah got the message from Pamela and relayed it to Maya. "Take the next exit," she said.

What she didn't tell the woman was the second part of Pamela's message. "The closer we get, the greater the chance they'll know we're coming."

"How?" Leah had asked. "How is that possible? They already have Lance—he was the one they were tracking."

"Because of you, dear," Pamela had said, so matter-of-factly that it had made Leah feel silly for asking. "Because of you."

[27]

THE INSTANT the thing called Patrick Cain slammed the door on them, Lance scrambled across the floor to Emmett's side. The man had crumpled forward after hitting the ground and was lying facedown with his cheek against the floor and one arm twisted under him.

"Ed," Lance said, gently shaking the man, his voice groggy in his throat. "Ed, come back to me."

Lance remembered the way the Surfer had tapped Lance's temple before he'd been taken prisoner, how the single touch had sent Lance away, trapping his mind in an awful emptiness. He'd drowned in the blackness, similar to how he'd felt only a few moments ago, when he'd been pulled away from the hellish landscape the spirit had been tasked with showing him and then had somehow gotten trapped between...

Between what?

Because there had been more than just this, the present, and the nightmare-filled other place. There had been the third place, too. The place that Lance had been grabbed by when Patrick had been toying with him, trying to rile him up.

The place with the basketball game and...

And Leah.

And she was really there, Lance thought, remembering how, at the end, right before he'd been jolted back to this room, everything had changed and it wasn't as if another version of himself was looking at another version of her, but it was the real them, their true selves. He'd felt the connection between them snap into place, felt the electricity of their emotions for each other fill the empty gymnasium the same way the cheering crowd had been just moments before. He'd seen the spark in her eyes, the surprise in them. The same surprise he'd felt, too. The moment had been fleeting, their own shock wasting away the precious seconds. Leah, in her all her wonderful smarts and strength, had managed to get her message to him just before everything faded away.

"We're coming," Lance said aloud. "We're coming for you."

Is that why he was so upset? Lance wondered, thinking of how Patrick had come storming into the room.

He shook his head. *No. He didn't mention anything about who I'd seen, only where I'd been. And when I told him, he'd seemed ... happy.*

The memory of the way that grin had slithered across Patrick's face made Lance shiver. He pushed the thought away and focused on Emmett. The man's chest was rising and falling with slow but steady breaths, and when Lance placed two fingers to the man's neck, he felt a pulse, strong and sure.

His body is fine. But his mind...

Again, Lance thought of the blackness, the prison of nothing where Evil sent its foes. How long would Emmett be trapped there? Lance had no memory of how he'd emerged from his own imprisonment in that place, only that he'd been there one moment—a moment that felt eternal—and then had snapped awake in the back of the Plymouth Horizon.

One of them could have brought me back, he thought.

If that was true, what did it mean for Emmett? What if Patrick or any of the rest of them never returned to free Emmett's mind?

We're coming for you. Leah's words echoed in Lance's head, sudden and unexpected. And with them came a new idea. Lance looked down at Emmett's face, and one of the man's gray and wispy eyebrows twitched.

Lance felt the determination and strength begin to swell inside him, felt his veins become alive with an energy. He took a deep breath and reached out one of his hands. "I'm coming for you," he said. "I'm coming for you, Ed."

He cupped the back of Emmett's head with his hand and—

And there was nothing. In a blink the room fell away and the blackness flooded all. Lance couldn't see, but he could *feel*. His soul registered the energy of another. The strength inside Emmett burned a bright heat nearby, and Lance reached out for it with his mind, searching in the dark.

Ed! he called out across the wavelengths. *Ed, I'm here!*

Only silence followed for several seconds before, finally, *Lance?*

The word was accompanied by a flash of heat that Lance homed in on. *I'm here, Ed. Take my hand. Imagine my hand and take it. We'll go back together.*

Another beat of silence. Then, *I don't...*

My hand, Ed. Use your mind. It's strong. Imagine my hand and reach for it with yours.

Lance reached out, waited. Could feel Emmett's energy pulse and waver like a faulty current. The man was trying.

Good, Ed. You're close. Concentrate.

A sound like thunder rocked the blackness, the entire atmosphere warping with the blast.

The pulse of Emmett's energy weakened.

Ed!

There's something out there, Lance. There's a ... a red line, like a horizon. It's getting closer. Bigger. I can ... I can hear screaming.

Ed, stay away from it! Don't look at it! Focus, Ed! I need you to focus on me! *Your hand, remember? Give me your hand!*

Lance, I...

Your hand, Ed! There is nothing but your hand and mine. Here, I'm reaching out to you. Can you see it? Can you see my fingers?

Silence.

See my fingers, Ed! See them!

Miraculously, Lance felt a surge of heat from Emmett's soul, his energy and focus trying to regain its footing.

I see them, Lance. I see.

Good, Ed. Good. Now reach out and take them. Grab my hand and I'll pull—

Lance felt it, felt Emmett's energy mesh with his. Lance squeezed tight with his mind and yanked them both back.

Their souls sped away from the darkness, resurfacing from the black waters. In his mind, Lance focused on the GUEST HOLDING AREA, saw the two of them sitting on the floor. Steered them toward the image.

Close, he thought, tightening his grip on Emmett. *We're—*

Lance felt their souls jerk sideways, off course. He'd barely registered the change before that great white light sparked again, brilliant and hot and impossible. It blasted away the darkness and—

And the nighttime landscape rushed by all around him as the motorcycle roared across the asphalt, chasing the wide cone of iridescent glow thrown by the headlight. The helmet felt heavy and foreign on his head, the vibrations from the engine beneath him caused his muscles to tense.

But it wasn't Lance's head, and it wasn't Lance's body.

Lance sat in the back seat of Emmett's mind as the man cranked the throttle and the bike shot forward faster. After a small curve, which Emmett leaned into expertly, the bike like an extension of his actual body, the sight of a car's flashing hazard lights caused him to slow. When the bike reached the car on the side of the road, Emmett pulled the bike over onto the shoulder with it and killed the engine.

A pretty young woman was leaning against the side of her car, her arms wrapped around her body, a cell phone clutched in one hand. Steam was hissing from the hood.

Emmett stayed on the bike, not wanting to spook her or appear to be a threat.

"Evening, ma'am," Emmett said, flicking up the visor on his helmet. "Car trouble?"

The girl nodded, wary. She stood and reached a hand toward the driver's door. "Yes," she said, her voice quiet at first. "It just started smoking out of nowhere."

Emmett nodded to the cell phone in her hand. "Did you call somebody?"

Now the girl's voice broke, and she fought back tears as she said, "No service," holding the device up in the air.

Emmett took off his helmet and then unzipped one of the pockets of his vest and fished out his own cell phone. "Yeah, there's only one provider that seems to work along this stretch, and it's your lucky day because it's who I use. And your luck gets even better—I work at a garage in town," he said. "I'll call Sleepy, he's good with the tow truck."

The woman almost looked as if she wanted to protest—maybe out of fear or caution or ... well, you're not supposed to take candy from strangers, right?—but finally she nodded and said, "Thank you. That would be great."

Lance watched and listened as Emmett made the call, hearing Sleepy's soft and patient voice through an ear that wasn't his.

Emmett ended the call. "He's on his way. Probably twenty minutes or so. I'll wait with you."

Again, the girl looked uneasy, only now it appeared to be more out of not wanting to be an inconvenience. Before she could respond, a new set of headlights popped in the distance, coming fast down the road and accompanied by the roar of an engine.

The silver pickup truck slowed to a crawl when it was nearly beside them, almost seeming to linger a few yards behind, but once it pulled forward enough to be able to make out Emmett on his bike pulled further off the shoulder, the truck shot forward as if spooked, growling as it accelerated away in a blur of silver and a squeal of tires.

"Asshole," the girl said.

"Yep," Emmett agreed. "Asshole indeed."

The girl shivered and wrapped her arms around herself again. Emmett nodded toward the car. "Get in," he said. "It's fine. I'll wait out here for Sleepy. Won't be long."

Still looking slightly unnerved after the encounter with the truck, the girl stopped with her fingers on the handle. "Thank you," she said. "You've made me feel a lot better."

"My pleasure," Emmett said. "Happy to do it."

"What's your name?" she asked.

"Emmett Emmanuel Dean, but my friends call me Ed."

The girl laughed, like this was a joke, and the sound caused Lance to feel a flash of warmth spread through Emmett's soul, along with a tingle of regret struggling to break free.

"Well, thank you, Ed. I'm Melody. You're exactly the friend I needed tonight. Are you working tomorrow? I'd love to bring you some donuts or coffee or something as a thank-you."

More warmth, like sliding into a bath. But there was sadness too. Spilling over the edges and splashing onto the floor. "I—" Emmett started, but

(*"What's he doing?"*

"Are they together?"

"Can he really do that?"

"He can."

"That's impossible."

"It's not. Not for him."

"Amazing."

"It's better than we hoped.")

voices echoed around them in the night, intruded on the moment. They broke the trance, severed the connection.

Lance? Emmett's mind sounded scared again, confused.

I'm here, Ed. It's time to go.

Lance didn't have to search for Emmett's hand this time. They were already together, their souls and energy already entwined in this...

This place...

Lance gripped the man's mind with his and followed the sounds of those voices, watched as the hazard lights and the car and the desert night broke apart and flashed white and there was that familiar roller-coaster drop and—

The one burning fluorescent above them on the ceiling flickered and then buzzed loudly as Lance rejoined his body and the room came back into view.

Emmett coughed and gasped. Lance rolled the man over on his back and worked to help him sit up.

"What ... what happened?" Emmett asked, his eyes wide and frozen in disbelief. "How... she was ... she was..." He buried his head in his hands and sobbed.

"Yes," the thing called Patrick Cain said. "How? That's a great fucking question."

Lance looked up and saw the looming figures of Patrick, the Reverend, the Surfer, and the white-haired woman named Karina huddled together just inside the opened door.

Karina was holding the Surfer's hand in one of hers, and in the other she gripped a metal baseball bat.

[28]

LANCE WATCHED as the poor man's version of the Four Horsemen of the Apocalypse swarmed around he and Emmett and then stared down at the two of them like they were some previously unseen dinosaur fossils recently excavated from the dirt. Their faces were a mixture of fascination and wonder and awe.

But also happiness. Smiles that flickered with menacing affect. In Lance's experience, it was never a good thing when Evil looked pleased.

"Take him," the thing called Patrick Cain said, barking the order to the Surfer and Karina.

Lance braced himself, prepared to fight. To scrape and claw his way free from their grips. The moment felt heavy, pushed him down with a reminder of that great understanding he'd momentarily forgotten during everything he'd experienced in the last few hours.

This is it. This is the end.

Lance looked up into those four disgusting faces, and he

knew that his death was waiting wherever they planned on taking him.

Karina and the Surfer's hands parted, and the tall woman flicked the tail of her coat back the same way she had in the terrible memory Lance had experienced behind the eyes of the man who'd been beaten to death behind the Ferris wheel. She flipped the bat in her hand like a cocky slugger at the plate, so sure he was about to go yard, catching it by the fat end, and then she lunged forward, thrusting the skinny end into Emmett's gut.

The man fell back and wheezed, the air rushing out of him in a coughing fit as he struggled to regain control of his lungs.

"*Hey!*" Lance yelled, jumping up and leaping over Emmett's body. He went airborne, his sneakers catching Emmet's knee, anger and sudden rage fueling his body to function without his mind's consideration of his actions. He reached out, hands ready to wrap around the white-haired woman's throat.

But he didn't make it.

The woman, in a half-blink of the eye, was gone. Now standing two feet to the left, closer to Patrick. Lance had just enough time to think *Damn, she's fast* before the Surfer grabbed Lance's arm and a fistful of his hoodie and spun around, flinging Lance with the strength of an Olympic track and field athlete going for the gold. Lance saw the room spin and then blur with speed as his body was hurled through the air, and then there was a great jarring crack as he slammed into the wall above the bench where Emmett had sat and told his story. Lance slid down the wall and landed hard on the bench, his skull connecting with the metal. His entire body was electric with pain, and he tasted blood in his mouth, but still, he leapt back up, a middleweight fighter refusing to stay down for the count.

"Stop!" Patrick Cain's voice boomed from his body with

impossible volume, the room reverberating with the noise, Lance's vision wavering as the message struck inside his head as well.

Lance froze, and the room fell silent, the only sounds that of his own hurried breathing and Emmett struggling to his feet as Karina and the Surfer hauled him up and gripped him by the upper arms. Lance looked into the man's eyes, and what he found in them was not fear but a grim determination.

"It's okay," Emmett said. "This isn't about me, Lance. It never has been."

Patrick nodded to the door. "Go," he told his companions.

Karina and the Surfer dragged Emmett out through the door without a struggle, and as the man's image disappeared from view, he called back to Lance, "Remember, I deserve this! I've had it coming!"

Emmett's words evaporated, leaving only the hum of the fluorescents above. Patrick cast a sideways glance to the Reverend, who'd moved to lean against the wall by the door and cross his arms, making him look like a holy security guard. "You too," Patrick said. "Out."

The Reverend looked offended. He stepped forward and sputtered, "But ... I can help you—"

"Out," Patrick said again, and his voice left no room for rebuttal. The Reverend looked to Lance in disgust, as if somehow Lance had voted on the matter.

Lance smiled and shrugged. "Sorry. VIPs only."

The Reverend said nothing. Only gave Lance one last hate-filled look and then turned and left the room. When the sound of the building's outer door closing faded, Patrick sat on one of the benches, in nearly the exact same spot where the tormented soul had been earlier. He gestured to the bench across the room, where Lance had been sitting previously. "Have a seat, Lance. Let's have ourselves a fucking chat, shall we?"

Lance stayed where he was. The metallic taste of blood in his mouth had gone, but the adrenaline and anger inside him were still pumping hard. He felt jittery, off-balance. The image of the young man in front of him now pushing Leah's head into a lit fireplace only a few days ago made Lance's stomach turn. "Don't act like we're just two old pals who are going to talk things through and then hug this out," Lance spat. "We're not friends, and I'm never on your side. I'm not buying what you're selling, no matter how good a salesman you are. I'd rather die."

Patrick looked as though he was considering this. He nodded his head slowly, and when he looked back to Lance his eyes were like stone. "I understand what you're saying, Lance. So, since you're so honest, I can be honest too.

"You're right. We're not friends. Never will be. Truth is, I hate you. I *despise* you and everyone even close to being like you. I've spent all my time in this dimension doing nothing except hunting down and killing your kind. And I want to kill you too, Lance. I want to end your life and rip apart your soul and hold up the broken pieces and shout 'Here he is! Here's your savior, your chosen one! Is that the best you can do?' And then I'll toss the bits of you into the pit and watch the beasts feed on one of the great protectors."

Patrick's words had been cold as ice, and the truth of what he'd said chilled Lance to the bone. "Well," Lance said, heading toward the bench to take a seat. "You sure know how to sweet-talk a guy. I'm surprised you're still single." He held up his hands. "No, let me guess. You're putting your career first."

Patrick blinked. "Sarcasm ... one of the many human emotions I don't understand."

Lance shrugged again. "That's because you're not human. Well"—he winked—"at least not completely."

Patrick's eyes narrowed to slits, and Lance felt a spark of pride at the small victory. He had one button he could push with the guy, the button he'd found by accident that day in the BBQ restaurant's parking lot when Patrick had grabbed Lance's wrist. Lance still felt there was some importance to this button, he just didn't know what it was. In fact, he was beginning to become certain it was too little, too late. It was information he'd never be able to do anything with—other than irk the guy and take a few cheap shots. Which, if Lance was being honest, was fun, but ultimately unfulfilling.

Patrick Cain leaned back against the wall, crossed his arms. Lance did the same. He had heard somewhere that mimicking your interviewer was disarming.

"Fuck it," Patrick said. "Here it is. We brought you here to see if you were as powerful as we've always felt you to be. And I'm not talking about all the cute shit you do, like seeing souls and reading people's minds. That's the kiddie pool, Lance. Child's play. Because you see, all of that, it's mostly based right here in *this* dimension.

"Now, you defeating demons, that's getting a little warmer. More impressive. But even that, still, is not equivalent action to the sheer ripple effect your energy has, Lance. You don't understand because you're, well"—Patrick made a show of winking—"you *are* human. That's what makes you so fucking fascinating to us. You have a multidimensional energy, even though you —*this* version of you—are bound to only this dimension."

Lance said nothing. He was beginning to wish Hillston High School had offered a quantum physics class.

"You are powerful, and then some," Patrick said.

"You're too kind," Lance replied, trying to sound unimpressed.

"Powerful," Patrick said again, and that small grin twitched his lips. "You going off with our little messenger, over to the dark side, if you will—well, that was expected. Like I told you, if somebody was guiding you, we suspected you'd find the way. But, after ... when you left me and headed to your basketball game ... that was unexpected and fucking impressive, Lance."

Lance had no choice but to shake his head, ashamed at his own lack of understanding. His head was spinning, struggling to keep up. "I don't know what I did. I don't know what that was."

Patrick nodded. "It doesn't matter. Because I do." Then, "You did it again, just a few moments ago, with Emmett. You went with him."

"Went with him *where*?" Lance hated the way he was sounding now, almost begging for answers he didn't even know he needed. Begging the Evil thing in front of him.

"An alternate dimension," Patrick said. "Another version of the truth."

Patrick's earlier words reprised themselves. "*This* version of me," Lance whispered, the enormity of what those words potentially meant sucking the air from the room.

"Billions," Patrick said. "Billions upon billions of alternate dimensions, different versions of the same reality, each one unique. Each path and choice and decision mapped out with different turns and forks and endings."

Lance found himself nodding. "I've seen them," he said, and he couldn't believe he was spilling his secrets to the thing seated across from him like it was part of some twisted therapy session. "I've had visions of them, before we even got here. I ... I thought they were just ... wishful dreams. False memories I created, like a"—he shrugged—"a defense mechanism."

Patrick looked momentarily surprised by this but then nodded as if it all made complete sense. "And now that you're here, you're living them, Lance. Somehow you're moving your consciousness from dimension to dimension like it's as simple as..."

"As taking a bus," Lance said.

Patrick snapped his fingers and pointed. "Bingo. And this last time, holy *shit*, you took that old biker with you." Patrick laughed and held up his hands. "Incredible. Fucking incredible."

Lance stayed quiet, thinking about all of it. All the implications, all the possibilities. He felt a brief flicker of happiness, of *hope*, inside him when he realized something else had happened during one of his supposed trips to one of his alternate realities.

He'd seen Leah. And Leah had seen him, too. *Really* seen him. She'd been there with him, not just an alternate version of her, not at the end before it all went away, but the her from right here, in this dimension.

She can do it too, he realized. He looked across the room at Patrick, who was sitting forward now, elbows resting on his knees. *And he has no idea she was there with me.*

Lance cleared his throat, tucking his secret away, locking it up tight. "What do you want from me?" he asked. "You still haven't said."

Patrick smiled his ugly smile, adjusted his leather jacket. "I thought you'd never ask." He leaned back again, recrossed his arms. "There are spots like this all across the globe, places where the barrier between dimensions is thin. That's why the feeling is so strong, Lance, the one you felt as soon as we arrived. Evil is literally seeping into this dimension from another, from one of *ours*."

"One of yours?"

Patrick nodded. "Of course. This war you think you understand, the ... how do you humans like to phrase it ... the battle between good and evil ... it has spanned time frames unfathomable to your comprehension, and been fought tirelessly across all those billions and billions of realities. Some of those realities, we control. Others ... well, your side has put up a good fight."

"You know," Lance said, "you can speak very well when you put your mind to it."

Patrick ignored him. "That place you visited with the soul that was here, the place with that magnificent army we've been building and feeding for centuries, it's close, Lance. It's right at the gate, ready to be let out. We've just been waiting for the right time, waiting for the key."

"The key to what?"

"To the *other* gate. The gate to the dimensions your side has had protected and locked away. The ones we've never been able to reach."

Understanding washed over Lance, made him dizzy. "And you think I'm the key. You think I'll open the gate for you."

Patrick nodded.

"Never."

Patrick stood from the bench, headed to the door. "Now, now, let's not get ahead of ourselves. You haven't even let me make my sales pitch yet."

"I'm all ears," Lance said. "But you're wasting your time. You might as well go ahead and kill me."

Patrick stepped out of the room and started to pull the door shut behind him. “We just might,” he said. “And you’ll find out soon enough. But have you ever stopped to think just what might be in this for you?”

Lance said nothing.

Patrick smiled. “I think you know what I mean.” Then he closed the door, leaving Lance all alone, forced to do nothing except wait for the end to come.

[29]

The silence had grown infinite, and the loneliness had begun to suffocate him.

Lance's thoughts went wild. The thing called Patrick Cain's revelations had filled his mind with such enormous impossibilities that Lance simply struggled to find a safe space within his own consciousness. He could not grab hold of individual thoughts to try and arrange them in a logical order, could not work out scenarios or options or possible outcomes.

He was lost.

He could not do what Patrick was asking of him.

Could he?

And even if he could, if the Universe had somehow grown his strength to an unfathomable degree that would allow him—a mere mortal, a human being with a few supernatural party tricks tucked up his sleeve—to pry open a cosmic gateway that led to an infinite number of alternate dimensions and realities, would he?

No, Lance thought. *Because that would be game over.*

It would be a betrayal of all the good in the world, a betrayal of all the Universe had given him, and ... a betrayal of his mother. Lance refused to acknowledge that there might be a part of him that would ever hand over to Evil all the keys to the kingdom, not after his mother had laid down her own life to allow him to live, allow him to continue on with protecting the world from the things hiding in the shadows.

He would stay strong for her. And for Leah.

But they'll try to make me, he understood. *They will stop at nothing to try to make me.*

But ... so be it. Deep down, beneath all his optimism and confidence and cool-headed self-awareness, underneath the jokes and the jovial youthful ignorance he would put on for show, Lance Brody had always feared this day would come.

He'd always known he was too big to go unnoticed, too big not to be sought after and used.

He'd always known he would have a role to play, even if he would never understand what it might be until the moment was upon him.

That moment was now, and when it came time to choose which team he played for, he would not hesitate to stand by the side of Good, the side of Light.

His mother's life, and his own, would not be wasted. Lance would not be responsible for willingly bringing any more death into this world or others that lay beyond.

The hours ticked by in his head as his thoughts swirled as if caught in a hurricane. Lance sat on the metal bench, right where he'd been left after Patrick Cain had laid out his desires. He did not move. His legs and feet had long since fallen asleep, and his stomach complained with hunger, but he did not feel them.

He'd retreated from his physical body, pulled himself to exist only in his mind. He found himself wanting to leave that place, leave his storm of unpleasant thoughts and find another version of himself inside another memory that was not a memory, discover another of the realities that he now knew existed. Like an addict, he'd gotten his first few tastes of a life where he was truly normal and now he longed for the next fix, the next blast of happiness that came along with the idea of being able to live in blissful ignorance of all the Evil that stalked the earth, and his own obligation to expose it.

But he could not find that place, could not navigate the vastness of eternity in search of that great light that would grant him his peace, if only temporarily.

Instead, there was nothing but an emptiness inside, a feeling of desperation that would not be tempered. He was trapped in this room, alone, with what felt like only a short-lived future waiting for him on the other side of the door.

The door opened, and the noise of it sent Lance's consciousness back to the front of his present mind. His body awakened, rife with the painful pins and needles shooting through his limbs. He gritted his teeth against the fire and turned his head toward the door, found the thing called Patrick Cain leaning against the jamb with his thumbs hooked into the pockets of his leather jacket.

"Showtime, brother," Patrick said, motioning for Lance to come forward and join him. "Everyone's waiting."

Lance Brody took a deep breath, maybe the deepest breath he'd ever taken in his entire life, and then stood from the bench. He shook the last of the pins and needles from his legs and feet and then stood tall as he walked across the room to the door. He stopped, inches from Patrick, and stared into the thing's eyes. "I'm not your brother."

They held each other's stare, Lance staring down from his superior height, and Patrick staring up with a bemused smirk on his face. In that moment, Lance wanted nothing more than to crash his fist into the young man's face, to feel the crunch of bone and feel the warm spill of blood across his knuckles. He wanted to cause pain, to vent his helplessness out and use it to punish those who've caused it.

But he did not strike.

Because he remembered the simple touch of Patrick's hand to Emmett's neck, how it had instantly sent the man's soul into the ether.

He looks like a man, but he's not. Except...

And then Lance gave a smirk of his own, another acknowledgment of the secret they shared.

"Let's go," Lance said, nodding for the boy to move out of his way. "I'd hate to keep the people waiting."

Patrick studied Lance's face for another second, a sliver of uncertainty flashing, but then it was gone and he nodded and spun around and headed back through the lobby of the Guest Services building.

Outside, the air was cold and everything was tinted with a pale blue shimmer as the moon began to tuck itself away. Patrick stood and waited for Lance to join him, and when Lance did, the two of them walked alongside each other down what at one time must have been Arthur's Adventureland's main midway. Shuttered buildings and long-extinguished light poles watched silently from the wilting shadows. Abandoned food carts and souvenir stands stood by, frozen in their past, offering nothing more than a reminder that time never stops and the world will move on without you if given the chance.

Who will remember me? Lance found himself wondering. *When I'm gone, how many years will pass before the memory of me is gone? How long before it will be as if I'd never existed at all?*

"Have you thought about what I said?" Patrick asked from beside him, his voice echoing off the forgotten buildings along the midway.

In the distance, the Ferris wheel loomed over the park with its watchful eye.

Here's the church, here's the steeple...

"Lance?"

"Nothing," Lance said. "There's nothing in this for me. You won't convince me otherwise."

Patrick laughed, and a hundred laughs echoed around them like a pack of hyenas. "It's always been fascinating to me, how your side manages to convince you to put your own well-being aside for what you deem to be the good of the people. To suffer so others won't. It's like you actively chose to be unhappy."

Lance shook his head. "You don't understand happiness. You don't understand anything that's good. If you did, you wouldn't seek to destroy it."

"I understand plenty," Patrick spat, his voice rising.

Lance kept his head high, his gaze straight ahead, locked onto the Ferris wheel. Something about the sight of it was causing an uneasy feeling to stir in his gut.

Here's the church, here's the steeple.

"So do you want to know? Do you want to know what's in this for you? I'll tell you, since I know you're going to pretend you don't have any interest." Patrick paused, waited to see if Lance had anything to say. When Lance didn't humor him with a response, Patrick took two quick steps ahead and then stepped in front of Lance, facing him and blocking his way. "You can have the life you've always wanted, Lance. Don't you see that? If you open the door to all the other versions of reality, you're opening the door to all the other versions of *you*. There's a world out there where you and Leah can be together and your biggest worry will be whether the condom broke. There's a world where you get to go to college to play basketball and experience the world without wondering if a dead classmate is going to show up in the crowd. You can go to parties and let your guard down and not feel like your every fucking action is dictated by some bullshit guiding force that you feel some sense of obligation to. You can be *normal*, Lance. You can just..." Patrick shrugged. "Just be."

Lance stared over the boy's head, refused to look at him. Chose to focus on the Ferris wheel. He stepped around Patrick and kept walking, knowing in the way that only he could know that the Ferris wheel was where he was ultimately being led.

"You can choose a version where your mother is still alive." Patrick's words went for the sucker punch. Lance took the blow in stride, did not stop.

A short stone building that had once served as restrooms sat across the midway's path, marking its end. Lance went right, following the walkway around it, seeing the long-faded sign advertising that the Wheel of Adventure was just ahead. He rounded the restrooms and saw the entrance to the ride's queue, which was a zigzagging pathway dissected by metal railings that ultimately led to a ramp that would carry guests up to load onto the wheel's waiting gondolas.

Lance stopped, the sick feeling in his gut stabbing him with a sharp pain of remorse.

He stared at the gondola waiting at the end of the ramp. *Oh, Emmett*, he thought. *No*.

"Well," Patrick Cain said, coming up beside Lance. He looked on with something akin to admiration at the sight before them. "Time to make your choice." He pushed Lance forward. "Either way, you're going to do what you're told."

[30]

The Reverend stood off to the side of the Ferris wheel's base, in an overgrown grassy area that fed into the back edge of the park. Lance recognized the area from the vision he'd gotten from the spirit of the man who'd shared the room with him and Emmett. The Reverend's black garb seemed to absorb the blue hue from the dissolving moon, growing darker as the sky grew lighter. He eyed Lance with a wary expression, and Lance couldn't help but think the Reverend looked afraid, as though he knew something the others didn't, that maybe this wasn't such a good idea after all.

Can he feel something? Lance wondered.

Because Lance could feel something. The air seemed thick with apprehension, enough to choke on if you tried to inhale deeply, felt charged with an awful electricity.

It's them ... they're priming the pump, preparing to...

To open their own gate. All the hate and Evil and terrible things that lived inside these creatures disguised as man and woman was *excited.*

Quickly, Lance tried to reach out with his own energy,

searching for its source, wanted to know that he wasn't alone here, that the Universe was watching, waiting to fight alongside him.

He felt nothing but despair.

"Lance!" Emmett's voice cracked like a gunshot through the silence that had fallen over the scene. "Lance, you know me now! You know I'm ready for this! Don't you try to save me, you hear!"

Lance's gaze shifted from the Reverend and back to the horrible image that had greeted him from the Ferris wheel's main platform. The Surfer and his side chick Karina stood on either side of the gondola. The Surfer, as always, looked bored and uninterested with everything, though his eyes were locked onto where Lance and the thing called Patrick Cain stood. Karina was bouncing on the balls of her feet with reckless energy. She was smiling from ear to ear, bobbing her head to an unheard beat, gearing up to dance. In her right hand she still gripped the metal baseball bat.

Emmett Emmanuel Dean—Ed, to his friends—was tied sideways across the gondola between the two creatures. His wrists were bound together and his arms stretched tight and fastened to a rear support rail of the next gondola in line. The same was done with his ankles and legs, his back flat against the middle gondola's door, his torso drooping sickeningly toward the ground as his strength wavered and his weight was pulled down. He stared at Lance with a pained and strained expression, but his words remained absolute. "We give them nothing, Lance! Nothing! I made my mistake, and I won't make it again!"

Lance Brody had spent an entire lifetime doing what was right, helping those in need, and twenty-three years of instinct and habit was not something that simply vanished on command.

At the sight of his suffering new friend, Lance felt his body react before his mind had fully caught up. He took a fast step forward, meaning to leap over the railings of the ride's queue and...

And what? What can I possibly do?

The thing called Patrick Cain's hand darted out and grabbed Lance by the shoulder. There was no pain, but a sudden lightheadedness threatened Lance's vision, and he felt his body begin to tumble forward. Patrick pulled him back, jerked him upright. "No," he said calmly. "Remember, you are still human, no matter what you might believe. You can be killed." Patrick shrugged and looked almost bashful, like he was about to reveal his secret crush. "And there's still a selfish part of me that would love nothing more than to end your life myself. So let's not get ahead of ourselves, shall we? We both have a job to do."

Lance's vision cleared and his strength returned after Patrick released him, and through gritted teeth he said, "Let Emmett go. He's not part of this. It's me you want, you've said it yourself."

Patrick shook his head. "Wrong." Then he nodded to Karina, just once.

The woman squealed with delight, and her white hair splayed behind her in a fan as she spun around and smashed the end of the baseball bat into Emmett's stomach. The man did not cry out, but the air whooshed out of him in a surprised gasp, which was followed by a horrible coughing spell as he struggled for air.

The blow caused a bolt of guilt and sorrow to stab at Lance.

"He's our catalyst," Patrick said. "On two fronts, actually."

Another nod to Karina, and she struck again, this time

higher up in the chest. Emmett bit back a bark of pain, and even from where Lance was standing he could see the cords popping in the man's neck.

"You see," Patrick continued, "his suffering whets the appetite of our army. They can smell it, like sharks smelling blood in the water. It riles them up, draws them out. And when I open our gate, they'll pour out like a great flood and they'll feed on him and grow that much stronger. I know this, because we've been feeding them for years, one by one. And, Lance, they're always hungry for more. They've been waiting for this day, the day we let them feast."

"I can't do it," Lance said, desperation creeping into his voice. "I don't know how."

"Second," Patrick said, as if he hadn't heard him, "each and every second you refuse to do what you're told, every moment you continue to act as though you don't have the power—which, let's be honest, Lance, we both know you do—to reach out to your side and open those other worlds for us—for *you*, too, don't forget—is one more moment longer that our dear brother Emmett here has to suffer." Patrick slapped on one of his ugly smiles, a look that was even more menacing in the blue light of dawn. It made him look like a smiling corpse. "You don't have it in you, Lance. It's not the way you're wired. Compassion is a flaw of human nature and you're busting at the seams with it." He pointed to Emmett. "You won't let this man die on your watch. Not him." Then Patrick leaned in closer and whispered, "Because let's face it, how many have died because of you over the years? How many innocent lives have been lost while you march around on your crusade against us, seeking to destroy us no matter the collateral damage? Are you really that much better than us, Lance?"

Lance said nothing.

"Your silence speaks volumes," Patrick said. "But there's another question I want to ask you, Lance. Do you think the Universe will just stand by and let you watch as Emmett, one of its soldiers, dies at our hands?" He shook his head. "I don't. No, just like the man's suffering will call forward the darkness, I believe his pain will strike a nerve with your side, too. I think the gate will respond, like the herd coming to the aid of a single member in distress. It will strengthen the connection between itself and you and Emmett and ... well, that'll just make your job that much easier, won't it?"

Doubt, stronger than ever before, overcame Lance. He was incensed with anger, furious at who they thought he was. "Do you think I control any of this?" he shouted. "Do you think I *asked* for any of this? I have no idea how or why I do the things I can do. I never have. What makes you think today is any different than any other day of my life?"

Patrick's grin made Lance want to rip the man's head off. "Stop lying to yourself, Lance. You can feel it. You've felt it for years, knowing that you were headed to some greater purpose. You just didn't know it would be the other side that delivered you to it. You've been following your orders for so long that you stopped trying to figure out who was really giving them."

"That's bullish—"

"*Enough!*" Patrick's voice boomed across the land. "We're finished talking. You know what to do. Open the gate and you can have the peace you been searching for, and you just might save pathetic old Emmett's life in the process."

Patrick nodded to Karina again, and before Lance could scream a response, the woman zipped across the platform and leapt to an impossible height in the air, coming down fast and swinging the bat, connecting with Emmett's knee. The sound of bone and flesh breaking shattered Lance's heart, and Emmett's scream—because this time there was a scream, oh yes—reached something inside of him and pulled him forward. Lance leapt over the railings of the ride queue like hurdles at a track and field event and then bounded up the ramp in three quick strides.

"Leave him alone!" He lunged for Karina, hands outstretched, ready for blood.

The Surfer was behind him then, wrapping his bare arms tightly around Lance's torso in a great bear hug and pulling him away from the woman, who sneered at Lance and cackled that car-muffler laugh and then flashed across to the other side of the gondola and raised the bat high above her head like she was about to try and ring the bell at one of those carnival test-of-strength games, maybe trying to win a teddy bear. She froze in this position and jiggled her eyebrows, teasing Lance. She looked back down to the ground where Patrick Cain was moving around the ride queue and positioning himself next to the Reverend in the open grassy area beside the Ferris wheel.

"What's it going to be, Lance? Are you going to give it the old college try? Or does Karina here have to break every single one of this man's bones while you watch?"

Lance was breathing hard, his chest feeling tight against the Surfer's embrace, his heart hammering faster and harder than it should, ready to burst. And Lance wished it would. Right then, in that moment, death would be the easy way out. Death would end it all, stealing the terrible responsibility, the terrible choice, away from him.

Because there was no happy ending here. No choice would be the right one. Would he let Emmett die? Could he really be responsible for opening a gateway that would allow a great infestation of Evil to ravage countless dimensions, countless realities full of happy lives and bright futures, places where the Light shined bright and burnt away the encroaching shadows? Would he be responsible for dimming that Light?

Lance's world became suspended, stopped in its orbit with no clear direction of which way to proceed. His entire life, his decisions had been heavily based on deciding what was right and what was wrong. But now, his moral compass spun in spastic semicircles, changing course as rapidly as a deck of cards being shuffled.

"I...," he started.

Try. His mother's voice shocked his system, his body jerking against the Surfer's and his eyes going wide.

Mom? Mom, I—

Lance, listen to me. For now, just try.

And Lance let her words fill his veins with a calmness, soothing his soul. His heart slowed and his breathing leveled out and an inexplicable sense of some unknown plan being set in motion gave him...

Hope.

Hope that seconds ago had seemed dead and buried for good.

Hope that lit a fire against the darkness and ignited the demons that lurked there.

"Okay!" he yelled toward the sky, yelled for the world and all the Universe to hear. "I'll try!"

He leveled his gaze at Patrick Cain, and when he did the Reverend cocked his head to the side. "I don't know if—"

"*Shut up,*" Patrick hissed. "I told you he'd do it."

The Reverend took a step backward, looked over his shoulder, and then turned back to Lance, watching him with a different sort of interest than before, like one might watch a street magician to try and figure out how he was doing the trick in plain sight.

Patrick nodded to the Surfer and the creature let Lance go, stepping away but staying close. Lance looked to Emmett, saw the sweat beading on the man's face as he strained against the pain and his bindings. "Don't," the man barely managed to whisper.

Lance said nothing. Took a deep breath and closed his eyes and released his mind, detached it from all his worry and anxiousness, left behind the pain and the doubt and the anger, abandoned the helplessness and the fear, left it all behind until there was only...

The blackness filled everything, the void coming for him. Lance's consciousness slipped through the inky nothing.

Try.

His mother's voice again, echoing all around him, coming from everywhere at once.

Lance focused, sent all his energy into the invisible wavelengths, trying to conjure the image of that great white light he'd seen before, when he'd been plucked from the conversation with Patrick and thrown into the image of coaching a high school basketball game. He strained his mind, strained every fiber of his being to call out for that light, to be led to the gate and—

Lance!

Leah's voice now, a breath of the sweetest air imaginable.

And right behind the sound of her calling for him, the darkness blinked away and Lance was falling through nothing and everything and—

He was floating on a great ocean, a gentle current rising and falling in a lullaby rhythm beneath him, effortlessly moving him toward...

Toward her.

No ... the ocean *was* her. She was there, with him. Their connection linked, their souls entwined. *Leah!* he called to her.

NO! Patrick Cain's voice shattered everything. The ocean vanished and the darkness blinked past and—

And Lance was back on the platform in front of the Wheel of Adventure, his vision spinning back into focus, his ears popping, his stomach twisting in a sickened knot. But...

But she was there, he thought, feeling the warmth of her spread through him. Then, with a startling clarity, he corrected himself. *She's here.*

"I warned you!" Patrick Cain spat, his voice that of an angered beast. "I told you to shut her out, Lance! You really should learn to fucking listen!" Patrick nodded to Karina. "End him."

The woman's eyes lit up like spotlights and she squealed and laughed and Lance tried to stop her but she was just too damn fast. She leapt into the air again and Lance dove forward but was still several feet short when his and Emmett's eyes met clearly for the final time right before the bat slammed into the top of the man's skull.

"Ed!" Lance cried, falling beside the man. Emmett's body had gone limp, spasming occasionally as his brain's final signals fired in a tangled mess of confusion and defeat. "Ed, I'm so sorry," Lance whispered, reaching out and resting a hand on the man's bloodied check, trying not to look at the caved-in portion of his skull. The man's breathing was hitching and sputtering, and just as Lance felt the fresh boil of rage begin to bubble inside him, Emmett's lips parted and then looked as though they were trying to move.

"Ed?" Lance leaned in closer. The man's eyes were open but unfocused, rolling uselessly in all directions.

"She's ... how," Emmett managed. "Go ... together."

Emmett's eyes went still then, and his breathing stopped completely, until...

Until he hiccuped a single time.

And then a bright light splashed across the platform and Lance jerked up and saw a pair of headlights flying across the grassy area beside the ride, the sound from a small engine whining for all its worth.

Lance held a hand up to shield the light and was just able to make out the image of—

Is that a minivan?

It was. And it was speeding toward the Reverend and the thing called Patrick Cain at easily fifty miles an hour. The two of them spun around and threw up their hands, and at just the last second the van jerked to the left, slamming directly into the Reverend and just clipping Patrick.

Lance watched as the Reverend's body flew through the air, arms and legs pinwheeling lifelessly, before it landed with a satisfying splat against the Wheel of Adventure's metal frame and crumpled to the ground in a broken heap.

[31]

Maya's caffeine high eventually faded and her energy quickly crashed, her eyes narrowing to slits as she fought to keep them open. Leah noticed and put a gentle hand atop one of Maya's, which was weakly gripping the wheel. "Maya, it's my turn. Get some sleep."

For a second, Leah thought the woman was going to protest, but instead of speaking Maya nodded twice and pulled off onto the shoulder of the two-lane highway. As she climbed into the passenger seat, she asked, in a voice that sounded like she was already half-asleep, "Do you think he'll recognize me? When we find him."

In the miles of silence and darkness they'd driven, Leah had examined this possibility from all its angles. She was about to tell Maya that she did believe Patrick would recognize her, was counting on it, in fact, but when she'd finished adjusting the rearview mirror and then looked over to the passenger seat, Maya was already asleep, her head against the window and her mouth open, just like little Noah in the back.

Leah put the van into gear and pulled slowly back onto the road.

In Texas, the roads seemed to stretch on endlessly, miles upon miles of straight lines and flat surroundings. Leah fell into a quiet trance as she navigated the highway, the occasional flashes of oncoming headlights momentarily disorienting her, snapping her out of her thoughts. For two hours, the road continued unobstructed. And shortly after the moonlight had started to wane and the nighttime blackness had begun to be replaced by a soft blue that reminded Leah of crisp fall mornings back home, the road came to an end at an intersection. Leah stopped the van, turned to look in the back. Pamela Brody had not been visible the entire trip, had faded in and out of existence as Leah had occasionally turned to check on Noah, but she was there now, and as Leah was about to ask the woman which way to go, she noticed that Pamela's face was different. She looked worried.

"Pamela?"

For a moment, Leah wasn't sure the woman had heard her, and she had a brief flash of fear that her own strength, her own abilities might be fading away. But then Pamela's gaze settled upon her and she said, "Left. We're very close now. I can feel him so close and ... he's so scared. My baby boy is scared."

Leah felt the lump rise in her throat and she worked to swallow it down. She blinked away the prickle of tears and steeled her resolve. "He'll be okay," she said out loud. Whether she was talking to Pamela or herself, she wasn't sure. She made the turn and then stepped hard on the minivan's accelerator.

Fifteen minutes later, a shape rose into the sky along the horizon, and before Leah could even complete her conscious thought—*Is that a Ferris wheel?*—a different phrase involuntarily escaped her lips in a hushed whisper.

"Here's the church, here's the steeple."

The rounded image reached higher into the sky in the distance, growing larger and larger as she sped toward it, slamming the pedal to the floorboard. The sudden rush of acceleration caused her head to jerk back against the headrest, and Maya's head slid back from the window, waking her. She shot up in her seat, gripping the armrests and looking around them. "What's wrong? What's happening?"

Leah said nothing.

"Mommy?" Noah was awake now, too. And Leah tore her eyes from the looming Ferris wheel for just a second to glance at him in the back seat. He did not look afraid, only curious.

Such a brave kid, she thought, and then it hit her.

A feeling like the greatest despair imaginable, like being force-fed sadness in heaping spoonfuls. And there was anger and hate mixed in with the despair, a perfect cocktail of...

Of Evil, she thought as the chain-link fence surrounding what she could now see was an abandoned amusement park came into clear view. *This is it. This is the place. He's here.*

Leah gripped the wheel tight and was fully prepared to drive straight through the fence like a scene out of one of those heist thrillers her daddy always liked to watch, but then she saw the large gate in the fence was actually opened—either an oversight or a trap, she didn't care. All that mattered was that they were there. Lance was here and every second mattered.

Try.

Pamela's voice.

Leah glanced over her shoulder but saw that the woman was no longer in the back seat. But still, her voice rang clear and true in Leah's mind. It came again: *Lance, listen to me. For now, just try.*

Leah drove the minivan with the precision of a NASCAR driver along a curved sweeping road, roaring by a deserted parking lot and flying toward the front entrance of the park. And she could *feel* him. For the first time in days she could sense his closeness, feel the tingle of electricity that accompanied the power he radiated. The love they shared and that reached deep into their souls, connecting them.

She spied an opening near the front of the ticket booths where some of the kiosks had been removed. Without thinking, as if the entire sum of her actions had been vetted and predetermined, choreographed and rehearsed, she sped through it, the van's suspension squeaking and clanking as it bounced over the sidewalk.

Close ... he's so close.

"Leah..." Maya said next to her, her voice wavering with fear. "Leah, slow down!"

Leah had nearly forgotten the woman was there. She darted a quick glance over, saw Maya sitting back against the seat and using one hand to brace against the van's roof.

"He's—"

That was all she managed to say before a shadow fell across Leah's eyes and she drifted away. There was a sudden blinding darkness and a single flashbulb eruption of a great white light and then she was floating ... back on the gentle waves of her ocean, the Universe's current swelling beneath her and she *knew* he was there with her. She knew that somewhere on this vast sea, Lance floated too, making his way to her. The ripples across the water were his and the foam bubbling atop the waves were from him and she could feel the swelling in her chest as their connection reignited and she called to him —*Lance!*

But then a new feeling invaded. A resurgence of that despair and anger that she'd felt on the outskirts of the park. The blackness began to speckle across the water and the sky and it all fell apart and there was a voice echoing through it all—*NO!* —and she recognized it as Patrick's voice right before the blackness flashed again and she was back in the minivan's driver's seat. She swerved in surprise at reuniting with her body, slowed briefly to get her bearings, and then followed the path at the end of the midway around a low-set stone building in front of the Ferris wheel that climbed like a mountain into the sky.

She rounded the corner of the building and there they were —two of them. The Reverend and the thing called Patrick Cain. Two of the things that had caused so much pain and sadness in their world, in *her* world. Two of the things that had stolen Lance.

Leah was consumed with her hatred of them, her desire to destroy them. She stood on the accelerator with all her weight. The engine screamed beneath the hood and Leah screamed, too. A primal noise from somewhere inside of her she did not know existed. The van bumped off the pathway and into the high grass, mowing its way toward the two figures, who had just turned, stunned, raising their hands against the headlights and the speeding bullet coming for them.

"Patrick!" Maya yelled. "No!" She grabbed the wheel at just the last second before impact, jerking it to the side, causing the van to veer just slightly off course as the two figures tried to leap out of the way. The right-side fender clipped Patrick and he spun like a top and then fell off to the side, lost in the grass. But the Reverend had no such luck. The front nose of the van connected squarely with him, and his body flew as if shot from a cannon before it crashed into the Ferris wheel and Leah slammed on the brakes and the minivan skidded to a stop in the grass. Leah jumped out of the van.

And there he was.

[32]

LANCE WATCHED as the minivan skidded through the high grass, fishtailing briefly before it came to a hard stop, a cloud of dirt and debris billowing past it like the van's own soul had left its body. The driver's door flung open.

And there she was.

Leah jumped from the minivan and rounded the front, stopping in her tracks when she saw him. Their eyes met, just for a second, and the current of love that shot between them could have powered the whole park. Lance jumped forward, ready to sprint to her.

"Keep him back!" Patrick Cain yelled from where he was lying in the grass. "Keep him away!"

Lance saw Leah's head dart in Patrick's direction just before Karina appeared out of nowhere next to him and slammed the heavy end of the baseball bat into Lance's gut, knocking the wind out of him. Lance fell to his knees, a hoarse cry erupting from his throat, and then another blow from the bat struck him between the shoulder blades, knocking him forward. Karina's long coat flapped around him as she moved with such speed, sounding like a flock of crows taking flight, circling him. The familiar slap of the Surfer's flip-flops came from behind him, and then a foot was planted into Lance's back, pinning him to the ground. He craned his neck, lifting his head enough to be able to shout for Leah to stay back, not to come for him.

But he didn't have to. Because what he saw was Leah and another woman whom he did not recognize rushing away from the van and over to where Patrick Cain was lying in the grass.

"It's over, Lance!" Patrick called to him. "It's your fault she dies! It changes nothing! You can't win!"

Lance heard the words, but it wasn't their message he noticed. It was the fear that laced them, hidden beneath the anger. The same fear he'd felt days ago as they'd all ridden inside the Plymouth Horizon and Leah had first reached out to him. They'd all seemed afraid of her then, and now that she was here it was as if their nightmares had come true.

A little boy, no older than maybe nine or ten, jumped out from the rear of the minivan, and something about him was so striking that Lance had to do a double take. Lance swiveled his head from the boy and then to the woman running hand in hand with Leah through the grass. Recognition swarmed him, clicked into place alongside the secret that he'd picked up from the thing called Patrick Cain that day in the BBQ restaurant's parking lot.

Lance couldn't help but laugh as the picture formed. Maybe the Universe controlled the plan after all.

"He's still in there, Leah!" Lance called to her, which earned him a kick from Karina, the toe of her boot like a spear in his side.

Leah's voice shot through his mind like a newspaper headline: *I know.*

That was when the red glow began to replace the blue of morning, and the screams began to fill the air.

Leah wanted to run to Lance; more than anything she wanted to feel his embrace. But if she did, she knew it would all be over before it had even started. She had a job to do—to *try*—and her window of time would close fast.

It was already closing, because as she grabbed Maya's hand and told her to run with her, Leah saw the red glow begin to rise from the ground a short distance behind where Patrick's body was splayed in the grass. A deep burnt color began to spread out from the glow, as if the grass was being scorched, and from inside this boundary, the most terrible sounding screams began to reach her ears—some human, some not. Some were unlike any noises she'd ever heard before.

"Oh my stars!" Maya yelled, stopping and pulling back when she saw and heard what waited ahead. Leah gripped the woman's hand with all her strength and pulled her along.

"No!" she called back, struggling to be heard over the chorus of pain. Then, saying the truth in the only way she could think that would encourage Maya's corporation, she added, "We have to save your brother!"

Leah felt the hesitation from Maya hold for only another second before the woman switched course and ran freely again.

"It's over, Lance!" Patrick called out as they reached him. He was trying to prop himself up with his left arm and leg, inching his way slowly backward toward the scorching earth. His right leg looked broken, dragging uselessly through the grass. His right arm was resting limp across his waist, his jacket sleeve was ripped open and a sickly purplish color was spreading along his forearm. "It's your fault she dies! It changes nothing! You can't win!"

A second later: "He's still in there, Leah!" Lance called from the platform, his voice sounding impossibly far away.

I know, Leah instinctively shot back with her mind, smiling.

"Noah, get back!" Maya screamed from behind her. "Stay in the van!"

Noah...

"No!" Leah stopped and turned, beckoning for Noah to hurry to them. "Bring him!"

Maya shot Leah a look that could have cut glass, but Leah grabbed the woman's face in her hands and said, "Trust me, Maya. You've believed in me your whole life, don't stop now. This is all or nothing. If we lose, we're all dying. So we might as well all fight."

Maya didn't have a choice in the matter anyway, because Noah was already at her side, clutching her arm and staring down at Patrick Cain's broken body. He pointed and said, "We found him! We found Uncle Patrick!" Then Noah's face squished up in a funny sort of confusion and he said, "He's a kid!"

A monstrous howl shook the ground, and the red glow pulsed behind them and then a great shape began to reach up from some unseen hole in the ground, a slithering tentacle as thick as a telephone pole waving into the air before slamming down.

Leah opened her mouth to scream but the sound was lost among all the others.

Go! Lance's voice found her thoughts.

Leah yanked on Maya's hand and the three of them fell to

the ground beside Patrick. His eyes were black and empty, the glow of red reflected in them like droplets of blood. His face was screwed up in concentration, his brow furrowed, and for a moment Leah thought he wasn't even seeing them anymore.

She looked to the horror growing behind him, the Evil that was literally seeping from the ground.

He's doing that, she thought. *He's opening hell.*

"*You're nothing!*" Patrick hissed. He fell back and shot his good hand out and gripped Leah's wrist. His eyes bored into her stare, and the sadness she felt filling her brought tears streaming down her cheeks in an instant. Heartbreak threatened to overtake her, burning away all the good inside, tearing out all the love the way a dog might tear the stuffing from a toy. She felt her strength fading as Patrick's grip tightened and he pulled her closer.

She had to fight back, had to reach inside and find the young man who was still trapped, the man who Maya had never given up on, had never stopped loving...

Love.

The flicker of the emotion sparked a light in her mind, cleared away the thickening cobwebs of Evil long enough for her plan to reemerge.

Love.

"Hold on to me," she called out to Maya and Noah. "Both of you!"

She felt hands—one big, one small—grip either of her shoulders, and a renewed strength pulsed through her as their energies collected and joined one another.

Patrick Cain's grip burned her wrist, the pain white-hot like a branding iron. The screams from beyond began to move closer, and hundreds of dark shadows began to slowly rise up alongside the tentacle of the beast, humanlike silhouettes, an army of tortured souls.

Leah looked down into the black and red-tinted eyes of Patrick Cain ... and she saw the fear. She saw his shock at the fact that she had not succumbed to his strength, the power flowing from his grip. Leah leaned down, her face an inch from his, and he snarled like a scared animal. Snapped at her. Leah did not flinch. Patrick tried to scrabble backward with his good leg but refused to let go of Leah's wrist, which only caused him to lose his leverage and fall further back to the ground. With Maya and Noah's hands still on her shoulders, Leah inched closer and whispered, "We love you, Patrick. It's time to come home."

She pressed her lips to his.

[33]

Leah's ocean crashed angry waves all around her, but she was not in the water. Her feet landed heavily in wet sand, sinking nearly to her ankles. A hurricane roared around her, a torrential downpour of rain forming a thick curtain, blowing sideways on the jet-engine wind. The roar was deafening, the wind mixing with the still-present screams and growls from that other place, the place beyond the red where the thing that had taken over the body of Patrick Cain had begun to call for his army.

A fury of lightning began to electrify the sky, and when Leah looked up, raising a hand to shield against the onslaught of wind and water, she saw the top of a tall stone building reaching out of the gray mist of the storm, looking down on them with cold indifference.

"Oh my stars!" Maya exclaimed. It was then that Leah realized she was clutching the woman's hand. She looked over her shoulder and saw Maya just behind her, with little Noah a step behind, his hand clutching his mother's. A human chain. "That's Stonebridge," Maya yelled through the squall. "The Stonebridge Home for Children. That's where we grew up!"

Maya took a step back, craning her neck to look up at the gray slab of building. "How is that possible?"

Her words were scooped up by the wind and thrown away, lost to the sea.

This is the link, Leah thought. *The link between us. He's trapped in there!*

"We have to go in!" Leah called against the storm, pulling Maya behind her. The three of them moved toward a large wooden door with iron rivets, a brass knocker hanging from the center like something from a Dickens story. When they were just a couple feet away, as Leah was reaching her hand out for the door handle, a massive gust of wind screamed from their side, knocking the three of them off-balance. Noah went down to one knee, and Maya let go of Leah's hand to turn and help him up. As soon as she did, the entire building began to flicker, the storm's noise growing softer as this world faded. "No!" she screamed, snatching Maya's hand back, just as the woman pulled her son from the wet sand. "Don't let go of me! Not even for a second! We're strongest together!"

Maya looked at Leah with uncomprehending eyes but quickly nodded her head, pulling Noah along. They reached the door together as somewhere in the distance a roar from something bigger than the storm shook the ground. Something angry that they'd gotten this far. Leah grabbed the handle and tried to push it down, but it did not budge. It was locked.

A fresh wave of worry and fear washed over her as the rain pelted them, her plan all at once derailed. She tried the handle again, throwing all her strength into it. It didn't give at all, remained absolute in its rejection.

"Let me try," Maya said from behind her.

Leah would have felt foolish, if she hadn't felt so afraid. *Of course,* she thought. *This is her connection, not mine. Stonebridge was theirs.*

The three of them quickly adjusted their positions, Leah grabbing Noah's free hand and then letting go of Maya's, keeping the chain connected. Maya stepped forward and gripped the handle and it pressed down easily. She threw the door open and the three of them fell inside together, Leah kicking the door closed behind them, shutting out the storm.

But the noise from the storm was quickly replaced by the sound of something heavy pounding against another door, the frame rattling and squeaking as though at any moment the wood would fail and splinter and whatever waited on the other side would reveal itself in all its terrifying glory. Leah turned, expecting to find a foyer or antechamber, something befitting the entryway to an old stone building such as Stonebridge House. Instead, the link between her and Maya and Patrick Cain had created a simple square bedroom. Walls of a cold gray, and a rustic wooden floor. Two single beds were positioned along opposite walls, a narrow rectangular window cut out between them, the glass frosted, nothing but darkness showing from beyond it. A lamp flickered a warm light from atop a small bedside table, throwing weak shadows along the floor and the bottom of the walls. The rattling door that kept back whatever wanted in was at the foot of the bed where Patrick sat.

Patrick—the actual Patrick Cain, his consciousness as it had been when he was a sixteen-year-old boy and had been hidden away, trapped inside his own mind while a great Evil had taken over his body—stared in wonder at Leah.

No, Leah thought, *he's not looking at me. He's looking at her. His sister.*

"Maya?" Patrick said, and his voice was so gentle and soft, so unlike the cocky and arrogant creature who had used his voice as its own for so long, it almost seemed wrong, like a dubbed-over version.

But it also seemed so right.

Leah turned to Maya, and the shock at what she saw nearly caused her to let go of the woman's hand.

The Maya in the room with them was no longer middle-aged, no longer the only version of the woman Leah had ever known. Instead, she was the teenaged girl from the Polaroid she'd shown Leah at her house, the image snapped on the high school bleachers, with a silly Patrick making bunny ears behind her head. Leah could actually smell the girl's perfume, could pick up a hint of the fabric softener used on the Spirit Day tie-dyed T-shirt she wore.

Leah looked at Noah, who either didn't notice or simply could not see the change in his mother. Instead, the boy's stare was fixed on Patrick.

"It's me, Patrick. We've come to take you home." The young Maya's teeth were bright white and her skin was smooth and her smile was the smile of a girl who lived only in the moment, not burdened with worry—of the past *or* the future.

Leah looked at Patrick, saw the young man's eyes slowly make their way across the three of them. "Who are they?" He nodded toward them. "Who's the little kid?"

"This is Leah," Maya said. "She's a good friend of mine. She showed me how to find you. And this..." She pulled Noah forward a few steps, positioning him between her and Leah. "Patrick, this is your nephew. His name is Noah."

Patrick's face stared for three, maybe four seconds. "*Nephew?* Maya, what trick are you trying to pull here? There's no way he's my—"

"We have to go!" Leah had to cut him off. She wasn't sure what condition she'd expected Patrick—the *real* Patrick—to be in when they found him, but it was already abundantly clear that his sense of time had been frozen, trapped along with him, since the day he was taken. The nightmare of this boy spending decades inside these four stone walls and not even understanding that time was passing him by seemed like the cruelest of robberies.

"We have to get out of here now," Leah said. "Patrick, you have to come with us. We can try to explain everything later, but—"

"Can't," Patrick said. "It won't let us."

As if to emphasize the point, the door at the foot of the bed shook violently with a *THUD!* After, the sounds of something scratching against the wood, trying to claw its way through.

"It never leaves," Patrick said. "Never."

"We'll go out the other door," Leah said, turning to point at—

The door they'd come through was gone, replaced with a solid stone wall.

[34]

Lance watched helplessly as Leah and the woman and the young boy fell to the ground beside the thing called Patrick Cain's body. He wanted to go to them, *needed* to go to them. He watched in horror as the red glow grew larger and brighter in the distance, felt an icy fear grip his heart as the tentacle of one of those great beasts worked its way free, ready to climb in this dimension and feed on the innocent.

Starting with all of them.

He struggled against Karina and the Surfer's hold on him, trying with all his physical strength to push himself up, get an arm or leg free from where he was pinned to the ground to wrestle the two of them off him long enough to make a run for it. But they were too strong. Karina seemed to be made of steel, her strength unnatural and unwavering. It was like trying to fight a boulder.

Now.

His mother's voice again, shocking him still. *Go to her now.*

Lance bucked against the impossible strength again, was

met with another kick to the side, the pain barely felt as he tried to focus on his mother's words.

"I can't!" he cried out.

You can. You're smarter than that. They can't hold on to your mind and your soul. Now go!

Lance felt the heat of embarrassment flush his face. Even in death, his mother was so much smarter than him, so much calmer and level-headed. He breathed in as deeply as his lungs would allow with the Surfer's foot still planted in his back, and then relaxed all his muscles, his body going limp against the platform's surface. He closed his mind to the sounds of those beasts and the screams of those tormented souls. He blocked it all out, breathing slow and steady, forgetting his body, forgetting the physical world. He searched for that ocean that he'd so briefly seen, her water on which he'd floated. The blackness flashed, and he was there, in the ether, navigating his way toward her love, toward that feeling that only she brought to him.

And then he could hear it, a great storm raging in the distance, and he knew it was working because underneath the wind and the rain and the howling of beasts he could still feel her, her light shining bright in the darkness.

I'm coming, he called to her. *Show me the way.*

He was falling then, his consciousness rushing through the emptiness of nothing, and then a hand gripped his, scooped him up and pulled him hard.

We're here!

Leah's voice whispered to him just as the blackness blinked away and a new world rushed into view, like a slideshow image clicking over in the projector.

Lance found himself standing at the end of a dimly lit hallway, the floors a dark wood beneath his feet, the wall ahead made of stone. A single frosted-glass window was cut into the wall's center, and beyond it he saw the red glow of something that could only be terrible.

Something terrible was inside, too. There was a wooden door just ahead to Lance's right, and Patrick Cain stood just outside it, pounding on the door with fists in an angry off-rhythm beat. He punched the wood two, three times, and then kicked it hard enough to rattle the entire frame, the entire hallway.

This was the Evil inside the boy, the monster that had taken over. Sensing Lance, this creature-version of Patrick spun around and hissed at him, his mouth unnaturally wide and full of razor-blade teeth stained blood-red, chunks of torn flesh stuck between them. His eye sockets were empty, nothing but gaping holes full of dangling veins. The boy's skin was milk-white with splotches of infected black sores. The ends of his fingers were tipped with talons, curved and jagged.

The creature bucked toward Lance and hissed again, bloody spittle flying from its mouth, and Lance...

Lance could feel the fear coming off the thing in front of him. He took a step closer, finding that he himself was absent of fear, a great swelling of energy and light building within him, like the greatest excitement he'd ever experienced.

"Be gone," he said to the Patrick-creature, the thing that had long worked to trap the real Patrick's mind. "You're finished here."

The thing hissed again and Lance took a final step forward, the excitement and energy inside him threatening to burst free, like an overdose of adrenaline and...

Love.

He felt her, on the other side of the door.

"Leah?"

"We're here," she called from inside the room.

Lance recalled Emmett Emmanuel Dean's last words to him, the pained whispers before the man had passed on. "*She's ... how*," and then, "*Go ... together*."

Together.

"I love you," Lance said. To Leah, to everybody. To the world.

"I love you too," came from the other side of the door and her strength joined his and that feeling inside Lance did explode then, his soul radiating a white glow that contained all the strength of the Universe. Lance turned away from the creature and reached a hand out for the door handle, and when the creature hissed its angry and afraid hiss again it shot one of those talon-tipped hands out and tore into Lance's wrist.

But Lance felt no pain.

The creature's hand began to sizzle for just a second before the entire thing caught flame in a brilliant flash, like a Fourth of July sparkler being lit. The flame eroded the creature's hand, and then wrist, and then arm, leaving behind nothing but a smoky emptiness in its place as it continued upward. The creature gave one final howl of hate and pain as the sparkling white flame reached its torso, and Lance didn't bother to even watch as it was fully consumed. He turned back to the door and pushed the handle down, throwing it open.

He stepped inside the bedroom, found Leah and the real Patrick Cain holding hands, along with the woman and boy. The four of them rushed to him, hand in hand, and when they fell together in the most powerful hug the Universe had ever known, they also fell from the bedroom, the blackness again blinking out everything, only to be sliced in half by the brightest white light any of them had ever seen.

A great roller-coaster drop sped them away, and Lance felt his mind's collision back with his physical form. His eyes shot open and he blinked away the blurriness, sucked in huge gasps of air, tried to settle his spinning head. That buzzing energy inside him was still here, and it made him jittery, his body electric with raw power like he'd never known before. He was ready to spring up, to throw his captors off his back and pounce on them like a rabid animal, wanting to rip them apart.

But he didn't have to.

Because that brilliant white light winked to life above him. At the sight of it, both Karina and the Surfer jerked back, freeing him, and Lance rolled away from them on the platform, pushing himself up to his knees and looking up to the sky. A mile-long slit had dissected the light blue canvas of early morning, like somebody had taken a scalpel to it. The two sides pulled away in a widening gap, and in the glow that emanated from the opened space Lance felt his soul sing, felt that energy inside him calm itself, become comfortable with its own strength, controlled. He closed his eyes, enjoyed the warmth, soaked up the goodness that was rejuvenating him.

A harsh scream broke his spell, and Lance sprang up to his feet. Thick iridescent beams of light shot from the white slit in the sky, full of only the most beautiful colors, colors he'd never seen and likely never would again. One of them struck Karina in the chest, and she stumbled backward with another scream. Her eyes grew wide with fear and confusion, and she looked to the Surfer as she fell onto her knees, her torso sizzling, the smoke tinted blue. The Surfer grunted and jumped back as Karina reached a hand for him, her screams begging him to pull her free as she burnt to nothing.

Coward, Lance thought, just as another beam flashed from the slit and knocked the Surfer off the Adventure Wheel's platform, his flip-flops floating in place for a split second before landing with a soft slap on the ground next to him as he withered away. And in that moment before the Surfer's physical body was eaten away, Lance saw a flickering of something else, the creature's true form, a slithering shadow that twisted against the light before it was torn apart, its pieces carried away on the wind.

Lance ran then, leaping from the platform's side and scanning the grassy area for Leah, finding her with the woman and the boy as they moved slowly across the land toward the waiting minivan, Patrick Cain's body carried between them. Lance headed their direction, his body light and lithe, reaching the group just as they'd managed to get Patrick inside the vehicle and the little boy had jumped in after. Patrick's eyes were closed and his body was limp, but he was breathing, Lance seeing the slow rise and fall of his chest.

Lance grabbed Leah and spun her around to face him, and upon seeing him her face was lit by that beautiful smile, the smile he'd dreamed about, and she kissed him and he kissed her back, hard, squeezing her to him, never wanting to let her go.

And the explosion from the sky sent a shockwave across the earth, the van rocking and Lance and Leah stumbling as a great force rushed toward the red glow.

And Lance did not let go, did not stop kissing her. Emmett's words in his head again, "*She's ... how. Go ... together.*"

The man had seen it all. In his last moments, one final

bubbly, the most important bubbly with the simplest of instructions.

Together.

Together, they were unstoppable.

A million beams drew together into a massive tornado of light that blasted against the red crack in the earth, slicing the great beast's tentacle in two and mowing down the tormented souls like a scythe. The screams were silenced, one by one, and the remaining tentacle was vaporized as it tried to slither back into its home. The tornado of light flashed even brighter, another shockwave shaking the ground, its intensity impossible to stare at. Lance and Leah turned away, listening as the wound into hell was cauterized, the dimension resealed.

The silence popped into place like somebody had corked a bottle. Lance and Leah finally tore themselves free from each other and looked to where the red glow had been, found nothing but a scorched line in the earth. They then turned their heads upward, where the slit in the sky had reduced itself in size, now no larger than a twinkling star winking down at them.

The star began to move, making an arched ascension downward, growing brighter and warmer as it came closer.

But the warmth was inside him, Lance realized. A strong and familiar sense of happiness that he'd not felt since...

The star settled a few feet away, its light blinking out all their surroundings, leaving just Lance and Leah alone in its glow. Lance stared easily into the orb of light as if there was no light at all, watched as a figure stepped from the luminance, and felt the overwhelming surge of love inside him as hot tears poured down his cheeks.

"Mom."

[35]

Pamela Brody's spirit smiled, and Lance would swear the halo of light surrounding her surged brighter, striking him deep in his heart.

"Don't cry for me," she said, reaching a hand toward his face. When her thumb grazed Lance's cheek to wipe away a tear, for the briefest of moments, no more than a microsecond of his and the spirit world colliding, Lance felt her, and her touch sent the lifetime of happy memories they'd created together shooting through his mind the same way one's life might flash before their eyes in the moment just before their death.

He knew better, but Lance reached for her anyway, his hand hoping to grab onto hers, to press her palm against his cheek, to feel that familiar softness, to pull her close and hug her. But his hand went through the image of her with only the faintest tingle, grasping at nothing but air. He looked into her eyes, and the sparkle still present there warmed him, and the tears did not stop but only came harder.

Leah grabbed his hand, laced her fingers between his and

squeezed, giving him strength. He cleared his throat, searched for the words. He found only one. "Why?"

And as he spoke the word, he found that he himself could not decide on its meaning. Questions stacked atop one another: Why did you let them kill you? Why am I the way that I am? Why is there so much pain in the world? Why did you leave me? Why...

"Why now?" he said. "I've missed you every single day. I've mourned you and cried for you and thought about you every second since that night. Why have you waited so long to come to me? Why did you make me suffer like that? *Why?*"

His sudden anger surprised him, and he hated himself for it.

Pamela Brody only smiled still, the same way she used to when Lance was younger and would get upset and she'd just sit there quietly and let him work it all out for himself. It was infuriating, but also perfect. Sometimes there wasn't an answer at all; a person just needed to be heard.

She looked at Leah. "Tell him, dear. He already knows, but he'll listen to you." She winked.

Leah spoke, but Lance did not turn to look at her, was afraid to let his mother out of his sight at all for fear that when he looked back she'd be gone again, this time forever. "She never left," Leah said. "She's always been inside you. You've felt her, and you've heard her, I know you have. A part of every child's mother lives on in them; it never dies. The bond you two have is unbreakable. Nothing can touch it."

Lance said nothing.

Pamela said, "They've never understood love, Lance. Love confuses Evil, flies under its radar unidentified. They fear it but cannot recognize it until it's too late. Its power is greater than they can imagine. Just remember, the light will always burn away the darkness. And you two"—she nodded to both of them —"your lights shine so bright."

Leah squeezed his hand again, and Lance said, "Yours too, Mom. Your light is the brightest of all." He smiled and pointed to the rim of light radiating around her. "I mean, literally."

He laughed, and Pamela grinned. Shook her head. She pointed to his chest. "I shine on from inside you, Lance. You carry my light now."

The three of them stood together in the grass, the moment golden yet fleeting. The light around his mother flickered, dimmed briefly before flashing bright again.

"It's closing," Pamela said. "It only opened because you needed it to, and now it's over."

"I really did that?" Lance asked.

"You both did it," Pamela said. "You could have only done it together. They were right in thinking you had the power, that the Universe would open itself to you if you called. But their arrogance blinded them to the reality of what that would mean. The thing inside that poor boy was strong—one of the strongest —and he's caused great harm, but..."

"But the light will always burn away the darkness," Lance said.

Pamela nodded.

"Is that really true?" Lance asked.

"It is if you believe it."

Lance shook his head. "That's not really an answer."

She smiled at him again, a knowing look. "The Universe is a strange and mysterious place, Lance. You know that better than most. Some things ... well, they can only be understood through experience and belief."

Lance sighed, and another question hit him. The memories

that weren't really memories. "Mom, are all those other dimensions really out there? Are there really a billion versions of me, versions who aren't ... well, are there ones that are normal?"

She nodded once. "There are. You know that. You've seen them. Evil's threat was real. They assumed they could pass through once the gate was opened and blaze their own paths of destruction."

Lance swallowed hard. Waited.

"Ask what you want to ask," his mother said. "It's almost closed again."

Lance waited a beat longer, unsure if he actually wanted the question asked. Didn't know what he'd do once he'd received the answer. Finally, his curiosity won out. "Could I really choose a different life? Do I really have the power to move into a different dimension and ... and not have to be this? Are there really places where you're still alive and we can be together?" He looked over to Leah and then back his mother. "All of us?"

Pamela did not hesitate with her answer. "Yes. Both of you can. But only together."

Lance went dizzy at the possibility, the idea that the reality he'd so longed for waited just beyond the veil, as simple as stepping across a threshold. He looked at Leah, but the look she returned to him gave him nothing.

But in an instant, he knew the truth. The answer as solid as the ground he stood on and his own love for her, and he made his choice faster than he would have ever previously expected. He shook his head. "No. This is our life. We can't abandon it." He thought about what his mother had said, about his and Leah's light shining bright, burning away the darkness. He thought about the way the Surfer had pulled away from Karina in her moment of anguish, what a coward the creature had been.

How many more hands would reach out for Lance in their moments lost in the shadows? "We won't abandon them," Lance said.

Leah moved in close beside him, gripped his arm with both of hers, rested her head against his shoulder. It was all the validation he needed, because the gesture told him she felt the same. This was their life to build on, and together they would shine bright for those who needed to see.

The light around Pamela dimmed again and this time stayed that way, the halo shrinking around her. She smiled at them with a look of proud satisfaction.

"Goodbye, Lance. I love you enough for a billion dimensions."

"I love you, too. Thank you. For everything." He shook his head and could not help the tears that came again. "For being my mom."

Pamela nodded and then looked to Leah. "Take care of each other."

Leah wiped tears from her own face. "We will. Promise."

Pamela turned to leave, stepping into the shrinking glow of light. Then she stopped and turned back to Lance, once last knowing look. "My sweet boy," she said. "What great things you've done."

And then she was gone, the light blinking out completely, only to be replaced by the sun rising on the horizon.

EPILOGUE

(11 Months Later)

Laughter echoed through the rooms of Lance Brody's home. The home he had grown up in and had shared with his mother, and the home he now shared with Leah, nearly one year after that horrible and magnificent night at a forgotten Texas amusement park.

"So I told him right there on the phone, I said Lance, don't do anything stupid," Marcus Johnston said, leaning back in his chair at the kitchen table. A table he had sat at a thousand times before, an image Lance had at one time grown certain he would never see again. Now, Lance swelled with happiness at the sight of his old friend, sitting at the same table and swapping stories just like the old days. Days that, in actuality, weren't so long ago but were also a different lifetime altogether. "But you know what he did?" Marcus asked, already laughing, pausing a moment to lean forward and take a bite of pie.

"Something stupid," Leah and her father both said together from across the table.

"You're damn right he did," Marcus said, slapping the table hard enough to rattle the empty plates. "Hiked all the way out to that teacher's house in the middle of the night and crawled around the guy's backyard looking for clues like a half-assed spy!"

More laughter from everyone, including Lance. "Hey, Mom drove me most of the way that night. I only hiked the last bit."

Marcus chuckled and shook his head, his face growing somber in the kitchen's warm light. "Your mother...," he said, trailing off. "She was something, wasn't she?"

"She sure was," Lance said.

Everyone was quiet in that moment, respect being paid. Then Marcus cleared his throat and smiled at Leah. "Well, Leah, I must say that this might be the finest Thanksgiving dinner I've had in a long time." He made a chef's kiss gesture. "My greatest compliments."

Leah blushed. "Thank you." She looked over to her dad, who was leaned back in his chair with his arm stretched out along the back of hers. "Mama taught me a lot of it."

Her father winked at her, and the light glistened in his eyes. "She was always a hell of a cook. I won't say it was the only reason I married her, but..."

Leah rolled her eyes and they all laughed again, and Lance could imagine no sweeter sound.

Later, after helping clear away the dishes, Lance and Marcus stood on the front porch, the crisp November air chilling their breath. They each leaned against the railing, looking out onto the quiet street, watching shadows move behind windows and smoke snake from chimney tops. The sky was thick with cloud cover, and snow was in the forecast.

"It's good to have you back, Lance," Marcus said. "I mean, really back. For a while there, I..."

Lance nodded. "I know."

After that night in Texas, after *everything*, Lance had known it was time to come home, but when he'd gotten back, it hadn't felt the same. It hadn't felt real. He'd spent a long time trying to move on like everything was back to normal before Leah had finally sat him down and helped him to understand. "It'll never be the same," she'd told him. "But that doesn't mean it's wrong. You have to stop pretending this is your old life, stop looking back. Look ahead. Look at us." They'd been seated at one of Downtown Joe's outside tables and she'd grinned at him and taken his hands in hers. "Never forget the memories," she'd said, "but don't stop making new ones."

As if reading Lance's thoughts, Marcus said, "She's special, that one."

"More than you know."

Marcus nodded. Clapped Lance on the back. "Love is a powerful thing, isn't it?"

Lance smirked. "More than you know."

The two men stood silently together for several more minutes, a lifetime of trust and friendship between them. Eventually, Marcus turned and headed for the door. "Getting too cold for my old bones. You coming?"

Lance pulled up the hood of his sweatshirt. "In a few."

Marcus slipped inside, the sound of Leah laughing at something her father was saying sneaking out into the night.

Lance glanced over his shoulder to make sure Marcus was

gone, then looked back to the street and waved. "Happy Thanksgiving, Ed."

Emmett Emmanuel Dean's spirit sat atop the most immaculate motorcycle Lance had ever seen. The man gave a thumbs-up. "Same to you, friend. Glad to see you happy. You've earned it." Then he winked, cranked the throttle to a soundless engine and shot away, off to explore endless miles of cosmic blacktop.

Lance had never seen a ghost on a motorcycle before, and as he stood from the porch railing he once again wondered at just how little he understood about anything. He had solved many mysteries, but he knew that one day the Universe would call on him again because countless others waited. And wait they would, because now...

The front door pulled open a tiny bit and Leah's face appeared in the crack of light. "Lance, the coffee's ready."

He turned and smiled at her. "The greatest words ever spoken."

Because now there were friends, and new memories to be made.

One cup at a time.

AUTHOR'S NOTE

Thanks so much for reading **DARK CHOICE**. I hope you enjoyed it. If you *did* enjoy it and have a few minutes to spare, I would greatly appreciate it if you could leave a review saying so. Reviews help authors more than you can imagine, and help readers like you find more great books to read. Win-win!

If you'd like to stay up-to-date on what I'm working on, there's a link on the following page where you can sign-up for my newsletter. I promise you'll only hear from me about new projects, sales, or giveaways. We all hate spam.

If you'd like to check out my Patreon page (patreon.com/mrobertsonjr), I'm offering lots of perks, early-access to projects, and behind-the-scenes content to supporters.

THANK YOU to the following Patreon members for your support:

Chris Cool, Deana Harper, Debra Kowalski, Diane Benson,

Diane Porter, Judi Mickelson, Karin Anderson, Kathy Oudinot, Linda Crisp, Lisa Fazalare, Martha Gilmore, Mike Gagliardi, Rebecca Curry, Tami, and Tanya Wolf. — I appreciate you all very much!

Thank you again, I hope you enjoyed, and please take care!

-Michael Robertson Jr

For all the latest info, including release dates, giveaways, and special events, you can visit the page below to sign up for the Michael Robertson, Jr. newsletter. (He promises to never spam you!)

http://mrobertsonjr.com/newsletter-sign-up

Follow On:

Facebook.com/mrobertsonjr

Twitter.com/mrobertsonjr

Instagram.com/mrobertsonjr

Patreon.com/mrobertsonjr

More from Michael Robertson Jr

SHIFFY P.I. SERIES

Run No More (Book 1)

LANCE BRODY SERIES

Dark Choice (Book 7)

Dark Holiday (Book 6)

Dark Rest (Book 5.5 - Short Story)

Dark Woods (Book 5)

Dark Vacancy (Book 4)

Dark Shore (Book 3)

Dark Deception (Book 2.5 - Short Story)

Dark Son (Book 2)

Dark Game (Book 1)

Dark Beginnings (Book 0 - Prequel Novella)

OTHER NOVELS

Cedar Ridge

Transit

Rough Draft (A Kindle #1 Horror Bestseller!)

Regret*

Collections

Tormented Thoughts: Tales of Horror

The Teachers' Lounge*

*Writing as Dan Dawkins

Printed in Great Britain
by Amazon